I0618459

Fresh Cuts²

The Skinning Volume

CHOPHOUSE
BOOKS

Fresh Cuts 2: The Skinning Volume

©2016 Chophouse Books

These are works of fiction. Names, characters, businesses, places, events, and incidents are either the products of the author's imagination or used in a fictitious manner.

All stories are copyright of their respective authors as indicated herein.

The Dolls ©2016 Joan Reginaldo

Toof Fairwy Twouble ©2016 Dean Fearce

Dirty Little Secret ©2016 Dawn Del Sontro

The Skin ©2016 Joan Reginaldo

Complexion ©2016 Gordon Hilgers

While We Sleep ©2016 Dawn Del Sontro

And So the Flies ©2016 Dan Tompsett

Soda Flies ©2016 Joan Reginaldo

Glamazons vs. Red Plaids ©2016 Dean Fearce

Twitch ©2016 Ernest Ortiz

A Mile in My Shoes ©2016 Joan Reginaldo

ISBN: 978-0-9969744-2-4

Edited by Joan Reginaldo

Cover art by Dean Fearce and Joan Reginaldo | Photo by Joan Reginaldo

Published by Chophouse Books | chophousebooks.com

Acknowledgements and Dedications

Dirty Little Secret—For Mike, my most patient husband. He jokes about sleeping with one eye open, but never shies away from my shenanigans. No matter how many times I've threatened your life, I do so with nothing but love.
While We Sleep—For Chase, Ryan, and Madison. My lovely children, who don't blink an eye at my weirdness and sometimes like to give me ideas.
I love you awesome weirdos.
—*Dawn Del Sontro*

To the Black Hats Writers Group, Ernest and Joan,
and a shout out to Joan for her immense talent and editing expertise
in helping to bring all of these stories alive.
And of course, for giving Dean Glamazons!
—*Dean Fearce*

To K.
—*Gordon Hilgers*

To all the writers who believe they are not skillful enough
or have missed opportunities. Don't give up.
Thank you again, Dean and Joan,
for letting me be a part of your lives and for this wonderful opportunity.
You guys are the reason I keep on writing.
To my family and friends, I know I don't always show it,
but I do appreciate all the good things you've all done for me.
—*Ernest Ortiz*

To Futurehusband and Grimlock. You guys keep me crazy.
Thank you to Black Hats Writers Group for challenging, frustrating,
and putting up with me.
And thank you to Robert Bevan, who keeps believing in me.
—*Joan Reginaldo*

My writing comes from a mild form of insanity I have.
—*Dan Tompsett*

Contents

INTRO TO *The Dolls*

When life is unbearable but suicide is not your thing, where do you go to escape the accumulation of moments, each with its own special hurt?

Drugs, alcohol, porn—pick your poison, your escape, your trip to the crossroads of Desperation and Denial Avenues toward the total annihilation of self.

Almost.

It's been said that addiction isn't a medical issue but a spiritual crisis, a longing to return to the mystic realm, the other side of darkness where we dwell beyond the physical manifestation of our reality.

Nothingness.

But, that also might not be to your liking, the loss of self, all personality, ego. Where's the drama in nothing?

Filipino mythology is full of mystical magical creatures, most of whom will do you harm, especially if you believe. Belief gives them power. Belief that's passed down in every whispered warning, to every generation, weaving an indelible blanket of darkness no amount of baptism could wash away.

So there we have the triumvirate.

Desire to escape. Something to hold. Willingness to believe. And of course, our mantra out of this moment of pain.

Anywhere but here, anytime but now, anything but this…

— DEAN FEARCE

The Dolls
by Joan Reginaldo

IT WAS A STROKE OF GENIUS putting all these women into one group therapy session; I spend one hour and forty-five minutes listening to them nicker and neigh like six nosy nags, and at the end, bill for six separate sessions. Cha-ching!

The idea to put them to a task was even more brilliant. By concentrating on detailed work, it frees their minds to wander beyond the pale. Much like taking a shower or going for a long walk helps writers get over their so-called "writers' blocks."

I stroll behind the women sitting around the large round table.

The shape makes it difficult for any one woman to dominate the conversation. There are no corners to hide in, or push anyone into.

On my infinite circle, in my practiced nigh-subliminal murmur, I say, "Let this doll take your burden. Give it your fear and frustration, your anger and anguish, the sadness of your soul. Create a vessel for your emotions while you take the power of its purity. Create your own salvation. Use your power of creation to create a gift for a child in need."

The women bow their heads over their work. Their oily scalps, visible in their parted hair, gleam like wet roads.

I stop talking and the only sounds are hands on cloth, fingertips on plastic, and the mouth-breathing of intense concentration.

Then one woman starts speaking with the erratic speeding-and-stopping of a person who has learned English late in life.

She launches into the same old complaint of suspecting her husband is cheating on her with one of their mutual friends. Half the women lean in and feed her suspicions in gleeful schadenfreude. The other half lean back, tired or frustrated with her weary tale.

I'm behind one of these frustrated women so I look at her work over her shoulder.

"Very nice, Diane," I whisper. "Looks like you're almost done."

The toddler-sized doll she's working on has dark brown hair and alderwood skin, pink cheeks and full red lips. Sensual, almost, if not for the eerie black holes where the eyes are supposed to be. It's always unsettled me, that sight. Sweat makes my armpits slick. I should shed my lab coat but I like it as a barrier between me and the other women. It prevents our doctor-patient relationship from dissolving into friendship.

"Why haven't you put the eyes in yet?" I say.

Diane glances up at the edge in my voice. My patients, past and present, always make dolls that look similar to themselves. Diane has made a doll that's nearly her opposite, but with one unsettling similarity: her pale blue eyes are just as empty as the doll's.

"I don't like the colors today," she whispers back, pointing at the plastic tray of pea-green eyeballs staring up at the florescent lights. They look like slime-filled warts on a toad's back.

"They're the only ones that came in the order," I say. "They'll send different ones in the next shipment."

"Fucking Chinks," she says. Another glance at me. "Oh, sorry, Doctor Galvante."

"No offense taken," I say lightly through a tight smile. "I'm Filipino, not Chinese."

"Right," says Diane. Her smile is as vague as her knowledge of Asia.

"Would you like to share anything today?"

"Not today. I just came to finish my doll."

"Thank you for your thoughtfulness. But...can I ask why you made the doll look so different from you? Does she look like a mother or sister? A girlfriend or lover? Would you like to share your doll's story?" It would give valuable clues to Diane's anger issues.

Her vague smile sharpens into a fox-like grin. "Sure I'll share something. I want brown eyes for my doll. I don't want green eyes. I want the brown ones we had last week."

"These are the only eyes we have today." I become aware that our voices have risen above the group-therapy murmur and the other women are now watching our power play. What the hell is Diane trying to do?

"Diane, these group sessions are about establishing harmony," I say to the women around the table. "It's about exploring our pasts and righting wrongs that were done to us, but more importantly, taking responsibility for and righting the wrongs we have done in the universe. What have we realized—" I spread my hands over their heads as if I'm bestowing this magic realization all over again, "—about the world when people start using phrases like 'I want' and 'I need'?"

"It's selfish?" Jessica Nutters says in her wispy little-girl voice.

"It's more than that," says Vicky Delacruz, gazing around the table, dark eyes as beady as spit-shined bullets. "When people start using I phrases, the conversation becomes all about them. You lose focus of the harmony in the world. You take and demand without a thought for the deficit you're creating. You—"

"Let's keep it positive, Vicky," I say.

She stumbles to a stop. Vicky is on the brink of her own personal epiphany. I recognize the signs: agitation, passion, discontent. She no longer feels comfortable in the world she's constructed. It fits like a coat she's outgrown. Soon she'll have to emerge from, or suffocate within, her cocoon. One hopes she makes the right choice.

I lead the conversation to the outcome I want.

"The universe provides for us," I say. "For example, I have a burning desire to help. And all of you, with your innumerable, wonderful differences, needed someone to illuminate a few steps in your life paths. The universe somehow brought us together. It provides what we need, which is sometimes not what we want. We are always in the middle of our own personal Hells. But only in retrospect do we see how we got there, and in doing so, we see the way out."

The women nod at phrases I memorized off Facebook memes. It's mostly the presentation: me with my arms spread wide, standing purposely in front of the window so the light makes it hard to see my face. For a moment, we all believe.

A car horn bleats outside, breaking the spell. I check my watch. Three o'clock.

"Looks like I kept you a little over time," I say. "Instead of putting the finished dolls for the foster kids in my office, you can just leave them on the table. And Jenna…" I wait until my newest patient makes eye contact with me. "Unfinished dolls go in the cupboard in the back. No one else uses this conference room. It'll be safe."

When the limb-less, bald, and eye-less dolls are put away, we join hands hastily and say our parting mantra for mental and emotional self-preservation: "Anywhere but here, any time but now, anything but this."

Then a flurry of scarves and coats and purses leaves the room.

I'm pleased to see four dolls on the table. In a strange twist of fate, their feet happen to point in the four cardinal directions. The north doll has blonde sausage curls and squinty blue eyes, and it's wearing a simple white dress. West doll, in a tomboyish buffalo check shirt and overalls, has short black hair and blue eyes. South doll has straight red hair, brown eyes, and it's wearing a jaunty yellow jumpsuit. The last doll is Diane's dark-haired doll, now dressed in jeans and a green sweater, pointing in the direction from which all things begin. The east doll.

Diane never put in the eyes. Did she forget to put the doll in her cubby? It stares with tenebrous sockets at a ceiling already growing dim in these short winter days. I can't stand the sight so I hastily pop in two green eyes.

At once the room seems a little brighter and I feel a little better. More tired though. And I'm glad when elderly Mrs. Dychingco comes in backwards, dragging her cleaning cart into the conference room.

"Hi, Mrs. Dychingco," I say to alert her to my presence.

She jumps anyway, whirls around, glances uneasily at the dolls the table. "Oh, I didn't know you were still in here, Doctor Galvante. I'll come back when you're done."

"It's fine. I'm done. Our group ran over time. Sorry, I should be the one apologizing for messing up your routine."

Mrs. Dychingco's smile is small but warm on her round, pock-marked face.

"Would you mind getting some boxes from my office?" I say. "Four... No, just three. They're right on my desk. Plain brown boxes."

She leaves, then comes back. I have to cross the room to her because she won't come within six feet of the dolls.

"I know, I know," I say. "Still our secret, right *Lola*?" It's not the first time I use the Tagalog word for grandmother to cajole her into silence.

She shakes her head and clucks her tongue in disapproval as I shroud the dolls in tissue then lay them inside the toddler-sized shipping boxes.

"Be careful," she says. "It's not good to use things that...sick people have made." She speaks softly to me even though I'm much younger and, traditionally, she has the right to chastise and rebuke me however she sees fit. But I'm a doctor, and American-raised. Two things which, in her mind, elevate me enough to warrant respect reserved for men and presidents.

I blow my bangs off my forehead as I lay the last doll into her cardboard sarcophagus. I've tried to tell Mrs. Dychingco what I'm really doing, but only obliquely because I'm worried she'll let it slip to one of my colleagues sharing this psychiatric clinic. Maybe it's time to be more plain about the truth.

"I'm righting a wrong," I say. "What I'm doing... It's to restore balance in the universe."

She closes the door, then stands in front of me, lips pinched and arms folded.

"Those women," I say, gesturing at the door Mrs. Dychingco just closed, "are the bored, depressed, ignored, domesticated wives of tech employees that have moved into our town. Tech workers who offer three, four times as much rent, cash in hand, to live here, because they love the small-town feel of our city. They're killing us with their love, Mrs. Dychingco! They're driving out people who have lived here for decades. Second and third generation, some even fourth-generation families. People who are descendants of the original 49ers. Some of them are young enough to start over some-where else. Some are lucky enough to have kids or relatives they can move in with. But many of them can't do either. They leave their homes unwillingly, then haunt the area like living ghosts, sleeping in their cars, moving from abandoned lot to abandoned lot. They're old or infirm, childless or with adult kids who don't want them, or kids who've died serving their country. They're unable to start over elsewhere. Their lives are here. It's not right. Don't you feel it?"

I set Diane's doll by my purse so I won't forget it and start taping up the three packed dolls. "I sell these dolls to other rich women. I call the dolls hand-made, one-of-a-kind, and all profits go to charity. None of those are lies. Who do I hurt? Those women, they'll pay hundreds, multiplied exponentially by how many trendy words I can attach to the dolls. And that money, which means nothing to them, means the world to those whose worlds they've taken. It means food, clothing, fees for a place to park their car-home for a week, shoes, medications for illnesses that only develop in the homeless. I am doing what I can, even if it's not enough."

She shakes her head again but her arms drop and her look of skepticism softens into sadness. "Are you doing it to help them, or to help yourself feel better?"

I stack the boxes, place Diane's doll on top, and head towards the door while saying what I think is a pretty good "last word" to end the conversation. "Isn't charity always a little bit of both?"

Then I have to gesture with my head for Mrs. Dychingco to open the door. Twice, because the first time she doesn't get it. Then I wait for her to open it. All this ruins my dramatic exit but in the end, I'm glad to leave her presence. She always makes me feel like I have to justify myself to her.

The post office is full, hot, humid, but thankfully it has two large sliding doors that are constantly swooshing open and shut, letting in a snappy, refreshing breeze that smells like a mélange of burgers, pho, and burritos from nearby restaurants.

I slide my boxes along the counter as the line moves forward.

Do I need stamps? Maybe I should get some stamps. God, what would I even use them for. Those ode-to-comic-book-heroes stamps look cool, though. I'll get a booklet of those. Are they still called book—

The Imperial March emits from my purse. I've gotten an email in a professional account. Either patient-related or...

Hm, it's about the dolls. One doll, specifically.

The email is from Emilia Zhang, the woman whose name and backstory I purchased to market the dolls. Very chic but approachable, adequate hints and touches of past trauma, a spiritual renaissance, self-taught but mentored by ethnic-sounding grandparents. I don't even know how much of her backstory is true, but so far it's held up to internet searches. People love her and her dolls. She loves the passive income.

The one unstated rule we have in our relationship, for mutual safety and deniability, is no direct contact unless absolutely necessary. I'm next up for the postal clerk windows so I only scan her email.

Something about issues with one of the dolls...something moving or not moving...damaged mouth. There's no mention of the customer demanding a refund though, so I tap out a hasty reply: "Remind the customer that the dolls are collectibles and not meant to be played with, don't move them too much, don't mess with their faces, etc. Offer 15% off next purchase and free shipping. Thanks."

Then I put the issue out of mind as I'm called up to the next open window.

"Hi, Doctor Galvante," says Marcus, the young heartbreaker with dark curls and dimples. He takes my packages. "How's it going? What's with the Mini-Me?"

"Huh?"

He nods at Diane's doll, tucked under my arm, and says, "Looks like a mini version of you."

Well shit, now that he points it out, it kind of does. Only the doll has green eyes. Mine are brown. I glance at my jeans and green sweater, which aren't the same but are eerily similar to the doll's clothes.

I hope Marcus doesn't connect the doll to the boxes I'm shipping, which I ship regularly, and which I've told him contain all sorts of boring things like yarn, socks, little toys from the dollar store, which I ship to the children of old high school friends. The usual chintzy adult-selected presents for preteen birthdays.

"A friend bought it for me," I say. "Because she thought it looks like me."

Marcus finishes weighing my packages and gives me the total. "Need any stamps today?"

"Sure. Those comic book stamps."

"How many?"

"Uh, how are they sold. Booklets? A book?"

He snorts. "They're sheets now, Doc. You buy them by the sheet or roll. Ten on a sheet."

"I'll take that."

He gives me the stamps on what looks like a short bookmark. I give him the cash and a pleasant goodbye. As I'm crossing the threshold of the post office, the Imperial March plays again. Another email from Emilia Zhang. I step out of the way of a hassled hipster carrying his folding bike.

By the end of the email, I don't know whether to laugh or scream.

"HA HA HA," I tap an email back to Emilia. "YOU TOTALLY GOT ME! Seriously, tho, Emilia. Are you okay? Your email is a little...unsettling. Dolls don't move on their own, hon. Did you take something again? Should I come over?"

I read and reread the last line of her long, blabbering, nearly nonsensical email: THeY KNow, they know, ttheyknowthetknoqthetknow \ and they're getting at me. at me. at me.

I send her a text in case she doesn't check her email right away: I'm coming over. Now.

She's close. Her apartment is just six blocks away at the other end of the main street bisecting downtown. Close enough to walk to, and during dinnertime, when this area is gridlocked with out-of-towners trying to get to the sushi bars and falafel bistros, it's faster to walk than drive. The sun has fully set, but there's still enough light for the redwood trees to cast a jagged-teeth silhouette against a blood-red sky by the time I reach her top-floor condo. Emilia answers the door, wearing gray sweats, a gray sweatshirt, and a pink beanie, which flattens her jet hair against her fever-flushed forehead.

Inside is sweltering. The muggy heat smells of body odor and uncleaned litter box. I put Diane's doll and my purse on the recliner near the door, then I go to the thermostat and turn down the heat.

"I'm cold," Emilia says, pouting.

"It's almost a hundred degrees in here," I say. "Are you sick?"

"Flu," she says.

"Goddamnit." I fish around in my purse, take out my anti-bacterial gel, and squirt a drop onto the finger that touched her thermostat.

"I'm almost over it," she says defensively. "That means I'm not that contagious any more."

"Yeah, but that also means you're taking meds for it still, right? What have you taken, Emilia?"

"Cold medicine I had delivered."

I scan her living room for medicine bottles. She's made a nest on her ash-gray sofa. Thick, knitted brown blankets and big pillows surround a cozy hole. On her apothecary chest/coffee table are a well-worn worry stone, whole-grain crackers, bottled aloe-water, laptop and tablet, rosary, phone, and a box of tissues, all within reach. A silver waste bin is between the table and sofa. It's half-full of Kleenex. And four empty bottles of over-the-counter flu medication.

"Those have pseudoephedrine in them," I say. "How much have you been taking? A normal person doesn't go through four bottles in the course of one flu!"

"It was a bad flu," she says. "The news said people died of it on the east coast."

"Yeah, old people whose immune systems were already taxed. Not young, healthy people like us. Emilia, tell me you didn't take more than what's recommended on the bottle." I push her towards the couch and go to her kitchen to get her a pitcher full of water.

"That stuff causes hallucinations," I say over my shoulder. "It's highly regulated for God's sake. I don't even know how you got four bottles at once." And the ammonia stench of cat piss and feces, confined in her apartment, can't be helping. The fat orange source of said piss and feces is on top of the fridge, tracking me with disinterest belied by its twitching tail.

I bring the pitcher of water to Emilia, who has tunneled into her blanket pile so only her face and hands, illuminated by the cold white light of her open laptop, are exposed. She looks like a newly dead corpse rising from a grave of freshly-turned earth.

The heat of her fever is a radiant warmth as I sit next to her.

"Here," she says, turning the laptop so I can see.

The video is already playing. The point of view is from high up. Higher than an average ceiling. And the room is better than an average room. A personal library or study of some sort, with a big, ostentatious table in the middle of the room. There's a computer screen on the table's corner. The computer seems to be on because it gives a sheen to the leather of the wood-framed rolling chair behind the desk. And beyond and around the desk are walls and walls of books. It's too dim to read the titles; the only light besides the computer screen comes from a flickering source under the camera. But I'm sure I could read the titles if the light was strong enough. That's how good the camera is.

Everything is still. The two indications that this is not a looping video of nothing, nor a still shot or lagging image, are the erratic flickering of an off-screen fire, and the time stamp in the lower right corner ticking seconds towards midnight.

Something's about to happen, though. Emilia sinks into her blanket-grave until only her dark eyes show. Her pupils are dilated enough to let a pencil through.

From the depths of her blanket-grave, she murmurs an incomprehensible warning.

I turn to ask her what she's said, almost missing it. Movement behind the desk.

There it is again!

What...

The chair. Turning. Slowly. By itself.

The tropic heat in the apartment plummets to bone-chilling clamminess. The hair on my nape stands on end. I shiver, watching the chair rotating on its axis until it's facing away from the desk. Turned by unseen hands.

"Impossible," I whisper hoarsely. "A fucking prank or something. Who sent this?"

"Keep watching," Emilia whispers back and I realize she hadn't had the heater on high to battle the cold of winter nor the chills of the flu, but the chill that comes from witnessing something supernatural, otherworldly, perhaps even something truly, evilly inhuman.

The chair spins slowly the other way, back toward its original position. And something is sitting on it. The toddler-sized doll sitting on the chair is pulling on the desk's edge, turning the chair to face the desk.

"Impossi—"

Something grabs my left arm and I scream, look down, see only Emilia's bony fingers squeezing me tight.

"Are you seeing it?" she says from the depths of her blanket-grave.

"Yeah," I say. "Someone's just pranking us." It'd be easy to hide behind such a massive desk, rotate that big chair without being seen, position a doll and its hand so it looks like it's pulling itself into position.

But it would take Jim Henson-talent to make a doll pick up a pencil between its fat, single-jointed fingers, and punch precisely at the computer keyboard. Its large glossy eyes reflect the white rectangle of a document but I can't make out any words.

"It's one of ours, isn't it?" says Emilia.

"I think so."

"Do you...know anything about it?"

I shake my head. We've been pulling this racket for almost three years now, shipping several dozen dolls per year. Each one is different, and it's like meeting people at a party; it's hard to remember names and distinguishing features if there's no attachment formed.

"Impossible," I say again. It's impossible to recall specifics.

The only distinguishing thing about this doll is it has a punched-in, broken mouth. That means it has a plastic face. The earlier dolls my patients made were rag, then yarn, some clay, then, once I had enough seed money to buy doll-making supplies and a contract with some small businesses for things difficult to obtain or process—like realistic hair—we started making plastic dolls.

This creepy doll, plastic, would've been made about a year ago at most.

"You keep saying impossible," Emilia says. "But the way you're saying it makes me think you know something is pretty plausible about all this."

I look at her, then break eye contact, remembering Mrs. Dychingco's warning about the dolls. If it's a prank, it's a poorly-timed one because the doll keeps pecking at the keyboard. The time for denouement is long over, the joke, growing stale.

Then a noise comes from offscreen, startling me; I'd thought the film was a silent surveillance video. The doll seems shocked too; the pencil falls from its grip and clatters to the floor. It slumps against the chair as if its invisible puppet strings have been severed.

"Amanda?" calls a male voice. "Amanda, I'm home. Uh, where you at, hon?"

A tall man with dark wavy hair, wearing a dark suit, comes in while he's shrugging off his suit jacket.

"Amanda," he sings. "Where are you?"

Then he pauses at the sight of the doll in his chair, chuckles, leaves the room with his suit jacket tossed over one shoulder.

His voice fades out.

Emilia reaches over and fast-forwards the video. The flickering orange light dies down until the room is dark except for a sickly bluish light coming in from unseen windows. Then room lights flash on. Everything is illuminated more crisply than before. The doll is still in the chair and, in normal lighting, looks harmless. The man from earlier stands at the threshold. He hasn't changed out of his shirt and suit pants, which look rumpled now. His hair is disheveled. His gaze darts around the room. Still looking for Amanda.

He takes his phone out, dials, leaves the room but his shadow remains across the threshold.

"Hello, yes. I'd like to report a missing person. No. Uh, just a few hours, but... I understand, but... Listen, please, listen to me. The balcony doors in our bedroom are broken. Things are on the ground—makeup, perfume bottles, picture frames." With a quivering but soft voice, he lists his observations, adds hastily, "Obviously, uh, something's happened. Please send help...

"I don't think so. I've been in the house for hours now... I appreciate the concern, and I'll call a neighbor, but I don't want to leave in case... All right, I'll wait outside."

Emilia fast-forwards the film again. The doll stays still the entire time, even when the man, accompanied by a smaller but older man in a green jogging suit and two uniformed cops come into the room. Emilia doesn't let up on the fast-forward, saying, "It's not important until..."

She lets it go. It's only the man and he drags his feet as he crosses the room. He moves the doll to his desktop, lays it down gently because it's probably Amanda's doll, and collapses into his chair. He leans forward and hides his face in his hands for a moment.

The doll sits up in front of him.

When the man raises his face from his hands, he yells out in fright.

"Dan?" calls a man from offscreen. "You all right? Dan!"

The older man comes in, freezes, confused. "Dan?"

Dan, the man looking for Amanda, scoots his chair back. The doll lifts its arm to point at the computer screen.

"This isn't funny, Dan," says the older man.

"What the fuck, Mike," says Dan at the same time.

Mike, the small older man, strides to the desk. His jogging pants make *wish-wish* noises. He waves a hand over the doll's head.

"This is a pretty elaborate joke to play on an old man," says Mike. "Amanda? You can come out now! Very funny and more than a little weird. How you doing this? Magnets or something? You kids..."

Dan leans forward and presses a key on the keyboard. His face pales with illumination from the reawakened screen. His eyes glide back and forth quickly, reading. Then he stares at Mike.

"What?" says Mike.

"Uh, it's some kind of ransom note or something," Dan rasps.

"Let me see it," says Mike. Gaze firmly on the doll, which he gives wide berth, Mike circles the desk to stand beside Dan. He reads silently, then aloud a few times, repeating phrases as if trying to grasp their meaning.

Then Dan mutters, "I see words I know but I can barely understand what they mean. 'Contact Emilia Zhang'? Who the fuck is that. 'I have your wife. I will kill her if Emilia Zhang refuses to come. I will kill her if she's not here within the week. I will kill her if you tell anyone about this. I will kill her if you contact the police.' Well, that's that then, right? The police were here already. I didn't see this note. I didn't see this note!"

"And what's with the fucking doll?" says Mike.

The doll topples over, then drags itself to the keyboard. It jerks its hand toward Dan.

"I don't understand," Dan says in a hoarse voice. "What do you want from us?"

"I think it wants that pencil on the ground," Mike says, retrieving it. Grasping it by the eraser, he leans over Dan and gives the pencil to the doll.

Again, the doll pecks at the keyboard.

"Bring...me...Emilia...Zhang," reads Mike.

"This is some kind of sick joke!" Dan roars as he rises, right hand swinging to deliver a backhand blow to the doll.

Mike gets between them. "Don't! This is your only link to Amanda. Don't sever it."

The doll types one more thing, then collapses with a thud on the desk. It seems to lose a bit of luster, a bit of color, and somehow, I'm sure that whatever presence animated the doll has fled, been vanquished, extinguished, or fallen asleep, at least for the moment.

And I'm just as sure that what I've seen is impossible. As impossible as Mrs. Dychingco's implied meanings when she warned me about using dolls made by "sick people," as impossible as the many things I've seen and experienced and learned on my visits to the witch doctors in the unmapped territories of the Philippine rainforests. And I'm just as sure that I have to go in Emilia's stead. There's no way she can go in the state she's in. Besides, she's just the front-woman, the brand. Our online doll empire is ninety-nine percent me.

I wait for instructions or a video plea but the tape ends.

"An elaborate prank, right?" says Emilia, lowering the blankets around her head to her shoulders, emerging from her blanket-grave.

"Did he send a note? Their address?"

Emilia opens a file on her laptop. It's a long, rambling, frightened and frustrated letter from Dan, first apologizing profusely in case it's a prank, then pleading with Emilia to come, then threatening lawsuits, of all things. People use the weapons most familiar to them. From this note, I gather Dan is some kind of lawyer, or someone my gamer friends would call Lawful Good. He is ill equipped to deal with the Chaotic, perhaps Evil nature of this situation.

In that thread, I'm obligated to go. To bring balance to the universe.

This is my fault.

"Can you book me a flight to..." I double-check the email, "LAX? This is from Beverly Hills."

"At least it's not too far," says Emilia, coming out of her cocoon some more. She looks relieved.

"You didn't think I'd make you go, did you?"

She gives me a weak smile. "Wouldn't be the first time I got sent to the slaughter."

"Yeah, well..." I get up and retrieve my purse from the recliner.

Emilia screams.

"What is it?" I freeze, frightened by the fear in that shriek.

"One of the dolls...is right...behind you."

My eyes feel like they're going to pop out. Everything is clear and sharp and suddenly very, very cold. I turn only my head.

And come face to face with myself.

Relief makes me so lightheaded I collapse on the apothecary chest/coffee table.

"This is just a doll one of my patients made," I say and pick it up, shake it between us to show it's completely flaccid like a... well, like a rag doll.

"Oh, who's that one going to?"

"Me, actually. Thought I'd keep this one. Has a lot of...personality, don't you think? And doesn't it look like me?" I put the doll up next to my face and grin. "Twinsies!"

"You're fucking crazy. Give me your credit card. Aisle or window?"

———

Before the flight, I shower and change at Emilia's place and borrow her largest slacks and blouse to fit my curvier frame. I put on some basic makeup, then blow dry my hair and pull it back into a low, polished pony tail. My only shoe options, though, are the heels I wore to the psych clinic that morning or a pair of tennis shoes Emilia got online that turned out to be a size too big for her but were too much of a hassle to return. A pair of bright pink tennis shoes. Emilia says they barely show because her slacks hang long on me, so I choose those over the heels.

I also borrow a plain canvas duffel bag that probably costs ten times what I'd think reasonable, which I fill with my jeans and sweater from the day, a spare outfit of slacks and a merino wool sweater, a pair of Emilia's yoga pants and matching sweatshirt, some of her panties, and my heels.

"Don't think you're leaving your creepy doll here," says Emilia.

"It'll probably just be for a day," I say, exasperated. "And there's no more room left in my carry-on."

"If you leave it, I will douse it in nail polish remover and burn it in my bathtub."

"Fine! God!" I take out half the clothes and stuff my doll inside.

After syncing our phones so she can track me, I leave for the train to the airport. The hour-long flight gives me no time to do anything but worry so I practice some self-guided meditation to calm myself with thoughts of "anywhere but here, any time but now, anything but this."

By the time the plane's wheels touch ground, my state of mind is as calm and still as a thick tome in the basement of a vast library.

I even manage a cheerful exchange with my Uber driver, who seems keen on driving into Beverly Hills. We both rubberneck at the mansions we pass.

In the Bay Area, estates hold houses like cupped flames, far from the road and neighbors. One could drive miles and miles down a one-lane dirt road and unwittingly pass half a dozen billionaires' homes. Here, despite some effort at privacy hedges, many of the houses can be seen from their front gates.

"Here's your stop," says my Uber driver. "Oh man, you didn't tell me they're having a party."

Every light is on in the two-story house, every path and walkway glowing with safety lights, and the front door is open, letting a trapezoid of illumination spill down the front steps and pool on the gravel driveway.

"I don't think it's that kind of party," I mutter. "You can just drop me off here."

"I can go all the way up to the house if you can get them to open the gate," he says.

"Here is fine. I can get in through the guard entrance." I nod at the wrought-iron door, which has been left open, as if expecting me.

"Suit yourself," he says morosely.

I get out and he drives off as soon as the car door loses contact with my hand. The spray of gravel would've drawn blood if I'd been wearing a skirt.

"Anywhere but here, any time but now, anything but this," I say to myself as I enter the estate of Daniel and Amanda Stoffer.

⟨∞⟩

As soon as my foot touches the gravel walkway on the other side of the gate, a feeling of trepidation stiffens my muscles. I shrug, roll my neck in an attempt to shake it off, but the feeling of being gripped doesn't leave. It only makes me scuttle faster towards the brightness of the open door. My duffle bag bangs against my thigh.

A tall silhouette darkens the threshold. I freeze just as I enter the light, unable to make out the face.

"Mr. Stoffer?" I say. "I'm...Emilia Zhang." For a second, I'd almost given my real name.

"Please call me Dan," he says as he steps out. Rote politeness seems to have overridden our fear. "Come in." He holds out his hand and I grasp it for a handshake but he yanks me inside.

"I came as soon as I could," I say. "Why is your door op—"

The intense smell of bleach gives me a choking answer.

In the foyer, against the wall closest to the door, there's a helter-skelter hill of gray luggage, speckled with something dark. Looks like they got shoved out of the way.

On the ground before them, the pale gray marble floor is as dull as etched glass, chemically scuffed by bleach. It's a man-sized etch mark, with a trail leading out of the room. At that doorway, leaning against the wall, is a mop with its head submerged in one of those big orange five-gallon buckets from Home Depot.

I piece it together: the doll has killed somebody.

"Did you call the cops again?" I say. "Is there a dead cop on the premises?" If so, I need to get somewhere with no extradition agreement.

"Uh, no," says Dan, running a hand through his dark hair. Auburn, a magazine would say. He's pale for a Californian, but fit. It's the pallor of someone who'd burn rather than tan. "I was just sitting down to dinner. Please join me."

Without waiting for a response, as if he's used to people agreeing with him, and people probably do, he turns his back on me and leaves the foyer. I take a quick glance around the octagonal foyer as large as a two-car garage. Three arched exits. One on the left, leading to a narrow hallway, a large one in the center, through which I can see into an entertaining room of plush beige sofas and low pale-wood end tables. Through the patio doors at the far end, I can see half of a large oval pool emanating the nuclear-blue of submerged pool lights.

I wonder where that library/study is—the one that was in the video.

I put my duffel bag by the door on the opposite side of where someone died.

"Mr. Stoffer, can we talk first?" I say, following him into the archway on the right, through a hallway that passes a dining room with a giant chandelier made of elk horns, and into a large kitchen. What real estate agents would call a gourmet kitchen. The thought crystalizes my initial impression of this house-that's-not-a-home. No personal touches. No painted family portraits on the wall. No cheesy souvenirs, no monogramed throw blankets, no personal-ized, engraved vases. It looks like Dan and Amanda Stoffer have just moved in or are in the process of moving out.

The only indication of life is the granite-topped kitchen island with built-in breakfast counter. Dan Stoffer is seated on a stool. Before him is a spread of old takeout boxes, frozen dinner trays, and plastic clamshells, like he pushes garbage out of the way to make room for the latest meal. Tonight's meal looks like noodles, fried rice, and pungent morsels in a reddish-brown glaze.

"Mr. Stoffer, what was on that video you sent?" I say.

"Please." He motions for me to sit on the stool next to him. "I insist."

I sit two stools over and swivel to face him. He serves me noodles and brown morsels. Then he holds up a bottle of wine and gives me a questioning look.

"I don't drink when I travel," I say. "Water is fine."

He looks annoyed, like I'm spoiling his plans to roofie me. "You're no fun. OJ at least? Has added calcium! Women need calcium!"

Internally, I wince. "Sure."

He pours me OJ from the fridge, then hands the glass to me with a grin, "Bottoms up!" and chinks his wineglass against my orange juice.

I drink more than half, despite the chalky calcium taste, thirsty from the flight.

Dan takes a drink and grins as he swallows. The edges of his teeth are pinkened by wine.

"Where's the doll, Mr. Stoffer?"

"Call me Dan. Please." He mixes all the food on his plate into a beige mess, shoves a forkful into his mouth. Again he grins but this time with his lips closed, cheeks rising, eyes squinting in a nigh-grimace. He chinks my glass again, washes down his food with wine, eyeing me with disapproval until I drink my juice out of politeness.

"The doll," I say. "Where is it now?"

"Yes, how did it get into my house?" he says, suddenly menacing, muscles taut on his neck, tightening on his arms as he clenches his utensils.

I take the receipt out of my purse and put it on the counter between us. Anticipating his question, I'd printed it at Emilia's house.

"Your wife ordered it," I say. "Handmade by...me."

"What is it?" he whispers.

"Just a doll," I say. "Tell me where it is. Did you do something to it, Mr. Stof— Dan?"

"It said it would tell me where Amanda is when you got here," says Dan. He swirls his food around on his plate. "It said not to call the cops. It said not to tell anyone about it, and it would return Amanda to me. I obeyed."

He snarls the word; he's unaccustomed to it.

"Mike meant well," he says. "Mikey... He's always looked out for me. He uh, said he was going to go for help. She didn't want us to leave. She didn't have to do it but Mikey, he... He..."

Dan bows his head and covers his face. I look down to give him privacy in his despair. On the ground, I see that the bleach-etched scuff marks continue like an abrasion across the lustrous kitchen tiles. A scar leading towards the garage.

Despite the feeling of dread and growing surety, I hop off my stool and follow the trail to its end. I open the garage door and peer into the darkness, discerning only two large car-shaped lumps lit by streetlamp lights coming in through frosted garage door windows. I smell the unmistakeable mineral-metal scent of blood, a tinge of meat beginning to spoil, the bad egg smell of pierced offal. I feel for the light switch.

As white light floods the garage, I see I've interrupted someone in the process of dismembering the body of Mike the Neighbor. He's naked on a blue tarp. The cutting implement is a hacksaw. There are three broken, bloody hacksaw blades neatly piled at the foot of the body, and child-sized footprints to and from the broken body and the broken saws.

I'm glad I didn't eat any of the food. It'd be joining the mound of organs on the tarp. Lightheaded from the smell of blood and the sight of the...the body, I grasp the doorframe to steady myself.

"When Mike and I were having dinner, it drugged us, you see," says Dan. His voice is loud. Close.

I try to turn to see where he is, but everything moves so quickly. I feel like I'm falling, then I am, with the blue tarp rushing up to meet me. I am spun like a lost kite.

Then Dan's cloud-filled face is over me, talking in a loud reverberating voice. "It drugged us and killed Mike...I'm sorry."

I'm sinking down, down, and the garage is getting darker and darker. There's something important I have to do, but I can't remember... Something very important!

Flailing, I grab ahold of something warm and firm. "Don't!" I say.

"Don't what?" asks a warbling, rumbling voice.

"Don't... Don't..."...something.

I am beyond speaking. As I slip beyond knowing, I have one final, brilliant spark of memory from a fading childhood: Admiral Ackbar yelling, "It's a trap!"

I wake slowly enough to know, by the time I open my eyes, where I am, how much time might have passed, and why I'm here.

The doll squats with its back to me.

From its squatting height, I estimate it's taller than other dolls, as tall as a three-year-old. Its soft blond curls, bouncing with the effort the doll is putting into shoving the hacksaw back and forth over an elbow joint, and its plump plastic arms and legs, evoke Shirley Temple. It's wearing a torn white grocery bag as an apron. Its arms are through the handles and the back is sloppily taped shut.

"Where's Dan?" I say. Then I remember on the video, its mouth was damaged; it can't speak.

The doll turns and regards me with deep blue eyes. Striking, lapis lazuli beads that had cost a fortune to order but I'd seen them in the doll parts catalogue and had been curious about them.

And beneath those beautiful gems is a mess of jawbone and flapping sinew, attached to the top half of the doll's face by wires and springs. I try to get up to flee but I'm bound to something immovable and wedged between the wall and a white car.

"Emilia Zhang?" it says. It's the voice of a middle-aged woman, maybe forty-something. Its words are well-enunciated for such a horrible mouth, as I knew they would be. As long as a doll has a mouth, it can speak.

"Ye-yes."

"You made this doll?"

"Yes. Where's Dan? Where's Amanda?"

The doll laughs a rumbling, leonine laugh.

It rises and moves aside to show me a prone body in a pool of blood. It lifts the head to show me Dan's bloody face in a rictus of horrified disbelief.

"Uh, what are you doing, Amanda?" the doll says in a parody of Dan's speaking style as it moves Dan's head. "Why are you leaving me, Amanda? Uh, I'll do anything for you, Amanda. Idiot!"

Enough strength has returned for me to push and pull myself up to a sitting position with my hands tied tight behind my back. The way it digs into my wrists, feels like a zip tie or something thin with sharp edges.

I rock forward and whatever is behind me clatters like it's full of metal. A tool table maybe.

"Are you...Amanda?" I say.

The doll drops Dan's head with a squelch, spraying blood that almost reaches me.

"How do I get back into my body?" says the doll. Amanda. The missing wife.

"Was he hurting you?" I say. "Is that why you fled into the doll?"

"Fled? So it's real. I'm not crazy. You know what's going on. You can tell me, right?" She comes closer, brandishing the hacksaw, dotting the garage floor with blood.

I look from the blood to the saw to the bodies to the saw to her face and her menacing eyes and her stalking steps. Dan wasn't hurting her. She hadn't fled into the doll. She'd been lured by it. Something sinister in it had called to a need within her.

"I don't know what you're talking about," I say as she stops at the corner of the white car's bumper.

"Yes you do, Emilia Zhang. You know what's happening to me and how to stop it." She grips my hair, pulls up to expose my neck. I'm blinded by the overhead garage lights. I feel the hacksaw blade on my neck, the drip of something cool and viscous slipping into the hollow of my throat.

"You can't go back," I say.

"Yes...I...can!" she grits out. "I've always been able to get back into my body."

That means she's done this often. I can't let her get into her body now, escape, and leave me to explain everything.

"There's no way," I say. "This time was different somehow. You did something wrong."

"You're useless!" she says.

The pressure of the hacksaw eases but only because she's drawing it back for a killing blow.

"Wait!" I say. "Take me to your body. I might be able to do something."

Amanda laughs that rumbling laugh; I feel more than hear it. She lets me go and disappears behind the car. "Never mind, Emilia Zhang." I hear the car door open and shut.

The car comes to life with a throat-clearing roar.

"Amanda?" I say. Is she leaving? It's fine if she leaves; I'll get loose. As long as Dan obeyed her and didn't tell anyone I'll have time to get free and get away.

The car door opens and shuts, then she reappears a moment later but doesn't come closer.

"You'll tell me or you die," she yells above the engine's burr. "Let's see how you hold up against an impending death you can prevent."

She stands there, staring at me, and I rack my brain about what I might've said to change her mind. What clue did I give her?

"There's nothing you can do," I say. "You're trapped in the doll. Let me help you. Take me to your body."

She doesn't say anything, doesn't move, maybe trying to fake me out but I know she's in there and waiting. The garage ceiling gets hazy with exhaust. Moments later, it gets hazy because I can't focus on it.

"Tell me how to get back into my body," says Amanda.

"You can't," I say, barely able to summon the energy to breathe. "You...are done."

"And you...are dead. Well, going to die. Carbon monoxide will kill you while I watch."

I answer her with a stubborn glare. It'll take hours.

But black dots are starting to appear in my vision.

"In case you didn't know," she says, "carbon monoxide sinks in cool temperatures, like early morning in midwinter. Tell me how to get back into my body, and I'll leave you a cell phone."

The black dots are getting bigger and bleeding into each other. I'm losing myself. But it'll be on my own terms. I take a deep breath and the blackness engulfs me.

"Anywhere but here, any time but now, anything but this."

"What did you say?" Amanda says.

Anywhere but here, any time but now, anything but this.

I open my eyes to a different darkness. Then I see a hole of light. I poke my finger in the light and pull down. The zipper slides open.

There's not enough time to stop and meditate in this body to fully meld my consciousness into it. I have to do it as I go if I want to catch Amanda while she's still in the garage.

Stiffly, I pull myself out of my canvas cocoon, trip on the zipper as I take a step. I fall face first on the marble. It hurts like none of the other dolls have hurt before. Immediate and sharp. The good part is that it means I'm somehow magically attuned to this body. It fits me, I fit it. The bad part is it means I'll feel pain like the plastic body is my flesh.

Fine. It's all fine. The universe has given me an advantage, I think, to balance out Amanda's advantages: she knows this house, she's been in her doll body longer than I've been in this one.

I follow the sound of a car engine on idle which, because the house is so empty and bereft of things to absorb noise, clearly comes from one direction. The door to the garage is shut and the knob is out of reach. I drag a stool over, climb it to reach the knob, then pull. The door is heavy. I yank on it, hard, then jump through the gap, hoping it doesn't shut on my leg.

I make it through. The engine's noise covers the sound of my landing. Everything is taller than I'd last seen it, as brief as that view was. After a dizzying moment to adjust my memory to my current scale, I get my bearings. I bend my knees, then launch myself at Amanda, who's facing my abandoned, unconscious human body.

"Urgh!" Grunting, she teeters forward but doesn't fall.

Stronger than me. Taller than me.

I hold on tighter around her neck, pivot my plastic legs around her waist.

"Gerroff me, bitch!" she yells, stumbling closer to my human body. She's still holding the damn saw.

I swing my butt side to side, using my weight to take her off her course.

"Oh I get it," she says, turning in a circle to keep her balance. "It's the body, isn't it... If anything happens to it, you can't go back in. That's...it, isn't it?"

With a final swing, I let go and land in front of my body.

"Don't do this," I say. "You can still walk away."

"He wouldn't let me!" says Amanda. "I was trapped. This is all I can do. Why wouldn't you help me?"

I was trying to, but not the way she wanted. There's a saying from the Philippines: A person who doesn't remember where they came from will never reach their destination. A circle. A balance. Spending too long away from her body made her forget where it is and how to get back inside. And the body, bereft of a soul which now resides in the doll, has most likely succumbed to the natural decay of a body without a soul. She left Dan's cage and is now trapped in one of her own design.

"If you're here, then your body is up for grabs?" she says.

"It doesn't work that way."

"Let's try and see. What happens if I...touch it!" She lunges forward, swinging her hacksaw.

It burns a slash across my chest. I bend, hold a hand to the wound, cry out in pain. Fatal, if I'd been human. As a doll, it burns like a curling iron pressed against my chest, but I'll live.

More importantly, she doesn't know how to fight against another doll. I whimper to sell the act. She lunges again to finish me off. This time, I catch the saw with my right hand and pull her toward me. With my left, I strike at her shoulder joint, knocking her arm out of its socket.

She staggers first from the force, then in disbelief, gaping at the hacksaw in my hand and her right arm dangling from it.

I swing both at her head.

My reach is long.

But she jumps to catch the impact on her shoulder.

Amanda stumbles aside away from the car, then scuttles backward, disappearing behind it.

Crap!

I run after her, glance at the garage door—it's heavy, there's no way she could've gotten out in time—it's still closed.

Good.

Where is she then?

Where?

It's getting darker and harder to see in here with the exhaust blocking the lights and growing thicker every minute. Like walking in a fog. Can barely see two feet in front of me.

Amanda definitely has the advantage. She knows where everything is, the tools that can be turned into weapons, the corners to hide in, waiting for me to come within reach.

Still thinking like a human.

I get low to the ground where there's still visibility, packed with toxic, invisible, fatal carbon monoxide. Gotta get my human body out. Gotta end this now!

I shimmy under the car, careful to keep my plastic body and flammable doll hair away from the car's scalding undercarriage. My doll head only turns side to side on its axis, with limited motion up and down; I can only see to either side of the car, not in front or behind it.

Left. Right.

Right. Left.

Keep quiet.

I see her on my right. She's wrapped oily rags around her feet to muffle the sound of her plastic feet against concrete. She creeps along the edge of the car, heading towards the tarp and the garage door. I lose her behind a wheel. I wait. As soon as I see her foot again, I grab it and pull with all my might. She falls on her side with a clatter, scratches for purchase on the concrete floor, but I'm pulling even as my shoulders brush against the car's undercarriage.

Burns! Oh god, it burns and my flesh melts, but I pull her bigger body under with me.

As her doll-body squeezes in between the floor and the car undercarriage, she lets loose an anguished scream. The sweet smell of melting plastic fills the tight space. I pull until she's completely wedged in, then I shimmy out on the other side, ending up next to my human body. Using the hacksaw, I cut through the zip ties binding my wrist to the tool bench.

I check the pulse, just in case.

Strong but slow. The body feels warm, the lips bright red. I could move back in and find, belatedly, that I'm trapped in a body that won't start, like a car that's run out of fuel. I'll have to take my chances.

Keeping hold of my wrist, I close my doll eyes, think of the special words, and fill the words with my longing to continue the path I'd chosen: Here. Now. This.

I open my eyes and see my doll body a moment before it falls like a felled tree. It's hard to see, not for the darkness caused by exhaust, but how toxic my blood must be. It's hard to hear the car engine or Amanda screaming because of the blood rushing in my ears.

Priority: get fresh air. I crawl to the garage door, feel up the wall beside it, slap the button. The garage door shudders then starts rolling up. A blessed gust of cold winter wind reaches inside like a hand and scoops out the exhaust and fumes.

The next breath is easier. The one after that, easier still. Soon I see the car and the walls, then the gravel driveway and crisp blue dawn beyond. Amanda's screams have diminished to pained whimpers.

"Calm down, Amanda," I say. "I'll get you out, but we have to wait for the car to cool off, or it'll just scrape off your entire front."

I try to open the car doors to turn the engine off, but all of them are locked.

"Under...front...wheel," whispers Amanda.

I feel in the wheel well and find a magnetized key holder. The key within opens the car door. I remove the key from the ignition.

Amanda's head shakes like she's trying to wiggle out.

"Wait," I say. "When the car cools, it'll let your plastic body go. Try to get out now, and it'll tear off everything melted to it, like the top of a pizza sticking to the cardboard delivery box. Do you understand?"

"Why are you helping me?"

I lower the garage door for privacy, keeping it open about two feet for ventilation. Sitting and waiting beside her, I say, "I can't give you death, but I can give you freedom."

"What do you mean?"

"The only thing that will free you from the doll body is fire. I could douse you in acetone or vodka, set a match to you, but that fire would be agony. It is unlike anything you have ever felt as a human. I can't give you that death because it's a false one. You would be plunged into the eternal fires of Hell, ever-awake, ever-present, ever-suffering, with full knowledge of who you are and what you did to end up there."

I nod at the body parts she'd been piling up for God knows what reason.

"You need an exorcism," I say. "I will take you to the priest who helped me. Then you must atone to nudge the world into balance. After that... it's up to you."

Amanda doesn't say anything for a long moment, only blinks her brilliant lapis lazuli eyes. Then she talks softly as I wipe my fingerprints off surfaces in the garage.

She'd wanted a divorce but Dan had found a loophole in the pre-nup she'd made him sign; he would've gotten half her money, and he wouldn't leave without her signing over her half. What he held over her head, she doesn't reveal. Neither does she reveal why she wanted a divorce, but I don't care.

She grew powerless.

Entering the doll just a few minutes a day to try it out gave her some power back. Then she'd spend hours in the doll, spying on Dan, trying to get information to blackmail him into stopping his blackmailing of her. More and more hours tailing him until finally she couldn't get back into her own body. Could barely remember where it was, how long she'd been away, why she was in the doll in the first place.

One night, she'd tried to get Dan to help her. Awakened by the talking doll, drunk, still half-asleep and thinking it was a nightmare, he'd struck her and broken her jaw. Mute, she decided the only person who could help her would be the person who created the doll.

Me.

Well, Emilia Zhang.

While waiting for me, Dan and Mike the Neighbor had tried to leave. Amanda the doll had drugged their wine, killed Mike, and had Dan attach Mike's jaw to her head so she could speak.

She ordered him to call the police station and say that Amanda had come back, it had been a misunderstanding. And she ordered him to drug me when I arrived. He thought the drugs were only in the glass he got from the cupboard, the glass he would fill and give to me. She had slipped them into the wine as well.

That's how she overpowered the men enough to make killing them, in her doll body, feasible.

By the time she finishes telling me all this, her words are even and her tone is sad, not boastful. The car is cool enough for me to gently slide out her melted, shapeless body, and lay her in a Louis Vuitton duffel bag she'd asked me to retrieve from her bedroom closet.

"I can't believe I did all that," she says.

"There is some truth to calling something a crime of passion," I say. "Rage and despair draw evil like lightning to rods."

"Are you...are you really going to help me?"

I pull the zipper up over her body and I flash on the memory of pulling a zipper shut on a body bag.

"It's my job," I say with a sad smile.

"Thank you, Emilia. Really, I'm sorry for dragging you into all this, and thank you."

"Yeah, about that. Call me Nicole. It's a long story, but call me Nicole."

"All right."

"Where's your body, Amanda?"

She looks frightened. "But you said —"

"I'm not putting you back in. You can't go back in if the body is dead, and it probably is by now. It continues to live as long as it has the triumvirate of power: heart, mind, and soul. If it goes too long without one, it dies. But we should be sure, don't you think? You should say goodbye. For closure."

Frustration, confusion, and concentration ripple over her face as she struggles to remember.

"I can't remember," she says. "I'm sorry."

I shrug. "Don't apologize to me. We should get going, though. Anything else you want to bring?"

"No."

I retrieve my own duffel bag from the foyer, take the glass I'd sipped from, and go back to the garage. I open the trunk on the white car. It's Amanda's BMW. We'll take it to the airport and leave it in long-term parking. She doesn't mind being the prime suspect for this massacre.

From the airport lot, I walk to the train station and we take the train south, not north, heading for San Diego. I make a few calls to let the real Emilia know what's going on and where I'm headed, and to transfer my psych patients to my colleagues at the clinic.

While I'm at the food court in the San Diego airport, waiting for our flight, eating a dinner of Cinnabon and iced tea, I catch the news playing on one of the mounted flatscreens. Can't hear over the din of voices and steady stream of departure announcements. I don't need to hear to understand because it's an unfortunately common event in this day and age.

Body of a woman found.

A police sketch of a woman in her mid- to late-forties. Red hair with touches of gray, a long face with freckles, pale green eyes, and for some reason, the sketch artist drew her lips in a slight frown. Makes her look so stern.

I reach for the Louis Vuitton duffel to get Amanda out so she can see herself on the news and I can ask her if they got her mouth right, but by the time I unzip it, the news has moved on to more important things. A "Who wore it better?" segment.

"Is something wrong?" says Amanda.

"I...nothing. Do you want some Cinnabon?"

The plastic corners of her mouth pull up, baring the incongruous male human teeth on the masculine lower jaw. I'm getting used to her smile.

"Sure," she says.

I put a piece in her mouth.

"Where we going once we get there?" she says around the doughy morsel.

I think about how to answer. Then I say, "The place has no name. It exists between two cities, at an intersection of two rivers. Those rivers move constantly, depending on how much it rains during monsoon season."

"But you know where to go? You'll take me where I can get help?"

"It's my job," I say. To give help to those who ask me for help, power to the powerless, redemption to the fallen.

A job given to me by an ancient doll I found in the Sierra Madre forest in the Philippines.

INTRO TO *Toof Fairwy Trouble*

In an uncommon departure from Dean Fearce's usual stories with adult main characters, *Toof Fairwy Twouble* features a young protagonist. A child with the curiosity appropriate to his age, the mental acuity of an adult genius—and not enough life experience to temper either. Basically, me as a kid.

Throughout the story, I related to Timmy, and his parents, and his adversaries, and the situation he made for himself, and how that situation spirals completely and utterly out of his control. Boy does it ever spin out of control—which is how the best stories transcend from day-in-the-life-of to "you'll never believe what happened!" It's rare for a story to have so many elements that feel real, especially when half of it takes place in the Fairie Realms.

— JOAN REGINALDO

Toof Fairwy Twouble

by Dean Fearce

———⌘———

ONCE UPON A TIME, there was a precocious boy who lived in the valley of the city of angels. He had a mop of brown hair, bright blue eyes, freckles, ample curiosity, and an intellect well beyond his four-and-a-half years. The boy was intent, obsessed even, on discovering the secrets of life. By any means necessary.

With fortitude, resourcefulness, and an uncanny understanding of the scientific method, he embarked upon his mission with Mrs. Goodkind's serial killer cat, Tinkerbell, a mangy, yellow-eyed orange tabby he had ensnared in a hot-wired birdcage.

Beakers, the former occupant of the cage, was a green parakeet. Beaker's bloody feathers were scattered about the cage. Some had escaped through the bars, floated to the floor, and danced along the concrete in the wake of Timothy's footsteps. They were in the basement of the Kilmoore residence where Timothy Kilmoore, also known as Timmy, had established a laboratory in his playroom where he kept toys of little interest, including the model train set Santa had brought him last Christmas.

Beakers, sad to say, was no more. Tinkerbell had taken him to the brink of death with her play. Upon discovering her predicament of being lured by the bird, then trapped by Timmy in the bird's cage, she vented her rage upon the tiny, near-weightless budgie body of Beakers and finished him.

Timmy, satisfied with the setup and method of his experiment, stood over the cage and adjusted his safety goggles. He reached for the electrical switch to send one hundred and twenty volts of alternating current through Tinkerbell's quivering cat body to determine if it was true that cats had nine lives.

"Timmy?"

Mrs. Kilmoore, also known as Mom in the Kilmoore residence, called down to the basement from upstairs and interrupted Timmy's experiment with an unpredictable variable in the form of her retarded French bulldog named Sam, short for Sàmi.

Sam was afraid to come down into the basement, and for good reason. He may have been a canine nitwit, but he knew a four-and-a-half-year old psychopath when he smelled one.

Unfortunately, Sam's incessant yapping at the top of the stairs had spoiled the experiment by introducing a cat's natural born enemy into the clean environment.

"Timmy, I can hear you down there. Everything okay?"

"No, Mom, everything is not okay." Timmy scribbled all over his notes with the vermilion crayon he had used to record them in a notebook of wide-ruled paper. He liked to code his notes with bright colors like chartreuse, cerulean, and fuchsia.

"Well, come upstairs for lunch, then. We have toasted cheese and chicken noodle soup, your favorite."

Timmy shook his head in frustration, his experiment contaminated by dog. But, he was hungry. "Okay, Mom. Coming."

Timmy removed his goggles and the oversized heavy-duty rubber gloves he wore on his little-boy hands. Tinkerbell, her eyes already spinning in her head, had nearly chewed through the duct tape over her mouth. Timmy opened the cage, noticed the smell, and saw the poop.

"That's disgusting," he said, and he had an idea. "Let's see if there's more than one way to skin a cat."

He closed the cage, flipped the switch, watched as Tinkerbell's fur crackled with current and exploded into the equivalent of a feline afro. She twitched and danced. The little bell on her collar tinkled maniacally. Timmy observed until the circuit hit overload and the breaker for the basement broke the connection.

He flipped the switch off and went upstairs for lunch. Toasted cheese and chicken noodle soup were good, but maybe not his favorite. Beef noodle soup was probably his favorite even though tomato soup went better with toasted cheese, but Timmy didn't care much for creamy-style soups.

"Mom, you forgot to cut off the crusts," Timmy said, and wiped his chocolate-milk mustache on his shirt sleeve. The white shirt, now stained and somewhat tattered, worked well as a lab coat for Timmy, who had acquired the shirt from Mr. Kilmoore, also known as Dad.

"What's that smell? It's coming from the basement. Timmy? What in the gods' names are you cooking up down there?" She trimmed the crusts off the well-tanned toasted white bread layered with a thin slice of American cheese, then sliced the sandwich in half diagonally.

"Sam ruined my experiment," Timmy said. Timmy had a difficult time pronouncing the letter r, so experiment came out sounding like expewiment.

"Oh, I'm sorry, Timmy. Next time, I'll put Sam out back when you're experimenting."

Timmy kicked out under the table in search of the dog's backside, but Sam knew better than to park too close to Timmy's little-boy bluchers.

When he bit into a triangle of toasted cheese sandwich, Timmy yelped and dropped the sandwich. It felt like something had bit him back.

"What's wrong, dear?" his mother said.

"Somesin inna sammich," Timmy mumbled. His hand covered his mouth.

"Let's have a look," Mom said. "Open up, Sweety."

Timmy opened his mouth to reveal an un-chewed bit of toasted cheese sandwich spotted with a dab of blood.

"Oh, my," his mother said. She poked a finger in his mouth, wriggled a lower incisor. Timmy started at the odd sensation. "You have a loose tooth."

"I'm losing my teeth?" Timmy said. "I'm only four-and-a-half."

Mrs. Kilmoore laughed. "They're your baby teeth, Sweetheart. They have to fall out to make way for your adult teeth."

Timmy put an exploratory finger in his mouth, felt the loose tooth, wiggled it, did not like the sensation, and pulled the finger back.

"When it gets really loose, we can pull it out," Mom said.

"No, no, no," Timmy said, recoiling back in his chair. "It hurts."

"And when the tooth is finally out, we can put it under your pillow for the Tooth Fairy."

"Tooth Fairy? What's the Tooth Fairy?"

"The Tooth Fairy comes at night and takes your tooth in exchange for a coin she leaves under your pillow while you're sleeping."

"Seriously, Mom? There's a fairy comes at night to my room? To leave money for my tooth?"

"That's right, Timmy. And if you're a good boy, the Tooth Fairy leaves even more money. Especially if it's a really special tooth from a really special boy."

Timmy stared at Mom for a full unblinking minute, which was always disconcerting to Mrs. Kilmoore. She busied herself tidying up.

Finally, Timmy asked, "Mom, how do you know the Tooth Fairy will come to get the tooth?"

"Because it's her job. It's what she does, Timmy."

"Have you seen the Tooth Fairy? What's she look like?"

"No, honey, no one has ever seen the Tooth Fairy. I think they can cast spells and turn invisible to avoid detection."

Timmy understood spells and magic from his reading, something he'd been doing since he'd turned three. He got up from the chair, went to the stairs, and down into the basement.

Mom said, "Timmy, where are you going? You haven't finished your lunch."

Timmy ignored her.

The last time Timmy had tripped the circuit breaker in the basement, he had watched Dad open the breaker box to identify the broken circuit and flip the switch to bring back the power.

Timmy had a small step stool set up to reach the breaker box and returned electricity to the basement. He tossed a towel over the smoking hot mess in the birdcage—he'd bury that later—and went to the tool room where Dad had carefully hung a pegboard, then put his tools on pegs, and with white paint, outlined every hammer, screwdriver, and wrench so it was simple to identify where each tool belonged. Mr. Kilmoore was a good organizer.

Timmy sized up the pliers, found a pair small enough that he could get a decent grip on them with his small hands. He wiped the plier jaws with rubbing alcohol—Mom had taught him to be sanitary—then reached into his mouth, clamped the pliers to his loose tooth, and yanked on it. It made a little squelching noise and popped out.

The pain was sharp and blood spurted into his mouth. It tasted like the copper pipes in the basement Timmy had licked out of curiosity when he was a baby. Timmy ignored both the blood and the pain. He took the tooth upstairs.

"Mom, my tooth came out. Do we have to call the Tooth Fairy for an appointment or something?"

"Timmy, your mouth is bleeding. Oh, come here, Baby. Let me see what happened."

"It's okay, Mom. I'm okay."

"Oh, that's my brave little guy. How did it come out?"

"It just came out," Timmy said. He danced like he had to make a wee wee, but really he was anxious to get started on his new project idea. "Where should I put it?"

"Why, under your pillow of course. But first, let me wash off the blood."

"Okay, Mom, I have to do some research," Timmy said. "Don't lose my tooth."

"I wouldn't dream of it."

Mrs. Kilmoore was used to Timmy doing research. His intelligence quotient had tested in the ninety-nine plus percentile. Even though Timmy was only four-and-a-half years old, he was smarter than almost everyone else on the planet.

———— ✸ ————

A walk into Timmy's room, which was next to the upstairs bathroom in the Kilmoore residence, was like walking into outer space. The background of the walls was painted as dark as the dark side of the moon, except for the wall behind Timmy's bed where the sun shone perpetually on the stars, planets, and moons locked in orbit on the other five walls of space. There were six walls total if you counted the ceiling and the floor. Which Timmy did. Like so many of the gifted, he possessed a keen sense of three-, and even four-dimensional space.

After twenty minutes on the internet, it took Timmy the rest of the day to gather all the equipment he needed for his next experiment. The items were not rare or hard to find, but he had to extract everything from where they were hard to reach for a child. The story of his young life.

From the garden shed, he found netting material Mom used to keep squirrels out of the strawberry patch in the backyard. In the garage, he found a ladder, rope, and flexible wire. In the basement tool room, he found hooks, pulleys, wooden dowel rods, a drill, and a saw. He found a small hand weight in his Dad's study.

He went to work immediately. The noise eventually alerted his mother, who knocked on her little angel's bedroom door before she stepped into his room.

"Timmy?"

"Hi, Mom," Timmy said. He sat on his bed and smiled. "Want to see what I made?"

She noted the rope strung through pulleys that hung from the ceiling on hooks, and the netting underfoot. She took another step, felt something tickle her ankle. It was a trip wire. It pulled a trigger that released the counterweight that drew up the netting, which encircled her legs and cinched snugly around her waist. Rube Goldberg would have been proud.

"Oh, my goodness!" Mom said. She was much too heavy to be hoisted off the floor in the trap. "What is this?"

"It's a fairy trap," Timmy said.

Based on images found in illustrated children's books, Timmy calculated the size of an average fairy to be approximately six inches tall, and probably not more than three-hundred grams. He was confident now the trip-wired trap worked and would be effective in capturing a fairy of that size.

It was a good day's work for an over-achieving evil genius of his age and stature.

Time in the Fairylands did not flow the same as it flowed in the world of human experience. It's not to say time didn't flow, it was that the denizens of this otherworldly place experienced it differently than humans.

To creatures of the Fairylands, time was less of an enemy, and more a multi-edged tool, like a Swiss Army knife. Whatever job needed doing, time was handy for getting it done. Expert time management was a highly sought after skill, and there was great demand for those who could open time, serrate it, chop it, cut it, corkscrew it, and clip chunks of it into manageable, coupon-sized portions.

Time rules the human fools, as the saying went.

Alas, time, like many tools, was a multi-edged blade. Unlike humans, the Fairylanders rarely experienced regret. No need for it because they could re-tool time and always be in the present moment. But constant time shifting created a hazy tableau of an ever-changing now that might lead to the murkiest of potential futures that rarely arrived based on past events, that instead appeared in and out of existence like a wack-a-mole game. Tomorrow could be a day before yesterday that was already the day after tomorrow that had been previously lost to antiquity.

Fairylanders had evolved to withstand the rigors of mutable time, but most humans who'd ever found themselves in the Fairylands never lasted more than a day—a finite human day, that is—before descending into a hopeless vortex of utter madness.

Sinnabone was employed by the Department of Good Fairy Works. She was a Hominem Tooth Extraction Specialist, also known as the Tooth Fairy. She could spin and screw time like no one else in the Fairylands. She had been certified at the near highest rank of Indigo Wizard in the Fairy Union, having advanced through the rainbow ranks in, well, hardly any time at all.

She would have advanced to the highest rank, that of a Violet Sorcerer, except for the circumstance of her lineage. She was a mixed union conception, that of a wicked ugly hobgoblin—though not a particularly nasty one—named Norton, and a sprightly pixie who answered to the name Crystalouise. Quite honestly, no one ever understood the attraction, but the heart wants what the heart wants, even in the Fairylands.

This day, the weather was perfect as it was every day in the Fairylands thanks to a mid-level Weather Engineer, an adept Green Mage who worked for the Department of Environmental Concerns. His name was Picklewick. He was a duwende of no particular importance, except for his skill with the weather, and to Sinnabone who had a crush on the introverted Picklewick.

Sinnabone had parceled out a nice chunk of time to get gussied up at the Beauty and the Beast Parlor and Spa. She lay prone on a beauty table with her face in the face hole while a beautician weaved an extravagant tail extension with a massive feathery plume onto Sinnabone's sad ratty appendage. Genetically, her tail was Norton's fault, as were the snout, fangs, bulbous eyes, and humongous ears that gave Sinnabone a gruesome gargoyle-like appearance.

It was true that Crystalouise had been a beautiful creature who possessed a magnificent wingspan. Everyone in the Fairylands admired her wings. They fluttered like a stunning butterfly but could race like a hummingbird. Crystalouise left a trail of magical iridescence when she flew, alighting from blossom to blossom.

Sinnabone had been born with a potent knack for time-space manipulation that was almost magical. From Crystalouise, she'd inherited wings, for which she was thankful, though they were membranous and furry, with the strength, power, and claws of Norton's hobgoblin physique. Crystalouise had been blessed with sleek sprinter wings. Sinnabone's wings were tougher, like the blue-collar ethic of a night-shift workaholic marathoner.

Sinnabone was a talker, and the beautician, a kind and gentle gnome named Gnaomi, listened, unperturbed by the burning stream of conversation…

"…boyfriend's a goblin, actually more like a duwende, really fugly, you know, fugging ugly, but sorta cute like that, but, he's not really my boyfriend, yet, I mean, we haven't, you know, but he's going to want me, don't you think? When he sees my big fluffy tail with those ginormous ugly peepers he's got, seriously, who could resist this tail? So don't mess it up else you get stuck in eternity diddling yourself in a dark empty bowl of gnomey poo-poo, if you get my meaning, and I think you do. Did you see the spores growing on that giant ogre getting the mani-pedi, ewwww…"

…flowing from Sinnabone's bat-lipped mouth like the river Phlegethon.

Gnaomi stepped back to get a longer view on Sinnabone's knobby backside. Not the best canvas for her work, but still, the tail extension was a masterpiece, a rare unicorn–centaur hybrid that cost more than Gnaomi's sweet little life was worth, which is why, even had she been tempted, she would certainly not "mess it up."

And a gnome messing anything up was a complete oxymoron. Gnomes took detail-oriented perfectionism to an exponential level. Gnomes were immigrants from the human world. They had fled to avoid the persecution of little people. They flourished in the Fairylands despite being without true technology, and were so pure in their intent, they weren't impacted by time flux at all. They were an industrious, hardworking, and self-effacing race of creatures.

And they were survivors. Gnomes owned the service-level economy in the Fairylands, and had a solid export business sending their dead back to the world. It was a win-win. No clutter of dead gnomes in the Fairylands while they continued their humble servitude as garden sentinels in their ancestral homeland.

Sinnabone spread her wings in front of the mirror, looking much like the grotesque she was, but now she brandished a lush new tail extension. She turned left and right, admired the tail as it swished and swooshed as if possessed by the soul of Cerberus. Her one-sided conversation continued without pause...

"...Grog, my boss, he's a filthy ogre, eats spicy faun feces. You ever smell spicy faun ogre farts? Terrible smell. He's always hitting on me. I'm so not available. When he sees this tail...does it look better pointed up or pointed down? Praise be to Leviathan, he'll be on me like fairy dust, you know he's got that burly ogre thing going, like, the big old horns, but the stench breath? Grog says I owe him another week, gotta log in my time today, but I'm four weeks ahead and only three days behind, so he's out of his scales..."

...as she turned, dropped three pearly-white teeth into Gnaomi's hand before she spider-walked out of the beauty parlor and took flight.

Gnaomi stared, flabbergasted, at the three human-child teeth. Flabbergasting a gnome is something most would think impossible. But three teeth? It was the most generous tip she had ever received.

Human teeth were valuable, and children's teeth were almost priceless. Life had become dependent upon them in the Fairylands since the first gnomes had brought them across the treacherous border regions from the world.

The composite structure of many human artifacts contained the chemicals that allowed the Fairylanders to advance their science and develop the technology that gave them mastery over time, space and their environment. The purest extractions of these chemicals were obtained from human baby teeth.

Humans had powerful dark magic, that was a fact, but they were idiots. That was the opinion of the Fairylanders who had a strong love-hate relationship with humans of the world.

Humans foolishly traded their teeth for worthless money. Money was toxic because it had no inherent value whatsoever, yet it allowed humans to perform the darkest of magic, that of getting something for nothing. The imbalance human magic created in the world was frightening to the Fairylanders because it put a wobble in the space-time continuum that would only lead them to a black hole of utter destruction.

Fairylanders had mapped the time-space coordinates to total annihilation of the human world, coordinates that were continuously updated and presented to Fairylanders in an easy-to-read info-graphic style, the results of which fluctuated wildly from moment to moment based on current events in the world. They called it the Social Engagement Linear Field Interconnection Engine, or SELFIE. Fairylanders were fond of acryonyms.

Often, humans were mere days from their final apocalypse. Preventing the journey of humans toward this final destruction was the totally self-serving prime directive of every creature that lived in the Fairylands.

The Department of Good Fairy Works was located in a tree that humans could only expect to find in an illustrated volume of fairy tales. The perception of scale—like time and space—was easy for Fairylanders to manipulate, but as a comparison, the tree was taller than the Empire State Building and as big around as the village of Green Springs, Ohio, which is 1.21 square miles in total area.

Branches on the tree were as thick as skyscrapers, the canopy of leaves so dense that Picklewick had to manufacture multi-tiered layers of sunlight to reach the mid and lower levels. The tree so dominated the forested landscape where it grew that many lived there all of their life and didn't know other parts of the Fairylands existed. It was, in the original sense of the word, awesome, and it created habitats and departmental offices similar to buildings in human-made cities, like Manhattan, or Tokyo, except in this case, the tree itself was the city.

The tree was called Oak. Basically, Oak was the Fairylands. The Oak mega-complex had been built by the industrious gnomes, of course, who had developed it without any forethought or planning, yet still managed to create an intricate interconnected living and working structure that fit the needs of its occupants, while it did nothing to diminish the grand majesty of the giant tree itself.

Down in the rooted bowels, the gnomes had created tunnels and warrens for the cave-dweller types like trolls, troglodytes, and other creatures that abhorred the light of the sun. They even built cave-like accommodations for the occasional sociable dragon, though their presence made the neighbors rather skittish. Dragons had voracious appetites and were known to really light up social gatherings.

The gnomes themselves, being wingless, occupied the ground level in perpetuity in exchange for their service. The middle portions of the tree were occupied by climbers and flyers, while the upper-level offices and apartments were leased to the strongest flyers that often spent their entire lives on the wing.

The top of the tree, the Penthouse, was occupied by a powerful and influential being, maybe the most powerful in the Fairylands, and in the world, too. The Fairylanders called him Aod, although he was known by another name to humans. He was an avid and experienced flyer, though he didn't possess wings, and was often called a jolly elf in the human world. In the Fairylands, he was known to be an angel with a dark reputation. Everyone agreed he had a creative flair for outlandish promotions.

In the Fairylands, his work was highly valued and appreciated, but he was such a creepy character, no one wanted to hook up with him. So, he kept to himself or hung out with his banshees and his hippogriffs, who he dressed up once a year to pull his chariot into the world and audit the human inventory.

Making an entrance at work had become Sinnabone's signature move. It made Grog, her boss, quite angry, which was most of the fun. Ogres are mad by nature so to make them crazy mad was like a blood sport.

Sinny would come into work high like a kamikaze flyer, then fold her wings back to dead drop to the window where she would open her wings wide to create an air brake and explode into the office like a frigging bomb, her chatter coming fast like a growling wood chipper gnawing through a tree limb.

"…knocked that tree toad back to a vegetarian epoch with his tongue wrapped around a pixie sprite for breakfast and boom! Touchdown…"

It always scared the Beelzebubs out of the office staff. Grog lost his bag of faun chips and they scattered across the floor. He proceeded to break stuff and swear like a centaur but the truth was he had such a mad crush on Sinnabone that he never followed through with his threats. For him, and her, though she'd never admit it, the entrance had become a flirtation.

"…filthy ogre eating deep-fried doo-doo, seriously, there's nothing delectable about deep-fried doo-doo…know what I mean? Seriously, who agrees with me? Greasy-fried poop, really? Ewwww…"

Sinnabone rambled on and sashayed around, her new tail job weaving a figure eight as if of its own blonde bombshell mind. The office staff had recovered from their scare and were greatly amused. They enjoyed her antics and the subsequent drama and destruction of the office space by Grog who had turned from breaking stuff to roughly penetrating a thick tree branch with his broken horn.

Maybe it wasn't anger, but passion, the titillated staff conjectured. They whispered, "*Get a toadstool, you two!*"

Grog roared and everything previously unbroken from his rampage threatened to fall and break from the vibration. "Shut yer yaps and get back to work you sniveling dweevils. Sinny, yer logged in three weeks out, but my reckoning says different. You owe me teeth, dammit! Get out there and collect!"

"…nastiest looking fangs I've ever seen are in your dragon-cracked head, you miserable abomination. What the heck did you do to my timeline? Was fine-tuned to the minute. I can't manage every darn thing, why is it my fault? It's always my fault when some hominem screws the Ooser with an unpredictable wrinkle. I'm an Indigo Wizard, not an Orange Sorceress, I can't predict the future you mold-encrusted heap a scales…"

"No excuses, Sinny. Don't give me no excuses. Gimme teeth. We got quotas to meet." Grog handed over a long scroll of overdue collections. "Now, go bust some jaws."

Sinnabone folded her wings, whirled like a top, and gained speed. It made it difficult to understand what she was saying, but it's safe to say the office staff had long ago learned to dial down the constant spray of her oral diarrhea.

Sinnabone's unique process for time manipulation involved physically spinning to touch various time coordinates to find the weak links of events past, present, and future that likely blew her schedule back into last week. This was the art of Sinnabone's mastery of time, that multi-edged tool, all made possible through advanced Fairylander technology from various human artifacts, most importantly baby teeth, though Aod would dispute that claim.

Aod's business unit involved collecting human things, but focused more on quantity not quality. All of which was part of the fabric of Fairyland, which spun the wheels of industry with freely given modern technologies via the Department of Good Fairy Works. Technology was available to all Fairylanders, much like fluoridated water in parts of the world. Or free wi-fi. Both, actually.

They called it Code. Code was everywhere. Like fairy dust.

Sinnabone stopped so fast it took an instant for her words to catch up...

"...there's the frigging wrinkle, three months out..."

...She grabbed the paperwork from Grog's claw...

"...got a place will fix them digits, nice mani-pedi would serve you well. And some dental hygiene, you snaggle-fanged beast..."

...She unfurled the scroll, scanned it quickly...

"...It's in here somewhere, gotta be a connection, there's always a connection, wrinkles don't just happen, wrinkles are made and hominem love to make 'em. Hah! There it be, and didn't anyone notice something new and special about me? What are ya, bunch a blind ghouls? What's a girl gotta do..."

...she arched her tail coyly, swished it with a seductive cat-like maneuver, then spun and grabbed the timeline to chase down the errant thread that had totally screwed her last three weeks in a single minute.

Timmy slept in his bed, one finger touching his tooth under the pillow. The fairy trap was armed and ready. He had run another string from the weight to his thumb in case he fell asleep. He tried to stay up as long as possible to observe and document the Tooth Fairy's capture firsthand, but his busy day had finally overcome his stubborn wakefulness.

When the trap was sprung, because, of course, it was bound to happen, Timmy dreamed a dream of Christmas. Even a precocious four-and-a-half-year-old super genius is not immune to the charms of sugar plums dancing in his head, sugar plums being a metaphor for the 2000X trine-ocular compound LED microscope, on sale for $2195. He hoped Santa would bring it this year.

Mr. and Mrs. Kilmoore weren't wealthy by any means, and had been shopping considerably downscale since Halloween for a microscope for Timmy. For all his smarts, the lad still hadn't grasped the concept of money. He would gladly trade you a dime for a nickel and think he'd gotten the better deal based on coin size.

Soon after the trap had sprung, Timmy's dream, which had begun with him watching Jolly Old St. Nick putting packages under the tree—and one package in particular that looked large enough to be a 2000X trine-ocular compound LED microscope—began to turn nightmarish when Santa winked at him with a glorious twinkle in his eye, patted him on the head, then grabbed him by the scruff and stuffed him into his sack.

Timmy fought hard in the dream, but Santa was too powerful, and as he cinched the sack tight, Santa's rosy-cheeked face turned into an empty-socketed, grinning skull. The bag smelled like rotten meat and Timmy dreamed he puked his dinner on himself.

Then he woke up, not because of the puke which covered his pillow, but because his parents had coming running when they'd heard him scream. Mom lifted her groggy boy gently, because that's what moms do.

"It's okay, Baby, it's okay. Everything's okay." She leaned over, brushed his hair with her fingers. "You must have had a bad dream."

Disoriented, not sure if it was day or night, Timmy saw bumpy clouds out of the eastern window as they turned purple-orange and surmised correctly it was early morning in the Kilmoore household.

Mom gave comfort. Dad studied the fairy trap. It was obvious he was impressed by the ingenuity and workmanship.

"The trap!" Timmy said, as everything clarified in that instant. He sat up. "I'm okay, Mom." From his vantage point, the trap appeared empty, but he needed a closer look. He scrambled up from under the blankets, and pulled the trap over to the bed.

Dad said, "So, you're trying to capture the Tooth Fairy? What do you use for bait?"

"Uh, my tooth?" Timmy said. Sometimes Dad asked dumb questions.

Mom cleaned the barf and Dad sat down on the bed. He and Timmy inspected the netting for signs of the Tooth Fairy. It appeared empty.

Dad said, "Hmmm, maybe it was a false alarm? You might have released the trap in your sleep." He pulled on the string and Timmy's thumb wiggled.

Timmy checked under the pillow. He pulled out a shiny new quarter. "I don't think so, Dad. It took the bait. But, how did it get out of the trap?"

Mom and Dad looked at each other. Dad shrugged.

Mom said, "Well, the Tooth Fairy has magic, so there's any number of spells she has to keep little boys asleep, and escape from clever traps."

Dad stood up. "Geez, Mom. It's almost breakfast time. I could eat a horse. How about you, Timmy, you hungry?"

Timmy nodded. His stomach was empty.

"Pancakes? Or waffles?" Mom said.

"Waffles," Timmy and Dad said in unison.

"Waffles it is," Mom said. "C'mon, Dad, help me mix up the batter."

Timmy sat on the bed, his magnificent four-and-a-half-year-old brain weighing the evidence against all the knowledge he could bring to bear upon it. Basically, everything he had gathered from the internet since yesterday. It was significant, but didn't offer answers. Even genius has its limits. Disheartened, Timmy went to eat waffles for breakfast.

After eating his fill, Timmy returned to his bedroom. His fingers were sticky—a common characteristic among his peers—with maple syrup. He released the netting and bundled it up into a ball in the corner. That's when something tickled his hand. He inspected his hand, but didn't see anything. He could feel something on his hand; it was round, and it tickled, but it remained invisible. He shook his hand like trying to shake off a booger, but like a sticky booger, it wouldn't let go.

Timmy went into the bathroom, climbed up his step stool so he could reach the spigots, closed the drain, and turned on the hot water. Soon as he put his hand in the water, he saw something. It was semi-transparent, about the length of a pencil, and looked like a dandelion stem with the head gone to seed. When he was a baby, Mom would pick them and tell him to make a wish, then blow on it to scatter the seeds to the wind so the wish would come true.

But this thing, it was something different.

"It's magical," Timmy said to his reflection in the mirror.

Something dark seemed to move in the shadowed reflections behind him. He turned to look, but the bathroom was empty. He turned off the water. The thing floated in the sink. It seemed to move of its own accord like a compass needle. When he took it out of the water, it turned nearly invisible. This was something remarkable.

Timmy put the thing—he was certain it was the Tooth Fairy's tail—on a towel to dry and took it back to his room. He tied a piece of string around it so it wouldn't get lost, then he opened his notebook, got a handful of crayons, and began to research illustrated fairy tales for pictures of fairy tails.

———— ✺ ————

The source of the fairy tail remained a mystery after Timmy's research. There was nothing like it to be found. Without any other insight or empirical knowledge into the nature of the creature he sought to capture, Timmy fell into theorizing; when you're four-and-half-years old and you can't find the story you're looking for, you make one up.

Timmy made up a story of an invisible Tooth Fairy that he'd nearly captured but had escaped his snare and left a part of itself behind. Now it was wandering around in Fairyland without its tail and it was sad, especially when everyone laughed because its tail was missing. Timmy believed the Tooth Fairy would return for its tail because tails—like money, according to Dad—don't just grow on trees.

When the Tooth Fairy returned to find its tail, Timmy wanted to make sure he caught it and there would be no getting free. He could use water to keep it from turning invisible. He could use syrup for something sticky to make sure it didn't escape from the trap. He would hot wire something with electricity because running current through anything alive would stop it, and it was just plain fun.

Lastly, he realized that to make sure the Tooth Fairy came when he had the trap ready, he needed another tooth. He checked each of the teeth in his mouth. There was the other bottom front tooth. It had a little give, but it was secure enough. He decided he would solve the problem of the bait after he built the trap, because that's when he would need it.

The birdcage in the basement would be the perfect holding pen for the Tooth Fairy. It would also be a good place to offer the tail, coat it with something sticky, run a current through it to stop the Tooth Fairy, and use a squirt gun to reveal the Tooth Fairy inside it. Not too much electricity, just enough to stun, not kill. Timmy's experience with different voltages on small creatures would serve him well. He would use the transformer from his model train set in the basement to modulate the current.

By lunch time—today, Mom served a can of little round macaronis with meatballs, one of Timmy's favorites—the cage was cleaned and hung from the ceiling in his bedroom. The fairy tail was coated with sticky maple syrup. It was hot wired, and hung limp and dripping sap in the cage. An arsenal of water guns were locked and loaded on Timmy's nightstand.

Timmy now faced the tooth dilemma. Never one to shrink from the advance of science, even if it meant personal sacrifice, he passed through the kitchen on his way to Dad's workshop.

"How was your nap, Sweetie?" Mom asked. She had a hot cookie sheet laden with warm snickerdoodles in her oven-mitted hand. They smelled like cinnamon, sugar, and butter; small chewy rounds of heaven. Mom liked to make cookies. Timmy loved snickerdoodles.

"Good, Mom," Timmy said. He had accomplished a lot during his nap time, but he hadn't managed to squeeze in a nap.

"What are you up to now, you little trickster?"

"Another experiment," Timmy said. "Mom, does the Tooth Fairy come for dog teeth?"

"Only children's baby teeth," Mom said.

"Oh, okay."

"No fires in the house this time, Timmy."

"Okay, Mom."

In the basement workshop, Timmy found the heaviest hammer he could lift. He also found a cold chisel. It was heavy, too. He decided the bathroom was the best place to extract the tooth in case there was blood.

Upstairs in the bathroom, Timmy stood on the step stool and stared at his reflection in the mirror. He rinsed the chisel in alcohol, then held it steady against his tooth. He lifted the hammer in the other hand and took a few unwieldy practice swings. The hammer was too heavy for a one-arm swing, but he was determined. He needed the tooth.

He reached out with the hammer arm as far as he could and swung it toward his face with no hesitation, but he wasn't able to contain the trajectory and the hammer swung wide. It threw Timmy off balance and he pitched forward into the sink and cracked his mouth hard on the porcelain edge. He cried out in pain. He dropped the hammer and chisel and cupped his mouth. He tasted blood and spread his already swollen lips to reveal bloody teeth, one of them clearly looser than it had been. Ignoring the pain, the tears, and the blood, he reached for the tooth and yanked it out. The empty tooth socket gushed blood.

"Mission accomplished," Timmy said, and went to find Mom for a small measure of motherly comfort. Maybe he'd have a cookie later.

Sinnabone hung like a bat from the ceiling and rampaged. Mad, angry, pissed, and murderous only began to describe her mood. Even Grog cowered spellbound by the stream of invective that flowed from Sinnabone's upside-down grimacing face.

"…going to turn him into meatloaf and feed him to the Minotaur three times a day, and feed the Minotaur poop to those ghetto cave ogres in the Dismal Swamp, and that's just for starters, little crumb snatcher tried to pull a trap on me, and got my tail? #&^@$% is going to regret this for the rest of eternity…"

When Sinny had calmed, Grog, who hated to do it, but he had to cover his ass, said, "You gotta file a report on the artifact left behind, Sinny."

Even with all of Sinnabone's skill manipulating time, the one immutable law in the Fairylands was never leave an artifact in the human world. The law existed for two simple reasons. The first was anything left behind offered proof of the Fairylands' existence, and would create a mad human frenzy to cross over and turn it into a theme park. Secondly, Fairylander artifacts created an odd time wrinkle in the human world and there was no way to rewind it and un-leave the artifact.

"…#@$&% artifact my fuzzy butt @#$&^ %!$#% #&$@%! report that you $!#^&★ &^#@$%…"

"I'm just the messenger, Sin," Grog said. "We gotta follow protocol."

"…#^@$&% protocol up your @#$&^ %!$!# here's a message for your @#$&…"

"Okay, okay, you can go back to get it, but we need to file the report, and it's gotta be a legit collection stop, even if we gotta wait for the kid to lose his next tooth."

"…#&^@$% boiling oil and bolt cutters @#$& #&$ legit my @#$&…"

"Don't matter to me how he loses it. You do what you gotta do, Sinny. I got your back," Grog said.

Everyone knew that was total hooey. Ogres don't have a shred of loyalty. And, it was common knowledge Aod had spies in every office of the Department of Good Fairy Works. It was already assumed by everyone in the Tooth Extraction Office that Grog was the leak. No doubt Aod already knew about Sinnabone's leave-behind breach.

Grog unfurled Sinnabone's claws and re-wrapped them around a scroll. "Here's your collections, Sinny. Maybe you'll get lucky and the kid already lost another tooth."

"…kid's going to lose a lot more @#$& teeth and a lot more of his #$&^@ mind after I get done with his #@$% reality timeline…"

Sinny released her grip on the ceiling, flipped in midair, and landed on her toes. She opened the scroll, reviewed the list, and was struck dumbfounded for an instant in which she actually didn't say anything, not a word, her stream of consciousness empty except for the slight huffing of her breath…

"…"

The elves, gnomes, goblins, and pixies in the office waited…

"…Hallelujah! #&%@ little @$&%, I got him now, @#$&^@ Hallelujah! What are the odds? The kid went and lost another tooth. My luck has turned the worm. Sinny will have revenge. That kid has no idea, not even a clue, will never know what's going to hit…"

Sinnabone danced and chanted, then spun in a whirligig move and winked out of the office to chase down her tail.

After Mom and Dad tucked Timmy into bed, and made sure he'd put his fresh tooth under the pillow, they kissed him good night, turned off the light, and closed the bedroom door. Timmy was much too excited to sleep. Things had lined up perfectly this day and he was certain he would catch the Tooth Fairy this night.

The sticky tail hung in the cage. Timmy had wired it through the model train transformer so he could control the voltage. He'd also tied Tinkerbell's jingle bell to the end to alert him to any tail movement. Timmy sat on the bed with his high-powered water gun and waited patiently for his destiny to appear.

When Sinnabone arrived in Timmy's room, she was ready for the little trickster's tricks…

"…fool me once, shame on you. Fool me twice shame on me, you little rat, first thing is to shut you up so no one else in the house is alerted, and then we'll deal with your timeline…"

…all said in a sub-aural frequency which hominem couldn't hear. It was easier for Sinnabone to talk softly than it was to not talk at all.

Timmy knew something was going on when he felt a splash of wet and the taste of salt water. Something slimy was in his mouth. It moved, pulled, grasped. It was a horribly wrong sensation. Timmy dropped the super-soaking water gun and ran to the bathroom. What he saw in the mirror shocked and frightened him. It changed his worldview dramatically.

Where his mouth had been there was now a large purplish-black octopus. Its tentacles curled and waved, and its suction cups attached to his face. They pulled and released, leaving red hickey marks along his cheeks. He wanted to scream, but the body and head of the octopus filled his mouth. He tried to pull the octopus out, but it felt like he was pulling out his own tongue. It was horrifying, a nightmare made real. Timmy felt the overwhelming confidence-shattering crush of a world well beyond his experience.

Tinkerbell's collar bell tinkled back in his room. Timmy had a brief hope that if he captured the Tooth Fairy, he could make it change him back. When he saw the tiny winged creature—it looked like a bat—lighting up in the cage like a blinking Christmas light, his hope plummeted into dread.

He turned off the transformer and the bell stopped tinkling. The bat-like fairy turned invisible. Actually, being invisible wasn't true magic, or an invisibility spell. It was a subtle tweak of time that allowed Sinnabone to be not quite present in the present.

Regardless, Timmy was frightened. If he had killed the Tooth Fairy, he would be doomed to live as a tentacle-mouthed freak. When he reached into the cage and felt the furry body of the Tooth Fairy, the room blinked out of existence. Timmy felt himself spin so fast in a tube of whirling pictures it made him want to puke, but he wasn't sure if he could throw up with a mouth full of octopus. He shut his eyes tight, held onto his head, and hoped it would stop soon.

And it seemed he got his wish because the spinning stopped and his stomach calmed down. Someone talked fast, like a mile a minute, his mother would have said, and it was all swear words and naughty language...

"...little effer electrocutes me and by Typhon, it didn't feel terrible, but the little creep grabs hold of me right when I jumped back home and now what the %$#@& we going to do with the little hominem? Grog, you want to feed a family of ogres with this slimy crank that stole my tail, which, thank the Scylla, I managed to hold onto even while this creepy kid felt me up and I..."

...and Timmy realized the bat-like creature was talking about him, that he was the slimy crank, and he was sitting inside a very small space inside a tree, surrounded by ogres, goblins, elves, and sprites who stood as tall as his knee caps. They looked as surprised to see him as he was surprised to see them, all while tentacles writhed in his mouth.

"Oh, Sinny, you screwed the Ooser now," Grog said. "You brought the hominem back to the Fairylands. This ain't gonna be good. Ain't gonna be good for any of us."

The staff of the Tooth Extraction Office in the Department of Good Fairy Works realized at once they would soon be visited by the biggest poop storm ever, so they vanished, disappeared, evaporated into thin Fairyland air. Grog and Sinnabone stayed. As anyone with half a brain knows, there is no way to escape Aod when he comes looking for you. And he was most certainly going to pay a call on Sinnabone and Grog.

Fairylanders were smaller creatures than humans, Timmy realized, and he wasn't hopeful he would fit through the door to the outside world. Right now that, and the octopus that was his mouth, occupied most of his thoughts.

When the temperature dropped unexpectedly—it got very cold, very fast—the ogre went into a corner and sat, and the bat-like Tooth Fairy hung upside down from the ceiling. She talked non-stop but it was quiet talking. The only reason Timmy knew she was talking was because her mouth continued to move.

Santa Claus appeared. He looked huge and fat outside the window in his jolly red suit with the white trim, and his bushy beard and eyebrows. Timmy felt elated that things would be okay, but then he remembered his recent nightmare with Santa. He felt less confident about the current situation. Santa got small and came inside the office through the front door. Apparently, he didn't always use the chimney. Nor did he always wear the red suit. He had shrunk down with what Timmy perceived as fairy magic and now wore a dark suit, his well-trimmed beard a salt and peppery gray. He looked like a businessman, albeit a very small businessman you could put in your pocket.

Timmy had lots of questions, but no way to voice them with a mouth full of mollusk.

Santa Claus pointed to Timmy's mouth "That's a neat trick. Who pulled that one off?"

"...really simple, actually, just a matter of finding the divergent moment in time when the two species split and reunite the DNA in the pattern you want to achieve to solve the problem, in this case, the squid lips shut the kid up and, obviously, make some drama, and an interesting effect for funnsies, no? not to mention scaring the Beelzebubs out of the little blighter for causing all the trouble he's caused. Now he's back here and it's my fault, no doubt, but the circumstances were extenuating..."

Santa chuckled, but it lacked the mirthful bowl-full-of-jelly belly effect.

"Brilliant piece of work, that kraken mouth. Sinnabone, you are an artist," Santa Claus said, though realistically, no one would look at him now and think Jolly Old Elf. He produced a large sack and approached Timmy. St. Nick and the sack appeared to get larger, or Timmy appeared to shrink. The tentacles in his mouth turned various shades of red and green as they writhed and curled in response to Timmy's anxiety.

Santa grabbed the now perceptually much smaller Timmy by the scruff and stuffed him into the sack. "Let's take this discussion upstairs," he said, "before we lose any more control of the situation."

Timmy expected the smell of rotting meat inside the sack, and he wasn't disappointed.

———— ❧ ————

High atop Oak was the Penthouse. It was the House of the Dark Angel, the North Pole, the Last Stop on the Road of No Return. Many names it had, but only one purpose. Aod, short for the Angel of Death, lived and worked in the Penthouse, where the industry of processing souls and recycling their organic materials was carried out. Not the actual work of processing souls and all the dead rotting meat of their bodies—that happened in Purgatory and then Hades.

The Penthouse was the Angel of Death's business office and living quarters, and the space was very stylishly furnished in glorious, top-of-the-line vintage mid-century modern, like stepping into a posh midtown Manhattan ad agency in the human year of nine-teen-hundred fifty-six.

Timmy was released from the sack and deposited in an original Wishbone chair. It was upholstered in a bright and cheery red, of course. Timmy knew the man in the suit was Santa Claus, and this was the North Pole, but this place looked nothing like the pictures from the illustrated storybooks Mom used to read before Timmy started reading himself.

The Angel of Death sat behind his huge Danish Modern teak desk with matching credenza. He smoked a Lucky Strike, his ankles crossed with his wing tipped broughams comfortably perched on the edge of the desk. He pushed the toggle on the office intercom, ordered a dirty martini for himself.

"Anyone else care for a drink?" he asked.

"…sugar water would be great, I got a sweet tooth. The hominem, they live on the stuff, but you know, they suck all the joy out of everything including the sweeteners they use, and they…"

"Sugar water, it is," Angel of Death slid in sideways before Sinnabone gathered verbal momentum.

"Blood and spinal fluid, fresh or frozen, don't matter," Grog said, "but don't make it special if it's a problem."

"Not a problem, at all," Angel of Death said. "We have a well-stocked larder for all manner of tastes. And how about you, little Timmy? Anything to drink?"

Soda pop, Timmy thought, because he couldn't speak. *Mom doesn't let me drink soda pop.*

"What flavor? Hmmm, I'm guessing you'll be a root beer fan. How about we start there?"

Timmy's eyes got wide, first because there was a beer soda pop for kids at the North Pole, and secondly because he realized Santa could read his mind.

"Yep, that's true, Timmy and we're talking root beer, sweet and syrupy, nothing alcoholic. You're underage, kid."

Kris Kringle had his dark side. And that was the ironic beauty of the whole Christmas concept he'd launched into the world. He was never turned away, always invited into every home. The Angel of Death had a free pass, a get out of jail free card in the spirit of the holiday he had invented. It was pure marketing genius.

"What should I do with you miscreants?" Aod said. It was a rhetorical question.

Someone was always dying, and Christmas was always in the back of everyone's mind, so the Angel of Death always had an agenda. To be clear, Aod didn't actually take lives, per se. He was the middleman, but he was adept at hastening the process along when needed.

All Timmy could do was stare and make choking noises. When the drinks came, the sight of him as he tried to negotiate his root beer past the writhing tentacles to his gullet proved to be disheartening to Sinnabone.

"…holy hags and harpies, that's painful to watch the little fellow with his soda pop. Methinks it time to back and forth him for a small space of peace to enjoy his sweet drink before his fate is sealed…"

Timmy was wicked thirsty and had the worst fishy taste in his mouth. He had also surmised the consequences of his actions were that Santa Claus had put him on top of the Naughty List.

Living hominem were unwelcome in the Fairylands with their bombastic and wicked pretensions. Their first and last thoughts were inevitably to rip everything down and build timeshares.

Once humans crossed over from the world, it was easy enough to dispatch them on a dragon quest, or an ogre hunt to rescue a fair elven maiden. You know, to make it an adventure for everyone. Dragons and ogres were always hungry. They enjoyed the fun. The hominem would predictably lose their minds quickly, so it all worked out for the best.

Sinny did her whirligig move, reached back into the Paleozoic with Timmy's evolutionary timeline knowing full well…

"…he'll be crazier than a midget berserker so he won't suffer much not knowing the reality of his situation when we feed him to the ogres, a bit less cruel though it's not to say he doesn't deserve to suffer, but why make him suffer more than necessary, seems a bit over the top…"

Back and forth millions of years wasn't a common leap for an Indigo Wizard. It was a tricky maneuver even for Sinnabone, who had risen higher in skill in the Fairy Union than her status indicated. There was speculation that her almost unnatural talent and vast leaps might have contributed to her somewhat strange behavior—like the never-ending vocalization of her thought stream. But the Fairylands were populated with such erratic beings and creatures. It made little difference, and was part of the local color.

When Sinny and Timmy reappeared, almost instantly, in the Penthouse, Aod sipped his drink. Grog had already drained his vat of bloody Mary, as his drink was known.

Timmy grabbed his soda and chugged it down. It resulted in a resounding belch much bigger than expected from his now even smaller frame since he had been made perceptually smaller by the Angel of Death, a Violet Wizard with a specialty in the craft of per-ceptual distortion, and discerning the thoughts of others, great skills to have as Santa Claus.

Everyone laughed, even Sinny, while she was going on about the wonders of the Paleozoic era…

"…the primeval seas are full of the interesting creatures and you wonder how some of them ended up in the Fairylands and others in the world. The question I have is what the heck?"

Her focus shifted to Timmy…

"…What's the deal with the traps? Why were you trying to catch a Tooth Fairy? What would you do with one anyway? Did it not occur to you we've run into nasty little hominem before? That we have experience with your kind? Was it for the money, the dark magic? They say it is at the root of all evil…"

Grog said, "If you have sumpin' to say, say it, kid. She ain't gonna shut up any time soon, and it's almost lunch time." He drooled. A puddle of it had formed at his gnarly feet. He made no attempt to disguise his intention. "Hominem hash and brain gravy," he mumbled.

"I wanted to capture the Tooth Fairy," Timmy said, "and learn about tooth fairy magic."

"He speaks, and seems unaffected by the time flux. Sinny, as this happened on your watch, you have a responsibility to help resolve the situation. Do you have any last thoughts before we, you know, ahem, carry on with our day?" Aod said.

"…would be good to give him a fighting chance, maybe a riddle challenge with a troll? Don't think he was purposely malicious, he was truly interested for the sake of science, not so much the dark magic, more imp-like than hominem, you know that behavior. A lapse in judgment one would suppose given the lack of experience and all, you know, due to youthful curiosity…"

"Why can't I just go back home?" Timmy said. "I'll be a good boy, Santa."

"…negative effects to the temporal interface, it becomes totally unpredictable, could throw the world into a death spiral or rip a seam into the borderlands and we'd be flooded with immigrants with not enough ogres to eat them all. This kind of disruption in the space-time continuum could wreak havoc for both worlds…"

Grog paced a dwindling spiral around Timmy's chair. His stomach growled like a Moloch's on steroids.

"Timmy, let me explain," Aod said. "Humans hover at the edge of an abyss of annihilation, you know, doomsday, for all the usual hominem reasons. We work hard to prevent them falling into that abyss because the market for human artifacts would eventually collapse and send us back to the Dark Times, before science brought the Illumination to the Fairylands. In short, we're addicted to technology and need humans to feed our addiction."

"...let me check, wouldn't hurt to check the SELFIE with twenty-minute updates before, during, and after, uh, you know, lunch. What could it hurt? We've all heard the legend the Angel of Death is actually a human, an ad man actually, crossed over in the Dark Times. It's been a boondoggle ever since. Am I right or am I right?"

"Sinnabone! That's dangerous territory. It's not in your best interest to pursue up or down the Angel of Death's timeline."

"...back in a sec..." Sinny winked out.

The hungry ogre made his move and Timmy cried out when Grog snatched him up and held him around the neck in a death grip with his strong scaly claws.

"Please remove the boy from the Penthouse, Grog. Blood stains are hell to remove from the upholstery."

Sinny winked back into the Penthouse as Grog headed to the exit.

"...by Skuld, we might consider the consequences of this boy's timeline based on the near future result of his imminent digestion. Grog, really? Going to run and eat? What I saw might ruin your appetite. It would probs be your last meal. You wanna bring about the Dark Times?"

But Grog was having a moment as his green lumpy tongue licked up and down Timmy's face. Clearly, not an enjoyable experience for Timmy.

"...Seriously, five minutes upstream of your swallowing the boy in three bites, you should learn to chew your food, point is, just five minutes after, the boy gives you the squirts and they hit the SELFIE fan. Makes a big mess in the world. So eat him now and suffer the Dark Times forever, except for an angry mob of Fairylanders that comes for you and makes it the shortest forever, ever..."

"Okay, hold up a minute, Grog. Put the boy down and let's reconsider our options," Aod said. "Christmas comes but once a year. Maybe the world has sent us a present."

"Like delicious human suet pudding with sweet kidney sauce," Grog said. His reluctance to release the boy was palpable in the Penthouse, like the breath of Typhon.

"Grrrrog? Do what I tell you."

Grog put Timmy back down in the Wishbone chair where the boy used his shirt sleeve to wipe the slime from his face.

"Was just a little marinade, to tenderize the thing," Grog said.

"…more disgusting than a bucket of mermaid piss…"

"Sinny, what if we returned the boy to the world?"

"…didn't look like an option either. The SELFIE showed you Aod, but out of focus. And when…"

"If he stays here?"

"…and that's the funniest outcome of all, because the SELFIE went on reset, but there were some changes, can only be positive outcomes. And not just for us Fairylanders. Hominem, too. Full disclosure here, Aod? It's not all rainbows and unicorns. You might not be happy with the *what ifs* and the *what fors*. Things aren't a bucket of nymphs for everyone here."

"If being Santa Claus has taught the Angel of Death anything, it's sometimes you got to take one for the team." Aod drained his martini, ate the olive. "Timmy, my boy, let's talk about your future here in the Fairylands, shall we?"

———— ⧟ ————

"…funny thing is, Gnaomi, can I call you Gnaomi? Thanks for getting me in on short notice, course, I could have rearranged your whole timeline, but lately, been letting the chips fall where they land. Not the faun chips, me and Grog, no, no, no, that was never a thing, but Picklewick? I think there's something there. Still hasn't seen my new tail since the accident. Did I tell you the boy is Aod's right hand elf these days? Just gave him conditional visiting privileges, you know, back to the world. Sappy kid likes to visit on Christmas Eve, says Mom leaves him milk and cookies. Guess his science is amazing, like out of this world amazing. Heard rumors that he figured a way to synthesize Code. Can you imagine? Synthetic code would change everything. Probably put me out of a job, but who cares, right? We could let those stupid hominem choke on their own teeth and it would be none of our concern. None of our concern ever again…"

INTRO TO *Dirty Little Secret*

In Dawn's *Dirty Little Secret,* when you mess with the wrong people, you'll get screwed in more ways than one. Dawn delivers a great tale where her character, the lowest person on the popularity totem pole, takes revenge to its extreme conclusion. It's always the weird ones. I'm sure it's something people have thought of doing during high school. Right?

— ERNEST ORTIZ

Dirty Little Secret
by Dawn Del Sontro

"Don't touch that!" Troy shrieked, his frightened voice octaves higher than my normal voice. I barely managed to refrain from laughing at his terror and tried to avoid looking at him as I brushed off wet leaves stuck to my knees.

"Oh God, Troy, don't be such a baby," I said. I turned away from him and hunched down to inspect what we'd found on our adventure in the woods. He'd brought me out here to so we could fuck in ways his girlfriend wouldn't.

I felt him behind me, his legs almost touching my back as he cautiously approached me, his flaccid dick grazing my back just enough that there was no mistaking what it was. He shivered but not from being cold. It was a nice autumn day. I hid my face so he couldn't see me stifling my laughter at his fear.

"Don't poke at it!" he shrieked again.

"Jesus, Troy. You are such a fucking baby." Again, I poked the bloody covered clump of…something…with a stick. It's not what I'd expected to see. I leaned close to try to figure out exactly what I was looking at.

It was a huge chunk of what looked like raw prime rib, the ends jagged and mangled like ground beef.

"It looks like…a part of a leg or an arm," he whispered, beside me now. He was close enough to me that I could feel his hot minty breath on my face. I could hear him fixing his clothing, finally calm enough to realize how stupid he was standing around with his pants down.

The stink of his breath and his tangible terror annoyed me so much, I needed to move away before I slapped him in the face. After I could breathe without the stench of gum, I poked at the "something" again. He was right. It was a section of thigh, about six inches thick of flesh, muscle and bone. Eerily resembling a rib eye steak, only made out of human instead of, you know, a different kind of animal.

The slab was covered with dried blood, leaves, dirt, and grass. We wouldn't have seen it except for the fact that we were lying almost right on top of it. I was busy with other things when Mr. Football Star screamed, jerked away, and almost lost his dick as my surprise changed my mouth from soft and sweet to shock and teeth.

"We need to go and, um…tell someone," Troy whispered. I stifled my snorting laugh.

"Why are you whispering?" My voice was loud in the silence of the woods. It's like all the animals and birds were holding their breath for something.

"Shhhh!"

"Why? What's going to happen? We wake up the chunk of meat and have it scold us?"

He looked at me and asked, "God, Sara, why you are so fucking strange?"

"Strange, Troy? Strange? I'm not strange enough that you won't fuck me now am I?" I snapped at him. "Your hot little girlfriend would be so disappointed with you before she moved on to the next football player."

He turned away to look back at the meat, but he didn't deny my words. My anger came fast. I knew this was our relationship when we started. I tutored him so he could play football, and he fucked me in all the ways I wanted. This is exactly what I had wanted when we'd started our "relationship," but up until now I hadn't realized that I cared as much as I did.

It had been months, this thing with Troy and I, and I realized that it meant something to me that I hadn't expected or even wanted. Since he'd started dating *her*, I'd become something he used when she was too busy for him. I was the smart freak that let him do things that the sweet innocent preacher's daughter wouldn't. I wasn't special anymore.

I stood quickly, my vision darkening for just a moment as my head adjusted to the change in height and my burst of fury. The stick dug into my hand as I clenched my fists.

He followed more slowly, stepping back a little to give me room or maybe to move away from the meat.

"Hey, listen. Don't be mad. It's just that, well, you know. You didn't want anyone to know about me either and now with Kimberlee around…well, you know how it is."

He was right about me not wanting to be seen with him but not for the reason he thought. When we'd first gotten together I felt like his special secret, now I didn't feel special. I just felt dirty.

Had he made any effort to treat me like a person I might have thought a little better of him and changed my mind. The past five minutes just solidified my opinion of him and cemented my decision.

Kimberlee. God, I hated her. I hated her blonde hair, too-white smile and pretentious way of telling everyone that she was not Kim, but Kim-BER-LEE. Kim (poke me on the nose) BER (poke on the forehead) LEE (her high-pitched laughter as she walked away).

When I didn't say anything, he pulled his phone from his back pocket, dialed, frowned, and walked away from me. Signal strength out here was horrible. I should know since I searched for hours for this particular spot. A girl doesn't want an unwanted call when she's misbehaving with the local football hero. It's a horrible mood breaker. Today, it would have ruined everything.

"No luck?" I asked innocently, actually batting my eyelashes at him for effect. He missed my effort of playing helpless damsel in distress, shook his head at my question and tried again.

With no connection, he shoved the phone into his pocket and turned to me, "Let's hike back to the road, I'll keep trying and you keep track of where the...uh...that...is."

I didn't reply, but looked at my watch. A snap and crunch of leaves behind me made me smile.

Perfect timing. Troy jumped and spun to look to the direction of the sound, his phone held in front of him like some kind of pathetic weapon.

His eyes widened in surprise before his shoulders relaxed and his hands dropped to his sides.

"Fuck, Luke. You scared the shit out of me. What the hell are you doing out here?" He let out a deep sigh and then suddenly tensed up again when he realized that he'd just been caught with the school freak, just minutes shy of his pants being around his ankles. He looked from me to Luke and back to me again. He opened his mouth to speak, but Luke beat him to it.

"What the hell are *you* doing out here with Science Sara?" Luke didn't bother to look at me and I ignored him. Science Sara. That's me. I used to hate that name, but now, it's my badge of honor. Anything was better than an over-pronounced name for a Barbie.

"Uh, well, see...DUDE, we found a body part!" Troy shouted pointing at the mess a few feet away.

Luke was more interested in the two of us. "A body part? Like your dick, man?" Luke asked and then heartily laughed at his own joke.

Troy muttered something stupid about projects and school and Luke continued to mock him. I ignored it all and went to retrieve my backpack where we'd left our things and put it on before walking past Troy. He didn't even try to stop me. No, "Sara, wait, let me walk with you." No, "We just found a body part, it might not be safe out here." He just let me go. Discarded me without a second thought or moment of hesitation.

It wasn't until Luke said "So, how's Kimberlee?" did I stop to turn to look at Troy.

To his credit, Troy didn't deny he was out there, fucking me. For a minute, I almost changed my mind about the entire reason we were out here.

But then he said, "Look, Luke, it's just Sara. It's nothing important. It was just for shits and giggles."

It. He called me an "it". What the fuck?

"Shits and giggles?!" I screamed at him, stalking forward, shaking with rage. Troy bent his head in shame and cleared his throat, but said nothing. He wouldn't even look at me and went as far as to turn away from me so he didn't have to look at me. That's why he didn't see when I yanked my pack off my back, pulled out my knife, and shoved it's long, serrated blade into his back as hard and as far as I could.

"Not important? NOT IMPORTANT?" I twisted the blade.

Poetic justice, really. He stabs his friends in the back, so that was the best he deserved.

Poor Troy fell to his knees with a gasp of pain and a hoarse cry. He reached for his friend, his raspy voice pleading almost too soft to hear, "Help me."

Luke came forward, still ignoring me, and grabbed his friend's hand. With his free hand, he reached around and grasped the knife, and shoved it in even further. Blood bubbled from Troy's mouth. His hands, white-knuckled, clutched at Luke's hand.

With a laugh, Luke yanked his hand free and shoved Troy to the ground. Then Luke held out his hand to me and smiled. I put my bloody hand in his and smiled. He pressed his lips to mine. I leaned in and tried to wrap myself around him, through him. His arms engulfed me, crushing me against him. The smell of his skin mixed with the scent of warm blood made me crave him.

Being in his arms made me remember why Troy had stopped being useful to me.

"Wait, Sara," Luke said against my lips. "We need to finish this," he motioned at Troy, "before we get carried away."

I nodded and extracted myself from his arms. The breathy groans from the ground drew my attention. "Still alive?" I asked, mildly surprised.

"Wow. I'm impressed. Kim died almost immediately," Luke said.

"Don't you mean Kim-ber-lee?" I enunciated each syllable in a manner so Kimberlee-like that I actually annoyed myself. "And speaking of the dead bitch, you were supposed to leave something a little more human-looking. That slab of her thigh, that was pretty obscure."

Luke smiled sheepishly. "Sorry about that. I was going to bring a hand or foot or something, but I ran out of time. I got stuck at work and then my mom made me help her. I grabbed whatever I could find."

I sighed but let it go. At least he had a good excuse. "That's ok. He still freaked out once he realized that it was human. You should have heard him scream." As we laughed, Luke pulled my pack from my hands and placed it gently on the ground.

He yanked it open and pulled out my knives and handsaw. "Let's see if we can get him to scream like that again," he said as I looked into the quarterback's eyes.

I picked up a saw and turned it on for dramatic effect and held it so Troy could see it spin, its blade a blur but still stained with good old Kim-ber-lee's blood. "Do you want to start or should I?" I asked.

Luke didn't hesitate. "You. He's been fucking you more ways than one. All he did to me was take my girlfriend."

I smiled. "That gives me an idea." Then I lowered the saw to Troy's groin.

INTRO TO *The Skin*

There is no way for me to give a fair and accurate assessment of the experience of Julia, the protagonist in Joan's story, *The Skin*. Julia is a young, beautiful woman of color. She's a wife and a mother, and was fortunate to survive and make an escape from the indifferent brutality visited upon the impoverished.

Even in the face of this caveat, I can speak earnestly to the horror Julia endures, and the strength of her will to make right the wrong she's been done. Because that, I believe, is the story Joan wants me, as the reader, to experience. It's an assumption, but nonetheless, that's where the story hits with a visceral gut check to a reality experienced when another yearns for her skin.

— DEAN FEARCE

The Skin

by Joan Reginaldo

THE WOMAN WAS BORN INTO a seven-person family that shared one bathroom, but she grew up in an area where first graders did pilates for PE; she didn't take for granted the ability to blend in. It was a survival skill that became a habit as much a part of her as the immutable color of her dark eyes. Eyes that were half open now. Not quite asleep. And even though relatives would say she could finally rest well, having achieved that slippery eel of a marriage to a rich man, and having produced three children who fortuitously came out as clones of their pale-skinned father, the survival habits of falling asleep in a room with bars on the windows kept a fraction of her mind always alert. Not alert for anything specific now, unlike then, when a certain timbre to a shout was the opening salvo for the crescendo of gunfire and sirens.

Now what kept her awake was the worry of something *missing*. Though it was night and a maple tree obscured her view of the gazebo next to the tennis court, she stared through the balcony doors as if she could still see the sharp crescents of dried glue on the gazebo handrails.

Someone had taken the Sacagawea coins she'd glued to the wood.

She'd felt foolish doing it when they moved in but she was compelled by a superstition that was part of her heritage. It was supposed to invite wealth to her home. Not that they needed any more, but she dared not risk the dread, the inevitability, of taking the blame if something went wrong and she could've prevented it so easily.

Her children and husband knew better than to touch the coins. The groundskeeper, Mr. Mendoza, or the cleaning service lady, Mrs. Andrada, must have taken them.

The woman barely spoke to the staff, avoided rooms or areas they were in, left notes as communication instead.

They reminded her too much of her own parents.

But the missing coins represented more than a mere note could convey. She worried about what she would say to them.

A sound from the hallway behind her caught her attention. Without changing her prone position, except to turn her head, she looked in that direction.

"Paul?" she said, calling out to her rambunctious, athletic ten-year-old. Her oldest.

No response came from the darkness beyond the open door. Not quite dark where milky moonlight, reflecting off the white walls in her children's rooms, made ghostly pools on the thick gray carpet.

"Miriam?" she said, calling to her sweet, peacekeeping middle child. Eight.

Now that she was a little more awake, she could see strange shadows in the hallway. Shadows that resolved themselves into the silhouette of a narrow table holding a pot of moon-faced orchids, and a painting at the far end of the hall, and a...a tenebrous column at the top of the stairs. The vacuum cleaner? Her husband's golf bag? She would recognize it in a moment, she was sure.

"Sam?" she said, calling out to her intense and solemn youngest child. Four.

No frightened child's voice responded. She listened a few minutes for footsteps or crying, but it was silent enough for her to hear the wind whistling through someone's badly insulated bathroom window. She turned her face back to the sliding glass doors of her balcony. The view darkened. A cloud must be passing between the moon and her house. The glass of the window turned into a mirror and the woman saw a reflection of her white sheets and the dark hallway beyond and that one unknown, unnamable drip of shadow which somehow seemed closer to the doorway of her bedroom.

She whirled around, this time fully facing the door with her left arm across her chest, left hand clenching her sheets to throw them aside, heart pounding, vision sharpening with surprise and fear.

Wide awake, she looked. The cloud between the moon and her house passed on. The shadow was a little larger, and it was no longer at the end of the hall, at the top of the stairs. It seemed closer.

She reasoned: every first floor door and window was locked, even here in this neighborhood, because the woman couldn't forget where she came from, couldn't outrun or outgrow the habits.

With every door and window locked, that shadow in the hallway was just a shadow then, wasn't it. And it hadn't moved, or if it had, it was due to the movement of the moon across the sky, rearranging the tableau.

The woman closed her eyes, held her breath, then let it out slowly through partly closed lips. She imagined her tension and fear seeping out with her breath. She was being silly. Afraid of a shadow, like her youngest. Maybe she should call her husband, Michael, who'd been away on his quarterly two-day business trip to Minnesota or Ohio or one of those other fly-over states. Then again, his plane had already landed; a meeting had been cancelled and he'd managed to catch an earlier flight. He would be driving now. The woman hated calling her husband while he was driving because he always picked up when she called. Always. And she'd never forgive herself if she called him because of a shadow and he picked up the phone and crashed headlong into an oncoming truck.

A shadow, for Chrissake!

She laughed a little again, opened her eyes.

And the shadow was at the foot of her bed.

The woman tried to scream but couldn't move, frozen in terror.

The shadow descended on her, hard. Wrapped around her neck, hard. It had substance after all. Hot and hard and it smelled like onions...sweat. A man. There was a man in the room, a room that had known no other men except her husband, and this man in it now would want what rightly belonged to her husband, and it belonged to her husband because he was the only man to whom she would willingly give herself.

This idea made her panic more, not less. It was not an insubstantial terror come to rob her of life. It was just a man committing a crime. A crime that had been held over her head since the moment of her birth when she came out with an organ that folded in rather than one that jutted out. A crime that many of her habits were supposed to protect her against. She spared a thought for what might have betrayed her now: a faulty door lock, a delicate window. Then she thought of only one thing: survival.

For her sake as much as her children's, for a man who would do this would surely not leave witnesses. And the children's doors were open. Sooner or later, they might hear a sound. Or the absence of sound. Or feel that something wasn't right.

The woman struggled and bucked but her legs tangled in the sheets which seemed to tighten and constrict the more she struggled.

The man above her, still clothed in darkness like he'd gathered the shadows as a shroud, rocked back to adjust his weight over her pelvis to pin her down.

Gave her just enough space to breathe out—breathe in—twist!

She reached to her right and scrambled her fingers over the nightstand.

Though she'd gotten another breath in, the exertion was quickly depleting her oxygen supply. It was already dark in her room but her vision grew dimmer. Her head felt like it was detaching from her body. Her legs felt like they were less and less under her control. Her fingers felt numb, twitching for some reason. She used to know why. Biology, something that had to do with electrical impulses. The electricity was turned off.

Everything felt very wrong and very right, like she was sinking into the natural state of things but she should be fighting it. She should be fighting tooth and nail about…something. A tiny part in the middle of her mind was still awake and wondering.

Why was the man not continuing? No clumsy fumble at her pajama waistband. Not lifting up her shirt. Instead, a slap across her face!

But she only sank into that *natural state of being* and that little awake-and-wondering part of her mind found it interesting that a person can be completely unaware of *breathing*, ignoring it until the mechanism stops, or a person can be completely aware and able to command *breathing* like when there's a birthday cake involved, but the in-between is the tricky part.

When the body's automatic breathing mechanism breaks, there's no way to restart it again. Not from the inside, at least.

The awake-and-wondering part grew less awake and less curious. It felt movement like the motion of being on a boat, but it no longer cared how or why. Then it felt something snap! And an inward rush of air made the awake-and-wondering spark flare like a backdraft.

The woman came to, aware, catching the end of the last thought, and suddenly, inexplicably free. She rolled sideways to get out from under the man who was no longer in shadows.

Landing on the floor beside the bed, she lunged for her nightstand, for the drawer, for the key inside her drawer that would open the locked box with bullets and a gun. It had been a good idea at the time—the key and the lockbox and keeping the bullets out of the gun—because they had kids and all, but now all she thought, as she brandished that useless key, was what a stupid idea it had been. Smart and stupid. They shouldn't have had a gun, shouldn't have needed it. Not in this neighborhood.

The man crept closer to her and now she saw him better in the moonlight. A man who looked as familiar as most white men did on this block. The usual haircut. The usual shave. But there was a hard determination in his pale eyes that vowed no end except hers, unless she ended him first.

But she only had a key and he was coming at her. With a knife. She saw it now. A silly thing she would've used for slicing apples. A blade only the length from her wrist to her fingertip.

Similar to the length of the blades on her haircutting scissors, still on the bathroom counter, because she'd just trimmed Miriam's bangs a few hours ago.

The woman turned and ran for her bathroom. She could see the scissors in her mind's eye and so she reached for it surely in the dark, felt the cool plastic loops slide into the hollow of her palm as she turned around, and for a moment paused the hesitation of a mother with children always underfoot.

What if it was Paul or Miriam behind her?

It was not.

The stranger lunged. The woman struck. Their blades crossed like lightning.

She felt the stranger's blade pierce above her gut. From the radiating dull ache, the blade felt bigger than it had looked, and it loosed something within her. Her muscles relaxed like the blade had been an epidural injection, of which she'd had three.

The woman looked down and saw a black flower of blood blooming on her pajamas. The blade slid out, followed by a burst of black blood splattering, thumping like fat raindrops against the stranger's chest. And next to the splatter was a dark flower too, from which the woman pulled her scissor blades.

A burst of blood followed, splattering the woman's hand that still gripped the scissors.

The man reached for her and the woman could neither fend him off nor draw him in. The wound he'd dealt was fatal but mostly painless. It had nicked the right veins and arteries. He knew what to do, having done it dozens of times before. He took more of her weight as her legs collapsed. He felt his own legs weakening from the mortal wound she'd given him.

They sank to the carpet together like two children sharing a secret.

The carpet smelled like blood and her favorite perfume. From below them came the sound of a door opening, then being carefully shut by a father who didn't want to wake his young children. Footsteps with the slightest squeak started heading towards the kitchen. The footsteps paused.

The silence of that pause joined the tomb-still silence of the house.

The footsteps reversed and headed, urgently, towards the stairs leading up to the bedrooms.

But the woman, his wife of twelve years, had died for the second time that night. And the man, a stranger neither of them knew, died for the second time in his life.

The woman found it difficult to wake up. She gave up trying to move her arms and legs which seemed to be encased in cement. Her eyelids were heavy and itchy with sleep. She could sleep in, just this once. The alarm on her phone hadn't gone off yet.

Or Michael had turned it off and taken the kids to school to let her sleep in. The light in the room was bright enough to turn her eyelids livid red.

But the sounds and smells were off. It was quiet in the room but many things clattered and clinked and squeaked beyond the bubble of silence. Occasionally, something chimed. There was no pattern to that music.

The smells were more familiar: the vaguely ozone scent of purified air, clove oil, and the tang of bleach. A hospital.

Because of last night.

Oh god, the kids!

"I know it's hard, Julia, but you have to wake up now."

The woman, Julia, startled to hear someone in her bubble of silence.

The other woman's voice was neither too loud nor too soft, but had the hard edge of authority that came from someone used to people listening.

"Open your eyes," said the woman in Julia's hospital room. "Try to move your fingers and toes. Count to five. Then move your hands and feet. Count to five. Then move your arms and legs."

She had the neutral no-accent accent of a news anchor, like she'd lived in many places and all those places had worn away at her words, smoothed off all recognizable edges and slurs.

Julia tried to move her fingers and toes. She couldn't tell if she succeeded. She still couldn't even open her eyes.

"You don't have much time," said the woman.

Julia tried to say, "Where's Michael? My children?" but it only came out as a low growl.

"Let me help you," said the woman.

A second later, a sharp pain under her left foot made Julia flinch and spasm. That's when she realized she'd felt weight on her arms and legs because she'd been bound to the bed.

"Get it under control," said the woman. "Then I can untie you. Fingers and toes, count, hands and feet, count, then arms and legs."

Again, Julia tried to say she was trying, but again, she could only produce a growling moan. At least her eyelids were starting to open. Still heavy but working.

The features of the room were distorted, like Julia was looking through old church glass. The woman speaking to her was just a white column with long dark smudges for hair.

"Fingers and toes, Julia," said the woman.

Julia thought of pushing off a diving board and felt her toes respond. She imagined gripping an apple and her fingers curled in.

"Good," said the woman.

Julia counted and flexed, flexed and counted, then did her hands and feet and arms and legs. Her body was as sore and languid and heavy as after an intense hot yoga session. As she worked on waking up, the woman did a half-circuit around Julia's bed. She cut off long white bands that had secured Julia's elbows, wrists, knees, and ankles to the steel rail all around the bed.

When Julia struggled up into a seated position, the woman said, "Good," and took a wide loop to where Julia couldn't see her, only feel her as she snaked hard arms under Julia's armpits.

"I need to get you into this wheelchair, Julia," said the woman. "Give it all you've got, all right?"

Julia nodded.

The woman counted down from three. On "one," Julia launched herself off the bed and into the wheelchair beside it, hoping and trusting the woman to do the fine maneuvering.

With a jolt that made her stomach ache, Julia landed in the seat. The woman pushed her swiftly out of the room and into the bustling corridor beyond. She took the turns easily, like someone used to pushing a wheelchair. Then they were in an elevator, then going down a hallway that felt fresher but warmer, smelled of eucalyptus and outside air.

Everything was a carousel blur.

The only moment they paused long enough for Julia to look around was when they were waiting for a cab in the taxi line.

The woman allowed a stoop-shouldered gray-haired couple to cut ahead of them for the next cab. Another cab rolled up, and the woman got the burly taxi driver to come out and help her get Julia into the rear passenger seat. Then the woman did something that Julia found odd. Instead of getting into the seat next to her, the woman sat down in the navigator seat. The taxi driver found that odd too, but the woman showed him something in her lap that mollified him.

Then they exited the parking lot. Julia, having had three babies at this hospital, was familiar with the speed bumps and turns of the route which she could not see through her still blurred vision.

When they cleared the hospital area, the taxi picked up speed.

The back of Julia's head and neck felt hot. She reached up to rub her nape. Then the back of her hand felt hot. Added to that was the feeling that something was *missing*.

The cab driver took the corners so quickly, Julia's head bounced against the door frame.

That, plus the heat, plus the unsettling feeling that she'd forgotten something—no, that something had been taken from her, *stolen*—made her feel ill.

"Hot," she wanted to say, but she feared that if she opened her mouth, she'd spew vomit all over the nice man's back seat. Instead, she clenched her fists and stared out the window to distract herself.

At some point, they'd passed the border of what Julia considered to be her town. They were in a quieter suburb. The houses were small, one story, with cramped yards fenced in by chicken wire, and an older model car in each driveway. Toyotas and Fords. No Teslas, no BMWs, not even an eccentric Jaguar or two.

They drove past the suburb and started up a slight incline into a heavily wooded area. The taxi driver opened his window but it did little to help the heat. Air coming in swirled sluggishly. Smelled dusty and undisturbed.

They continued up into the mountains, flanked by ancient redwood trees with trunks so wide, she could park a Hummer in one. Now and then, a sharp bend and clearing between the trees gave her a view of a steep ravine below. The sides were covered by more redwoods and some stalwart shrubs that formed a lush, dark carpet, thick enough to hide a body where it wouldn't be found for weeks, if ever.

Oh god, what's happening? she thought, finally clear-headed enough to be afraid.

Julia took stock of the situation. Was she being kidnapped? Preposterous. They were taking a cab for Chrissake. She felt foolish for getting in the car in the first place. Dimly, she remembered she was supposed to fight back, that it discouraged kidnappers and rapists who would abandon her and go look for meeker, weaker prey.

Okay, enough hindsight. What could she do *now*?

She was in the back seat of a car driving about thirty-five miles per hour. If she jumped out, she could survive if she rolled out of the rear tire's way. But she might roll off a cliff edge.

Could she take out the woman in the navigator's seat? Maybe. Yes. Maybe. But that might freak out the driver, who might drive them *all* off a curve.

And there was no way she'd try taking out the driver.

She'd wait until they got to wherever they were going.

Also, maybe she was jumping the gun. There was a slim chance, after all, that Michael set up some kind of surprise party or something. Her thirty-fifth birthday was coming up in a few weeks. Not a big milestone, and still weeks to go, but that'd make an even bigger surprise, wouldn't it?

She cupped that lie like a candle flame.

The taxi took one more turn and the road they were on ended in a roundabout surrounding a fountain that had been converted into a large container garden for drought-tolerant succulents. The taxi pulled up to the jasmine-covered bower over the entryway.

The woman told the driver to wait for her. Then she got out and opened Julia's door.

Julia got out.

The woman could've been her sister. Twin sister, even; the woman looked almost like Julia's reflection. But the woman had hard eyes and a furrow between her brows. And she was shorter than Julia, by almost a foot.

Still, the resemblance was uncanny.

"Why did you bring me here?" Julia said, finally able to speak without threat of throwing up. Immediately, she regretted it. Her throat felt raw. She tasted blood on her breath. Her voice was hoarse and low.

"Don't try to talk for a few hours," said the woman. "They intubated you. I had to yank the tube out. Sorry."

She didn't sound sorry.

The woman patted Julia down. Julia noticed her own clothes because of it: a blue sweater, crusty with dried mud or something, dark blue slacks, and black tennis shoes. She never wore tennis shoes unless she was going to play tennis. And this wasn't a tennis outfit.

"Why am I dressed like this?" said Julia. The pain in her throat made the question a stupid, unnecessary one.

The woman found a key in Julia's left pants pocket, unlocked the door, pushed it open, and gestured *after you* to Julia.

Julia nodded her thanks and entered the twilight stillness of the house. It smelled of electronics and new paint. She put her right hand to the wall, ventured a few steps in to find the light switch.

The rectangle of light she was standing in narrowed quickly.

The door slammed shut behind her.

Julia spun, hand groping the door for the doorknob. There wasn't one! Only a cold rectangle of metal where there should've been a knob. Julia groped up and down, following the seam between door and doorframe, digging her fingers into cracks. The only thing she found was a piece of electrical tape stuck over the peephole.

She looked out just in time to see the taxi finishing the circle of the roundabout, then dipping face first down the winding mountain road.

Julia rested her forehead against the cool door. Strength left her. She turned around, slid down the door, landed hard on her ass but barely felt it. Barely felt anything except the feeling that something was *missing*.

She sat in the dark for God knows how long. Gradually, the darkness took on a crimson slant, then a wine hue. Dusk. Sunset, maybe. The dark house grew colder, which gave Julia the impetus to get up, explore, or face the alternative: stay on the floor and freeze and starve.

As she rose, Julia did a more methodical search of the door. Hand over hand, searching for a knob or handle, latch or lock. This could be one of those new smart-houses she'd read about, and maybe simply touching a patch of glass or applying pressure to a button flush with the wall would open the door.

There was nothing. With her hands on the left wall, she shuffled into the gloom. The wine-dark room seemed to get brighter. The source of light was a slit on the floor about the length of a door. Julia left the wall and shuffled bravely across the expanse of the room to reach the door. She groped where a knob would be and sighed in relief when she found a cool metal ball. She turned it and opened the door.

It led to another room in what, to her, was turning out to be a luxurious prison. At least this one had a large window. Julia went to the window to look for a latch. It was as secure as a window on the seventieth floor of the Marquis Hotel. Good thing, too. Beyond the window, there was a perilous drop to the valley floor below.

The window afforded a breathtaking view of the tips of redwood trees, and an awning prevented direct sunlight from entering the room. The setting sun was at the perfect angle to come in between awning and window sill.

This meant that this window faced west.

Which meant that the front door to the house faced north.

Julia turned to find a clear acrylic desk against the wall opposite the window, and on that desk was an open laptop. Surely she could make a video call from it, or an emergency call. The mesh-backed rolling chair maneuvered easily from the desk. She sat in it heavily, bounced once, glanced at the screen frame for a brand but found none. She reached for the power button.

And stopped.

Her hand.

It wasn't her hand. This hand was paler, wider, thicker all around with stubby fingers. Potato-digging fingers, Michael would've said. With ugly square nails that were almost concave.

And yet it turned over when she wanted to see its palm. It curled its fingers when she wanted to see its nails. It splayed open when she felt a spasm of fear.

Then the laptop screen flared to life.

There was a man on the screen. A familiar man in a familiar room. The man was the stranger who'd attacked her…was it only last night? And the room…was the room she was in now!

Julia spun in her chair. Yes, this was the room in the video. She turned back to the laptop, seemingly synchronous with the man turning in the video.

A terrible suspicion rose in her mind. She lifted her hand. The man in the video mirrored her. Because it wasn't a video but a mirror. The laptop camera was showing herself, inside the man's body.

"No," she whispered.

The laptop image faded to black, then returned. Same room, same man, but different somehow, the way identical twins, raised far apart, have subtle differences. The man in the video had the face she wore now, but his blue eyes were hard and cold. Not cruel. Indifferent. Which was more sinister than cruel, in Julia's opinion. Cruelty came from envy or hate, and both emotions had a kernel of love in them. They could be redeemed.

Indifference was a lost soul. No, it was a soul that was missing something.

He adjusted himself in the chair, pushed the sleeves of his dark blue sweater up to his elbows, revealing tanned forearms with a fine down of hair.

"Hello, Julia," said the man. "Let's get this out of the way. You are not my prisoner. I am not going to do 'sex' things to you.

"After this video is over," he said, "you're free to leave. But I don't think you'll want to. Not yet." He paused dramatically.

Then his image faded to a photo of Julia. It wasn't a news blog screen-capture from the numerous charity events she and Michael attended. It wasn't from a marathon or store grand opening or any of the other highly-photographed events, all of which Julia would've remembered because they required a signature of release.

In the photo, she was wearing a black strapless dress. Her hair was up and adorned with a big white orchid. The Black and White Ball at the Santa Rosa Country Club. The photo wasn't from a press release; her back was to the camera, her profile was barely lit from a sconce. She'd just stepped out on the balcony for fresh air. Michael had joined her and they'd spent a few minutes necking like high school kids. Then he'd gone back into the ballroom to fetch her a drink.

That was three years ago.

Had this man been stalking her that long?

The photo slid left, starting a slow stream of slides. The images looked old-timey. Julia was no photography expert; with all the photography apps available, no one needs to be. But a secret, morbid hobby of hers was looking at Victorian postmortem photographs; she liked the formality, the flowers, the grand final gesture of having a photo taken when doing so was a luxury. She felt confident in discerning between real old-timey photographs and sepia-washed fakes.

What was on the screen were not postmortem photos of dead people propped up to look like the living, but they *did* seem to be taken during that time or slightly before. The scenes told par-ticular stories, most of them painful to see but Julia made herself look: a slave auction, a battlefield, a trio of women standing around what might be a dead stuffed dog. Some were neutral, even joyful: a wedding, a christening, a group photo of a ladies club.

She picked up no patterns, even when the photos started having color, and the people in the photos started smiling, and soon there were cars and planes. Then the people in the photos ceased to be *people* and became one person. An unsmiling child of ambiguous ethnicity, just obviously not Caucasian. There was one photo of her scowling, with a wispy ponytail, wearing a threadbare dress yellowed on the collar and cuffs, standing with other solemn children in equally droopy clothing. Then a few more photos of her. School photos in which she was never the primary subject but accidentally part of the background behind toothy laughing teens in bold plaids and vibrant skirts. Then a blurry photo of her in a vintage waitress uniform only it wasn't vintage, it was real, and she was waiting on a table of people her age, who were grinning at the camera while in various stages of shedding graduation caps and gowns.

"That's me," said the man's voice. "Before I put on the Skin." The photo faded and was replaced by the video of the man, leaning back in his chair with his hands behind his neck, elbows up in the air, then leaning forward towards the camera in the laptop, which gave the effect of leaning into Julia's personal bubble.

He plucked at his stubble-shadowed cheeks.

"This is what I mean by the Skin," he said. "You're wearing it now, so I don't have to go through all the rigamarole of convincing you that it *does* exist, it *can* be worn, and it can be *shed*. Seeing is believing, so now, you see."

The video paused, briefly faded away into the mirror effect, and showed Julia in the Skin, eyes wide with bewilderment. But Julia was pleased to note she didn't look too scared or confused. Then it switched back to the video.

"And since you see, hopefully you believe. That's part of the reason why I picked you. You still *believe*. Originally, I started with a dozen possible people."

The screen split into a grid of twelve photos. Julia looked through them quickly. All women. All people of color: two black, some that might have been Latina, three Asians, the rest she couldn't say for sure.

"From these twelve," said the man, "I narrowed it down to six who impressed me with their journeys. You need to earn the Skin. I'm not talking about winning some Emmy or Nobel Prize. I'm talking about the difference between how you were when you were five to what you'd become at thirty-five. Slum to Santa Monica. Ghetto to Guggenheim. In your case, boondocks to Bay Area. Or should I say, *bundok*." He smirked as he said the Filipino pronunciation, which was the basis of the English word. "Oh yes, I judged your journey with interest."

The screen showed a photo of Julia when she was in elementary school, androgynous in a bowl cut and her brothers' hand-me-downs, which she'd called "hammy downs" until a kind friend had privately corrected her.

Then a photo of Julia in high school, during a science fair. She was in a borrowed blue dress. The bowl haircut had grown down to her elbows. The photo framed her a little to the left of a tri-fold display board, presenting her experiment on semiconductors to an audience of distinguished-looking men in suits.

The two other kids she'd done the experiment with had tried to coerce her into giving up her share of the research credit. So she gave them the wrong time for the science fair, told them to come at eleven. Then she'd corralled the judges as soon as the fair started and was done presenting, by herself, by nine.

After that, the number of photos increased: Julia accepting beribboned tubes of paper at ceremonies, Julia at dances (wearing more borrowed dresses), Julia graduating, and Julia with a face-splitting grin, standing in front of Beatty-Moore BioSystem with a bunch of other interns. The intern to her right was Michael.

The laptop showed less photos of her, but the photos were sartorial or artistic magazine-quality shots.

The last photo—a staged photo designed to look informal with her and Michael playing soccer with the kids—was replaced by the video of the man.

"An enviable life," he said. "And I do envy it. And what I want, I take. But I *am* offering you a gift in return, Julia. A gift for people like us."

For a moment, Julia wondered what they could possibly have in common. Then she remembered the man claimed to have been a woman. Specifically, a woman of color, now wearing a white man's skin.

The man spoke: "I was given the Skin by a woman like us, and she got it from a woman like us, on and on to who knows when. I traced it back as far as I could from her memory, which wasn't that far, considering a few peculiar things about that Skin. Let me tell you about it now."

The man paused and thought. "I'll tell you my name but that's it because I want you to concentrate on your own journey and your own new life. My name was Mathilda Cooper. While I wear the Skin, I call myself Theodore Cooper. And in..." the man looked at his watch, "...a few hours, I'll be calling myself Julia Burbank. So now, Julia, let's get down to nuts and bolts.

"The Skin is incredibly tough and resilient. I'd go so far as to say it's immortal. I've worn it into volcanoes, irradiated areas, under the blast of a launched rocket. Don't scoff, Julia. Try it if you must. Lord knows everyone has to try it, if not for fun, then at the end...

"I'm getting ahead of myself. Julia, the Skin survived everything I tried, but it punishes you. It'll make you feel everything, *everything*, while it remains unscathed. I don't know if it's magic or alien or primeval, I just know that..."

Theodore leaned back in his chair and wiped perspiration off his forehead. "This is harder than I thought it would be. The excitement..." He stood, paced, shaking his arms and legs to loosen the tension. Then he sat down again.

"You will never age," he said. "Never get sick. Never die as long as you wear that Skin. And it's a *good* skin. Much better than the ones we were born into. Use it, Julia. Use it to become the person you could've been if you hadn't been born..." He gestured at her through the camera.

"That's my gift to you," he said. Then he leaned forward. There was a weariness in his eyes that looked decades older than his face. "What I'm taking from you, your gift to me, is your death. Like I said, the Skin makes you immortal. Honey, I don't think we're meant to live like angels. I believe there's a...a divine fire in us, but a fire with a set amount of fuel. The flesh we're born with has a 'Best by' date, and once we pass it, things get stale."

Theodore turned his gaze away from the camera and stared out the window. Afternoon light robbed his face of shadows, made it flat like a cheap painting.

"It's like being given a task that has no end," he murmured. "There's no anticipation of the *thing* that comes next. Goals become meaningless. Experience becomes meaningless. Art becomes meaning—"

He jumped a little, like he remembered the laptop was still recording. He turned his attention back to the camera and smiled sheepishly. Julia thought it might've been the first time she'd seen him smile. It was not quite even, with the left side of his lips rising just a little higher. It made Theodore look endearing and handsome to her.

"I'm tired," said Theodore. "This is the only way I know to take my rest. It's a gift we're giving each other, don't you see? So when it gets to be your time, Julia, you'll have to make a video like this one, store files for the one you choose as your successor, find someone worthy, and then comes the most distasteful but necessary thing: You have to find someone who wants to live as much as you want to die. Do you understand the trade? It'll only work that way."

The screen changed to that grid of twelve possible people, then to the six that Theodore had chosen. Then one by one, a red X appeared on three women's faces, followed by a brief glimpse of screen-captures from news blogs about women murdered in luxurious homes. Miami, Manhattan, Austin.

"They didn't want it enough," said Theodore, back on the screen. "But you did. Almost lost you because I squeezed too hard, took you by surprise too much, but I revived you and we tried again and you managed it. Fought back because of this, I think." He held up a photo of Julia's three children on the beach in their swim outfits. A photo she'd had tucked in the frame of her bedroom vanity mirror.

Seeing her children in Theodore's hand stoked a flame of anger within Julia, startling and comforting her at the same time, comforting her with something familiar about herself. A flame that burned as hot and large as a hydrogen fire, burning away the last of whatever drugs she'd been given at the hospital, burning away the disbelief and distrust.

Theodore's expression hardened back into its severe commanding expression as he pointed his finger, like a gun, at her children.

"Pay careful attention now, Julia. This will be for our mutual benefit. You understand the idea of rules, don't you? That they are created to protect people? Few rules come with the Skin, which is apropos of the idea of it, being the sex and skin color of power. Rule number one: Do nothing to disturb the one who gave it to you. They have earned their rest. *I* have earned my end. That is the rule that protects me. Rule number two: Do not get caught. No jail, no prison, no asylum. In the Skin, the worst thing isn't death. It's losing your freedom. If you get sent to prison and sentenced to life without parole, you will be there for a very long time. If they notice you never get old, you never die, they might try to experiment on you. You will feel *everything* and you won't have the escape of death. Don't let that happen. That rule is meant to protect you."

Theodore tapped the photo.

"Some motivation. A little insurance. Come near me, I'll kill them, and I'll frame you for it. Do you understand? You'll lose your children *and* your freedom."

He glanced at his watch and stood. "There's one door to this house and it'll remain locked until you figure out how to unlock it. That's the final test of your worthiness, one I'm sure you'll pass. Once you figure it out, you start a timer that will unlock the door in two weeks, giving you enough time to process what I've just told you, to heal physically, mentally, emotionally, to plan, to learn more. This laptop has access to two petabytes of information stored in climate-controlled cells under the cabin. Make use of them. And two months' worth of food in the freezers. *Bon appetit*, and I'll see you soon."

He leaned over. His arm bridged the span to the screen. The screen turned black.

The room grew dark.

Julia sat in the darkness, too stunned to be afraid.

I hope this is a dream, she thought, though she knew otherwise. There was so much to take in and process, she couldn't find a place to start. Part of her thought she should try to watch the video again, for clues or something. She moved to turn the laptop on. The ceiling flickered, then glowed; it was comprised of four square panels of built-in lights, like an upside down dance floor. Most likely motion-activated.

The brightness in the spartan room made the darkness beyond the window more sinister. An old worry prompted an old habit: Julia worried whenever it got dark and her kids were separated from her, at a friend's house or out with Michael. She touched the table, seeking the comfort of her phone, wanting to call them to make sure they were safe.

But she had no phone, and the laptop showed no apps to use to make outside calls. It wasn't connected to any network at all. She had no way of contacting the outside world, her husband, her kids…

Her kids.

If she could just focus on them, it would make the next moment bearable. And the next. And the one after that. She had to get back to them and get back into her own skin. But that was still thinking too far ahead.

When she was a kid, her mother once posed the riddle: How do you eat an elephant?

Julia had thought the idea preposterous. How could her poor family afford such an animal? How would they house it? Where would it come from? Once it was theirs, obviously her family could eat all that meat quickly. It was a luxury that would not go to waste.

Her mother told her to focus on just the words and their one simple idea: How do you eat an elephant?

The answer: One bite at a time.

Julia took her problem one bite at a time. She needed food to work. She found plenty of it in the freezers and fridge in the kitchen, which seemed designed for a bomb shelter. There was no stove, to minimize the risk of fire. Only a microwave.

In the cupboards were camping and survival rations. Plastic trays of dehydrated beef stroganoff that she could reconstitute with tap water and microwave. She heated one up and ate it, surprised at its pleasant chewy *al dente* texture which made up for it being slightly under-salted.

Cleanup involved rinsing the tray packet and folding it into a garbage compactor, and rinsing her one fork, which she left to dry on the counter.

Next, Julia needed sleep.

To the right of the room with the laptop, she found a smaller room with just enough space for a twin bed with an extra long mattress, like she used to have in college. She laid down and waited for the lights to go off due to her inactivity. She was asleep before that happened.

The next day, she rose and contemplated a necessary-verging-on-painful thing which filled her with dread. The adrenaline from her fear had worn off, which was why she hadn't felt it as keenly as she felt it now. The need to pee. She sat at the edge of the bed, elbows on knees, face in her hands, looking at the *thing* through her pants.

Julia had had a healthy sexual appetite. She hadn't let her Catholic upbringing shame her, hadn't let her poor background make her feel unworthy. Sex had been pleasurable so she sought it out in a careful and mature manner. She'd held plenty of dicks in various stages of arousal.

Just not one attached to her own body.

It looked hard, too. *Morning wood*, her husband would've said. It was cumbersome and Julia felt like she should hide it but from who? Her own eyes? The urge to urinate was starting to cause sharp throbbing in her abdomen. On the video, Theodore had said the

Skin couldn't get sick, but Julia didn't want to chance a urinary tract infection or an infected kidney. Covering the bulge with her pillow, she stood and left the room. The last door off the short hall from the front door opened to a small bathroom with toilet, sink, a large mirror over the sink, and a bathtub-shower combo.

Julia put the pillow on the counter next to the sink, unzipped her pants, pulled them and her boxers down, sat on the toilet seat. Without looking at it, she squished it down between her legs and peed. It felt like a spool of thread unraveling out of her gut and into the toilet.

When it was done, she tapped it brusquely to get rid of lingering drips, then pulled boxers and pants on but didn't do the zipper or button. She looked at the tub and shower combo against the wall.

Now? Or later?

Julia pushed the shower curtain aside then sat on the edge of the tub. It felt like her body, not like she was wearing a man-shaped suit over her skin. And the feeling of the tub edge digging into her butt was so familiar; she'd done this hundreds of times to run a bath for her sons or daughter. Her kids.

The sooner she ate this elephant, the sooner she could see her kids. She ran a bath of hot water and stripped in front of the mirror. The Skin's arms and legs were hairier than her husband's. Though the hair was blond, it was coarse and felt a little like soft toothbrush bristles.

The Skin had good muscle definition and Julia wondered if Mathilda—Theodore—had exercised to keep it in shape.

Julia's gaze slid over the Skin's penis, now deflated. She held her breath, forced herself to look at it. Nothing special. No distinguishing marks or memorable bends, like that one man she'd dated, whose penis had bent the wrong way due to a childhood incident when he'd slid down the stairs bannister, forgetting the decorative wooden ball at the bottom.

The pubic hair around the penis was ungroomed and darker than the Skin's arm hair. Michael kept his pubic area shaved for cycling events. On the Skin, the pubic hair formed a matted bush with a triangle pointing up and trailing to its navel.

Julia flexed and examined the ripple of muscles on the Skin's faint, disappointing six-pack. There was nothing distinguishing on the Skin's torso or back, no scars, not even where Julia had stabbed it. She remembered vividly the sight of Theodore's blood on her scissor blades, the hot spurt of it like ejaculate on her hand.

Lastly, the face. Unlike the body, the face had a lot of character and, to Julia, was a memorable one though she couldn't remember ever having seen it before. Then she thought of Mathilda in the Skin, calling herself Theodore. Theodore had a completely different personality. His eyes had been hard and cold, not bewildered and attentive, as they were now that Julia was in the Skin. Theodore's forehead and brow had been knit in a perpetual scowl. On Julia, the skin was smooth, the brows drawn up unevenly, how she'd used to look in her own skin. Theodore's lips had been frowning or sneering, pulled so tight across his face, the inside of his lips were white. On Julia, the mouth was neutral but at ease.

It was a face Julia would have been attracted to, conditioned as she was from a young age that the skin spectrum was a litmus test for morals and ethics and earning power, with the creamiest rising to the top. She was attracted to the face of the skin she wore because it was white, and she'd been conditioned to associate whiteness with security.

Julia knew this prejudice about herself. She turned from her reflection in shame. She eased her new body into the tub, displacing too much hot water because she'd underestimated her size. Water sluicing down the tub sides and onto the tile floor alarmed her at first; someone might slip; then she remembered she was alone and supposedly immortal so there was no reason to clean it up immediately.

Instead, she stared at the ceiling, planned her day, planned what she would do to get back to her children and Michael.

⸙

After the bath, naked, she went back to the tiny bedroom, wondering, and yes, there were bags of clothes under the bed. A pack of three white shirts, a pack of six white briefs, and two pairs of jeans. All the Costco house brand. The different quantities didn't give a clue as to how long Mathilda expected her to stay there. Behind all the clothes, a small paper bag with toothbrush, toothpaste, and a bar of Irish Spring.

Julia put clothes on then kicked everything but the paper bag back under the bed. After breakfast, she brushed her teeth. Then she sat down and opened the laptop.

On reflex, she checked the battery. Full, and it had the little lightning icon next to it. Charging. How? She tried to pick it up but it was somehow fastened to the desk top. Standing over it, she saw a power cord connected to the back, and the cord disappeared immediately into a small hole in the desk. Julia traced the cord down inside the table leg, into a power source under the desk, maybe. The desk proved immobile, so that had to be it.

From all that, Julia surmised a few things: Theodore wanted her to have access to the laptop. There must be something important on it, other than the petabytes of random information. And if Julia needed a power source for anything, this was the best place to access it without tearing out a wall.

She pulled up the mesh-backed rolling chair and opened the laptop. There was indeed something important in it. The way to activate the door timer. But it was a coding puzzle with numbers and shapes and diagrams, pages of step-by-step instructions with sudden-death consequences that would require her to re-start if she missed a step. After an hour or so, Julia figured out half the puzzle had to do with how to work the house's electrical system so it would unlock the door. The most important thing, the only other thing she figured out from the puzzle, was that a simple *disruption* in power would render the lock permanent; she couldn't just dig up the floor and cut the wires to the door.

So there went that plan.

Julia leaned back in her chair to take a break. She swiped through all the information she could access. There were a lot of videos, like lectures on physics, instructional videos on something called Muy Thai, even videos on artisanal bread-making and surfing. All things she could've accessed through the internet but Theodore had graciously downloaded and stored them for her.

There were fifty digital books for every video, and seventy percent of the digital books were nonfiction: history, politics, memoirs, and biographies of notables. The fiction was all romance and westerns, the two genres Julia least favored.

She spent a few hours gleaning what little information she needed, then focused on her plan. She stood up and stretched. The goldenrod hue of light was the same as when she'd head out the door to pick up Sam, her youngest, from preschool. Then they'd go to lunch at The Sea Witch Cafe. Then they'd do errands, like pick up groceries at Fruit Basket, before getting Miriam and Paul for their piano lessons.

Julia shut the laptop. She rolled the mesh-backed chair into the bathroom. With barely any effort, she picked it up, then swung it as hard as she could against the mirror. Theodore shattered into a hundred pieces. Julia paused, looking at a hundred blue eyes. She didn't have a name to call herself yet, and a superstitious streak made her unable to continue symbolically destroying Theodore without having *something* to replace him.

What, though? A female or male name? She only thought of herself in terms of *I* and *me* and *my*. On the outside, she looked male. On the inside, she felt...well, she'd never considered it before. She supposed she had been raised to be a *woman*. She'd learned the habits and social cues, good and bad, of a *woman*. But to call herself a woman trapped in a man's body felt literally true but not quite right. The confusion was sapping her of energy. She needed more time and knowledge to give the question of her identity the gravity it deserved. So she settled on the first bite of that elephant-sized situation: a gender-neutral name.

She'd never liked them; they were given to unkempt brats by parents too young and immature to be parents themselves. There was one she'd liked, from a horror story she'd read as a teen.

Reagan.

Reagan lifted the chair again, felt her white shirt tighten against muscles bunching up on her back and shoulders. With a grunt, she swung with all her might. The mirror shards rebounded off the wall from the force of her strike. Sharp stings flecked her arms and face then grew warm as blood gathered in the cuts. She put the chair down and removed her shirt. Blood streaked and bloomed on the white cloth as she wrapped it around the largest shard of mirror glass, which was about the width of a cell phone and the length of a wooden spoon. It would've been unwieldy in her old hand but it fit well in the grip of her new hand.

Using the mirror shard, Reagan started cutting the mesh off the rolling chair.

⁂

It was deep night by the time Reagan had sculpted away the mesh back on the rolling chair. It had been reinforced with wire, which took several strokes of the mirror shard to get through. When Reagan wheeled the chair skeleton back into the laptop room, the large window to the outside world was liquid black. An unfathomable pool. It showed nothing but Reagan's large, pale, male body. Her arms and face were covered in flaking brown blood. Wearily, she wiped a hand over her face. Her skin was unmarred. Rather, the Skin had been damaged but it had healed without her knowing it. Not even the faintest scrapes.

Reagan stripped to her briefs. She ate dinner, brushed her teeth and showered, then slept.

The next day, she didn't bother with the laptop anymore. She ate, brushed her teeth, then got to work.

Reagan picked up the rolling chair's skeleton by its base. She'd removed the mesh back and the fabric and padding of the seat last night. She was left with the frame: the wheels, attached to the seat, attached to two thick prongs that had supported the mesh back. Reagan tapped these prongs against the wall. The prongs made a dampened knock.

Reagan stepped back, lifting the chair away. The prongs had made two indentations and had scraped some of the beige paint off the wall.

Using those indentations to mark the spot, Reagan measured about four inches right. Again, she lightly struck the chair against the wall. The sound came back: hollow. Reagan struck the wall about four inches to the right of that: dampened sound. Solid. She repeated this all the way around to the shared wall and came up with an estimate: most studs in the shared walls were spaced about sixteen inches apart. Industry standard, going by the "how to build a house" books she'd looked through on the laptop yesterday. The studs for the outside walls, however, sounded closer together. Eight inches in some places, twelve in others.

She didn't know if that was enough space for her new male body to fit through, and figured that it would be better to test the whole house rather than waste work on a space that proved too narrow.

For the rest of the morning and early afternoon, she tapped and tapped around the house, seeking, not its weakest point, but the point which would allow her new, much larger body, an exit.

After pushing one of the freezers away from the kitchen walls, she found a possible space and prayed it didn't have pipes or wires running through it. She examined the wall, eyed the room, and nodded. There was enough space to swing her makeshift pickaxe, the rolling chair.

She grabbed it by the base again, but gripped the heavy disk between the wheels this time, pulled it to the side because there wasn't enough room to swing it overhead, and lunged into the attack. The two back prongs slid into the wall like a knife into crusty french bread. And stuck there.

Reagan yanked on the chair. It shifted a little, but the prongs were stubborn. She heaved back and forth. Out came a wedge of drywall and dense insulation material.

For a moment, Reagan thought the insulation was a sign of compassion; Theodore hadn't wanted her to freeze to death in the mountains. Then she thought something closer to the truth: it was a safety measure to prevent her screams from being heard by the nearest neighbor.

Reagan looked at how much she'd accomplished in the day. She showered, washed the briefs she was wearing, hung them over the edge of the sink to dry. Then she ate. Then she slept.

———— ∞∞∞ ————

The next day, Reagan worked on her section of wall. She learned that she hadn't needed the chair. Once she'd made a hole large enough for her to get a grip on the edge, she could pry chunks of drywall out. It felt like tearing apart a giant sheet of peanut brittle.

Then Reagan used two empty packets from dehydrated survival food as gloves to scoop out insulation. It was thicker than she thought.

She paused intermittently, listened to her fearful, ragged breathing to convince herself she was still alive.

That she still existed.

And she coughed up marble-sized, bloody, slime-covered insulation wads.

Then her hand brushed something hard. She nearly choked on hope and excitement.

Frantically, she dug through the insulation like a rat trapped in a ribcage.

Unlike drywall, the wall she uncovered wasn't powdery or smooth. It felt almost hairy, rough with splinters. Plywood, maybe. She paused, thinking.

The chair-pickaxe she'd been using would be difficult to maneuver within the small kitchen; her new height prevented a downward swing. And it would be difficult to maneuver between the two studs on either side of her; side-swings would clip the studs, absorbing most of the force. She would have to use her new body and hope it was strong enough to break through plywood and whatever was behind it.

She couldn't remember what was behind it.

Had she seen what the outside walls were made of? It was California; no one built with real brick or stone. Especially not on top of a mountain. The weather didn't necessitate it and it would split with the next magnitude-seven earthquake.

The only thing she could think to do was to shove her side against it. And she had nothing else small or dense enough to use as a battering ram.

Three, two, one, *ram!*

Three, two, one, *ram!*

She kept at it, switching shoulders when one grew sore.

Three, two, one, *ram! Grind!*

She felt the friction of something give. The next impact, something must've come loose!

The next impact, something crinkled near her shoulder. At the spot she'd been hitting. The plywood was cracked. Reagan held her arms out in front of her, locked her elbows, put her hands on the spot, and pushed like she was resuscitating the wall. The plywood gave way but pressed against a membrane. She cracked and pushed the plywood in and out until she made a hole about the size of her face. Then she grasped the membrane. Felt a bit thicker than garbage-bag plastic. And something jagged beyond it.

Reagan tore through the plastic. And the jagged thing beyond it felt like the displaced slats of house siding. She rammed her body against the wall again.

Three, two, one, *ram!* Crack!

Three, two, one, *ram!* Crash!

Sunlight poured in, blinding her. Frigid air whistled in, swirling up dust and insulation fibers.

Reagan blinked in the light and the cold. She hadn't realized how stuffy it was in the little house until she breathed in the cold, wood-scented air. Gulping deep breaths made her lightheaded. She leaned against the wall and tried to see out the hole as sweat cooled on her brow and bare chest. But it was too bright outside and her eyes, accustomed to the dark, irritated by insulation fibers and dust, watered and burned.

When she'd rested a bit, she finished breaking down the wall. The world returned to her in patches. In the waning light, she finished but she didn't leave immediately. Instead, she sat cross-legged right outside the opening.

It grew even colder as the sun sank beneath the horizon. Reagan shivered, crossed her arms easily over her new flat chest, but didn't go back into the house. Not yet. She enjoyed the contrast between the orange sky at the horizon and the intense indigo curtain of night about to fall on the serrated black tree line.

Night sounds were starting. Frog croaks, insect chirps, owl hoots. It was almost too crystalline clear to be real.

The air smelled more…the only way she could describe it was *earthy*. From the scent, she could almost taste dirt in her mouth.

It was peaceful and picturesque and Reagan felt both refreshed and weary from the exertion of freeing herself. She wanted to rest for a day or so, prepare her body for what was coming, but Mathilda had said solving the logic puzzle would set off a two-week timer for the door to open. The implication then was that Mathilda planned for Reagan to be imprisoned for at least two weeks. Something would happen within that time.

It would be best to leave as soon as possible.

And night would be a good time to travel. She didn't fear it any more.

Wearing the Costco jeans, her cleanest shirt, the socks and shoes she'd had on when she'd first arrived, Reagan left through the hole and traveled by moonlight. She brought nothing else but some packets of dehydrated survival food wrapped in the dark blue sweater with the stab wound hole.

On foot, the road winding around the mountain was wide and safe as long as she stayed on the inside. Not one for heights, she didn't miss the view.

At some points, there were helpful shortcuts where locals had hacked away errant bushes or staked saplings and shrubs to grow away from a trail.

It was still dark by the time she made it to the valley. Wary of looking suspicious, she rested only briefly at the curb of the first house she came to. She figured as long as she stayed off people's property and kept to the road, as long as she walked with purpose and didn't look too long at any one house, she wouldn't arouse too much suspicion. Plus, she was now in a white body which also had a respectable haircut. There was slim chance anyone would call the police about her.

Still, thinking of the trouble her brothers had gotten into simply for being at the wrong place at the wrong time and being the wrong color, Reagan kept to the lights and sidewalks.

After a few blocks, she arrived at a main street but the area was still unfamiliar. She only needed the name of the city or some landmarks. That would solve a lot.

All the boutiques were closed. Even the lights at Starbucks and Peet's were off. And the street didn't smell of urine. Those things marked this city as being rather well off. Not as urban as San Francisco. But big enough for a Starbucks, and a Peet's as well. That meant it was either big enough to be ride hail territory, or near a city that was. And she would soon find a twenty-four hour gas station.

Reagan followed the main street in one direction until she came upon an old sign marking miles until the onramp for the Pacific Coast Highway. That meant this was an older town; only old locals and old signs referred to Highway 1 as "Pacific Coast Highway," or PCH for short.

It gave her a point of reference. The PCH ran up and down the coastline. She was currently south of her town. The closest large park with a lot of ancient redwoods was south of the Bay Area. She was southwest and not too far from home.

Reagan veered away from the sign and kept following the main street to its end. Heading to the highway was no use. She could not traverse it on foot.

Up ahead, the street was brighter with artificial light. She was close. Past a two-story office building with an ivy-covered facade, she came upon a Shell station with four fueling pumps and a snack hut.

Inside the snack hut was a short Latino man with glasses, talking on his phone.

Reagan shook the remaining food packets out of her sweater, smoothed wrinkles out of the sleeves, then put the sweater on. The hole wasn't too obvious and the fabric was thick, the color rich, and the style looked expensive. She mussed her hair. Then, limping, she approached the snack hut.

The Latino man looked up, said something on his phone, put it down but Reagan wasn't sure if he ended the call. He leaned over to a slender silver microphone attached to the wall.

"Can I help you?" His voice was metallic as it came through the speaker next to the bulletproof glass payment window. His words had no accent.

Reagan slowed as she got to the payment window. She held her hands out to show they were empty. She slouched to look as small as her new large body could look.

"I'm sorry to bother you," she said.

Her voice surprised her. It had a lot of baritone. She took a shallow breath, concentrated on speaking from her throat and not her chest.

"Could I impose on you for a ride hail?" she said. "I got carjacked. And mugged too." She held out the sweater so the knife hole gaped.

"Oh my God," said the Latino man. "Let me call the cops." He picked up his phone, said into it, "Dennis, I'll call you back. Yeah, yeah, I will."

Crap! That was not what Reagan wanted. She also didn't want to resort to threats. That would definitely not inspire this man to help her.

"Please don't," she said. "I have a bunch of unpaid parking tickets. They'll come and try to help but they'll arrest me too."

The Latino man looked unconvinced. "You might need medical help."

"I'm okay. I just want to get home to my hu–wife." She'd almost said husband. "Please. A car can be replaced. And I can call my credit card companies when I get home. I just want to go home to my wife."

The man nodded. "Where do you live."

"Forty-two Laurel Court, Loyola Hills." She gave him the address of a neighbor down the road from her house, just in case.

The man thumbed it in and raised a brow. "That's a fifty-dollar ride on Uber."

"I'll pay you back," said Reagan. "I'll PayPal you money if you'll give me your email address. Or I could send it to uh, this gas station or something."

"Let me check the other companies."

Reagan watched him check three more apps.

"Uber's the only one with cars nearby," he said. "That okay with you?"

"Yeah," Reagan said quickly. "Anything. Thank you! Thank you so much."

"Seven minute wait," said the man. "You can wait here in the light." He took a pack of nuts from the counter and a bottle of water from the fridge behind him. These, he passed on the curved metal tray under the bullet-proof glass.

"Thank you," said Reagan. She wasn't hungry but she was thirsty enough to finish the bottle in one go. She ate the peanuts one at a time and pretended to be interested in the ads and missing dog flyers taped to the wall beside the payment window while the man called Dennis back and, in Spanish, told him about the weird encounter with the white man who got mugged. Dennis wanted him to call the cops, apparently, because the Latino man promised he would after Reagan left.

There were two newspaper-dispensing bins below the posters. One was for a free pop-culture magazine based in San Francisco. The cover was a caricature of Zuckerberg and Jobs. The other bin had a free local paper which caught Reagan's interest because it had a photo of her old face on the front page, above the fold.

"Wife of Beatty Biotech employee attacked in Loyola Hills Home."

With sad humor, she noted how she was described not as simply a *woman* but as a *wife*, not in her home but in a *Loyola Hills* home. The implication was that her attack was significant because of who she was married to and where she lived.

According to the article: The man who attacked her had left the hospital and was later found dead of his stab wound in an alley behind a dive bar, positively identified by the wife of the Beatty Biotech employee, who had miraculously survived and was recovering well.

Below the fold, a small article on a missing man, a cab driver, probably *the* cab driver who had driven her up into the mountain woods.

Reagan put two and two together: Mathilda, who was now wearing Julia's body, had lured the cab driver—the one who'd picked them up from the hospital and driven them up the mountain, a man whose fate was dictated by his position in the taxi line—to the dive bar and killed him in the alley. Case closed on the attack. The Loyola Hills community could rest easy.

Reagan was about to flip to that page when the ride hail car came. A blue late-model Honda with a fist-sized dent on the passenger side front bumper. The woman driver's smile faltered when Reagan opened the navigator door. As Julia, prone to motion sickness, she'd always sat in the front seat of ride hail cars.

As Reagan, in the predawn gloom, she supposed she made an unsettling figure for a female driver. She gave the woman a rueful smile, shut the door, and sat in the back seat. The car smelled like spoilt milk and there were linty cheerios and action figures under the front seats.

Reagan took a final look at the gas station. When everything was settled, she would look it up and send the gas station attendant two tickets to a 49ers game, one for him and one for Dennis. Then she rested and thought and planned during the half hour drive into Loyola Hills.

———— ✸✸✸ ————

The car slowed. Reagan sat up and noted the time on the car's dash. About six-thirty in the morning, and though the sky still seemed dark, it was bright enough to see down half the block to her house. The kitchen light was on, which was understandable. Michael would be getting ready for work.

The driver let her out a few doors down from her house, did a three-point turn, then rolled away with a wave through the window.

Reagan put her hands in her pockets and gazed in the direction of her house so that anyone who might look out their window would see a man who knew where he was going. A man who belonged on their street.

She wasn't too worried about them talking to the cops later. She'd be gone by then.

And she wasn't worried about the security cameras on every house. More than half of them were fake and no one watched the surveillance videos unless something really bad happened. It would be too late.

She wondered if they'd caught videos of her murder.

Only when she was close to her own driveway did she leave the sidewalk. She sidled up to the deep shadows between the fence and hydrangea bushes, crept close to the kitchen windows, and watched.

Michael was already showered, shaved, and wearing his slacks and a pale blue button-down with a mustard-yellow napkin tucked into his collar. Reagan took a deep breath. She could almost smell his soapy skin. Just her imagination, of course. The windows were closed.

Toast bounced up in the toaster. Michael slid off the stool at the breakfast counter, shuffled to the toaster, retrieved the toast, sat down again and bit into a piece, sipped his coffee, then stared across the room at a stack of moving boxes.

They were moving.

Of course they'd be moving.

Mom was attacked in that house.

Reagan realized the counters were unnaturally bare of small appliances. No rice cooker, stand mixer, juicer, blender, her potted orchids. Just the toaster and coffee maker.

That's why Mathilda had locked her in the house with that ridiculous logic puzzle lock. To buy her time to mobilize her stolen family. She'd planned it down to this.

Another light came on in the second story. The kids. Paul and Miriam getting ready for school.

Reagan looked into the kitchen again. Michael was at the sink, rinsing his mug. He took the napkin off his collar and wiped his lips and hands with it. Watching those hands that had caressed her face, those lips that had kissed hers, Reagan almost lost her resolve to wait. She wanted to knock on the window or yell through the glass that it was her, Julia, his beloved wife in the body of the man who had attacked her.

Then, like watching a nightmare come to life, Reagan saw her old body emerge from the darkness of the stairwell. Michael smiled gently at the imposter. Michael took Mathilda, now Julia, into his arms and hugged her, kissed her on the forehead. Reagan felt it on her own forehead. Imagined. Remembered.

Her knees buckled, unable to support the weight of her breaking heart.

She felt the sun on her back, the wet grass under her knees, the damp leaves on her face. Dawn came, and with the light she saw footprints in the soil around the hydrangea bushes. Police, probably, looking for clues or traces of the man who attacked her. Reagan searched the different shoe prints for what might've been Theodore's prints as he stalked her family. Had Theodore's heart broken for things he could not have?

That was no reason for doing what he did.

Reagan stayed hidden and watched the garage door scroll up. Michael's gray Toyota Highlander rolled out. Paul was in the front, a smaller version of his father. Miriam, dark-haired like Julia, was in the back. Sam was buckled into his car seat, barely visible except for a cluster of blond wisps that would darken into a mousy color between his parents' shades.

Their faces were white and somber as they all faced forward. Reagan wanted to watch them until they disappeared down the road, but she'd miss her chance. The garage door was already scrolling down. Hunched, she scuttled beneath it, huddled beside the door, watched the car to make sure it kept driving away. It did.

There were stacked boxes everywhere in the dim garage, labeled with the kids' names or for a specific room. She crept around boxes until she reached the door to the kitchen. It was quiet beyond the door. Reagan opened it slowly, silently, and listened. Nothing.

The hot water tank in the garage roared to life, startling her. That meant Julia was running water for a bath or shower. Reagan waited a beat, then stepped through into the kitchen. An upstairs door opened and shut. She waited for footsteps across the upstairs hall or descending the stairs but none came. Julia might've entered the bathroom for that bath or shower. Reagan didn't know how much time that gave her.

She took her shoes off and moved silently across the kitchen, up the stairs, and headed for the bedroom she'd shared with Michael. Her path took her past the guest bedroom. The door was open, the bed looked slept in, but the extraneous furniture—the vanity, the arm chairs and matching ottomans—was gone. Family photos and a silver salver with matching brush and mirror set that had been on the vanity were on top of a cardboard box next to the bed. Shower sounds came from the bathroom.

The kids' rooms looked mostly packed up.

When she got to the bedroom she'd shared with Michael, she'd expected it to be packed up too, but everything was intact inside. It looked exactly as she'd left it the night she'd been attacked. There was even still blood on the carpet. For a moment, it looked shiny, crimson, fresh. A trick of her mind.

The dried blood looked like mud had been lathered into the gray carpet. It had dried carpet fibers into stiff clumps which scratched her palms as she got on her hands and knees to look under the bed. Then she looked under the nightstand. Then she looked under the dresser. She didn't see it. Maybe it had been kicked into the bathroom.

She started to get up then caught a glint of something beside a dresser leg.

As she reached for it, she felt a tremor on the floorboards. And she didn't hear the sound of water moving through the pipes anymore. Julia might be done with her shower.

Time was running out. Though Reagan wore an "immortal" skin, Julia was unpredictable, and Reagan didn't want Julia to damage the skin they both wanted.

Reagan clawed her fingers through the carpet under the dresser. She found what she was looking for: the key to the box with the gun and bullets. With it in hand, she went to the closet and looked for Michael's gun box on the top shelf behind purses she'd meant to drop off at Goodwill. Now, in her new body, she didn't need a footstool or chair to reach the shelf. She moved the purses aside.

It was gone!

She stepped back and clutched the key hard in her shaking fist. Where would it…

Michael might have taken it to the guest room. If that's where they were sleeping now, after an attack, he might want it close at hand.

But the imposter Julia was in there.

But she'd *just* finished her shower. Maybe she was putting on lotion.

No time to waste on *maybe*.

Key out and ready, Reagan went to the guest bedroom. The bathroom door was still shut. There weren't many places to look but there still wasn't enough time to check everywhere. Reagan had to gamble.

If she was Michael, she'd keep the gun close. Really close. Under the bed. He'd sleep closest to the door. The side with the family photos on top of the cardboard box.

The space by the other side of the bed, where he'd insist Mathilda, in Julia's body, sleep, was empty except for half a dozen gold coins and a stack of self-help books on coping with trauma, attacks, robbery. Well-intentioned gifts or Julia's charade. Probably never opened.

Reagan got on hands and knees by Michael's side of the bed. The gun box was within reach.

The floorboards vibrated.

Reagan yanked the box out, slid the key in the lock, flipped open the lid.

A drawer opened and shut within the bathroom.

Reagan took out the revolver. She opened it and checked the cylinders.

The floorboards vibrated.

Reagan stood and strode toward the bathroom door as the doorknob turned.

She cocked the gun and raised it.

The door opened with a gust of humid, soap-scented air.

Reagan aimed the gun at Julia's forehead.

Julia was wearing jeans and her favorite green blouse. Julia looked calmly beyond the gun muzzle and met Reagan's eyes.

"No backsies," Julia murmured. "The Skin doesn't work like that."

Reagan regretted cocking the gun earlier; she couldn't cock it now, dramatically, to make her point.

"You stole my life," said Reagan.

"I *gave* you a gift," Julia said. "You should be *grateful*. You can do *so much* with the Skin."

"I did a lot with the skin I had —"

"You can *be* somebody. Cure cancer. Be the president. Save the world! Things you couldn't do—"

Reagan snarled. "It shouldn't have to be like that!"

"It would be easier!"

"And it shouldn't be! You don't get it. You're diminishing the value of the choices I made by saying that. You're diminishing the value of my life, of the life of every woman who's made similar choices, by saying it isn't enough. That I could've had more. You're diminishing me and the career of motherhood. Why was *that* life, in *that* skin, worth less?"

From the coldness in Julia's eyes, she remained unmoved.

"And is this what you really wanted?" Reagan asked, pressing the gun muzzle in the new furrow between Julia's eyes.

"Death?" said Julia. "Freedom from immortality? Yes."

But her eyes bulged with fear. The green blouse shivered with her frantic heartbeat.

Reagan pulled the trigger.

Julia gasped and jumped. The smell of pee filled the air. Julia's crotch darkened into a V.

"You had no right," said Reagan. "What made you think you could just —"

A strange look came over Julia's face. The fear shrank, replaced by something cold and calculating.

Reagan cocked the gun. The fear returned.

"Give me my body back," said Reagan.

"I *can't,*" said Julia. "I was telling you the truth. You have to find someone who wants to live as badly as you want to die. It has to be an act of mutual destruction. And you can't go back, only forward."

Reagan pushed the muzzle deeper against Julia's forehead. The skin around it whitened. Julia closed her eyes.

"I'm telling the truth," Julia whispered. "If I could undo it, I would… Just like the woman before me. I wanted *her* to take it back too. She couldn't, and I grieved for what I lost. I lived in the Skin. And gradually, I came to know its power. Real life power. You can t—"

Reagan pulled the trigger. Click.

Julia jumped, whimpered.

"Here's what's going to happen," said Reagan. "You're going to let me see my kids. I'll look for a way to reverse what you did, but this isn't going to be the arrangement you had with the previous woman. I'm not giving up my family. You're not moving where I can't find you."

"But —"

Reagan cocked the gun again.

"All right," said Julia. "But you can't just show up out of nowhere. We have to make up a backstory and a reason, a history…"

"Stick close to the truth. Keep it simple. You can do that much, at least, can't you?"

Julia glanced at the gun. "Fine. I can do that. I just need a little time. But you have to leave for now."

Reagan, whose arm was finally starting to tremble, let the gun drop, but slowly.

Without another word, she left. En route to the front door, something caught her eye on the bare kitchen counter. She swept the keys into her hand. They must have changed the locks on the house because the new house keys were so new, the metal was almost white. Reagan headed for the garage. She flicked on the lights, got in her BMW, frowned as she adjusted it for her new height, then started the engine.

Halfway down the road, she realized something was bothering her. Halfway out of town, she couldn't let go of the image of the guest bedroom. All the family pictures were by Michael's side of the bed like they were clutter. And Julia had given no goodbye kisses to the children. And Julia had literally pissed herself when faced with a gun.

What kind of person longs for death then balks at the face of it...?

Reagan gripped the wheel.

But maybe that's how anyone would react...

Could Reagan take away the only mother her children knew? Would she let them grow up with the feeling that something was *missing*?

The family pictures...

Her children...

Something *missing*...

The missing coins. The gardener and housekeeper hadn't stolen them. Mathilda, as Theodore, must have. They were the gold coins on the table on her side of the room. Theodore had stalked not her family, but her wealth. Like those rich women with the Xs on their faces. Miami, Manhattan, Austin. And those were the ones Theodore had bragged about. Who knew if there were others?

Reagan turned the car around.

She drove it into the car garage. She went upstairs, where, contrary to the plans they'd just agreed on, she found Julia packing a suitcase of clothes. Good. At gunpoint, Reagan coaxed Julia into the car. And at the mountain house where she'd been imprisoned, Reagan shot Julia.

And from three towns south, Reagan, wrote a postcard to Michael and the children to tell them she was sorry but she couldn't keep up pretenses any longer, she'd met someone else, and it wasn't their fault but she was leaving them. God bless.

Michael recognized his wife's handwriting.

Over the next two years, he and the children felt like something was missing. Then Michael met a new woman who fit into their lives like she'd always been a part of it.

INTRO TO *Complexion*

There's a sweet spot at the beauty shop where, if you sit down in that particular chair, you can see yourself reflected infinite times between two mirrors.

It's a thrilling feeling, akin to the stomach-dropping lurch in a swiftly descending elevator, a moment of weightlessness, of losing one's weight, one's mass, one's matter. And in that absence of mattering, what's left is feeling.

Gordon's short story—which is probably a poem in one of those infinite reflections, or probably a six-tome epic in another—hits that sweet spot between being trapped by the barriers of physical sensations, and being transformed, magnified, multiplied, and freed by those barriers.

— JOAN REGINALDO

Complexion
by Gordon Hilgers

WHY IS IT SOMEHOW SAD to be confused yet alone in that confusion?

Perhaps, friend, there is a moment when any kind of taxidermist goes blind, even as his scalpel knives deeper, careful not to damage the hide he (or she) is bent upon keeping, only to find even deeper beauty, and deeper still, hugging the bones a beauty that seems to rhyme with death itself.

Of course, I am no taxidermist, and my life has nothing at all to do with skinning animals. Yet this morning is chilly, and as I pull my coat tighter around me, the clouds above all stratus, a gray layer that blocks a sunshine which might warm, but might as easily not warm at all, I think about the horizon all around me. Sure. As in any large city, this horizon is jagged, a cliff-like mantle of jutting silhouettes of skyscrapers, treescapes I cannot quite see, even the nearby apartment complexes on this street, one laden with people in transition, none of whom seem, myself included, capable of completing the multi-faceted projects we tend to call our lives.

Years ago, when I was younger, the horizon seemed confinement. I wanted to see it all. I wanted to know how all these gadgets I simply have to have are made, and who makes them. But beyond that mere curiosity over what may hide behind the horizon, what behind the horizon may affect even fairly unimportant people like me, there was a longing connected to that curiosity, an ache that echoed the frustration of not being able to know a sort of wilderness of mystery lying just beyond the edges of my vision, and all this led me to a sense of being powerless that would set me to drinking, and once drunk, I would shout at the walls. Let's put that up to youth. I could not sit still. I lived in unrest. I wanted to go farther, deeper. But couldn't.

At least that's the skinny here as I make-way to begin my day's work. Now the sun is appearing, burning away the early morning cloud cover. Yet I am alone. The woman I love is hidden beyond this horizon, in another place, another town, out beyond the skin of the known world, at least my version, gone past a point of no return, and I miss her. Terribly.

Let's put this all into a different perspective: I know a woman who sells cosmetics. She's like a lot of women who, reaching middle age, discovering in the mirror one morning a slight trace of a crow's foot beneath an eye, each recoil into some sort of prescriptive means, in her case an array of expensive cosmetics which cover signs of age or promise to erase those signs of age, a means of forestalling the inevitability of aging, of losing one's beauty, a loss that is a permanent one, one more sign perhaps that life itself is transitory. This is frightening to many women, and the woman of whom I refer is indeed quite beautiful. While she wears little in terms of make-up, and simply does not need the cosmetics, she is also an actress, and once, she asked me how a photograph of her face, all made-up in rehearsal for a Shakespearian play in which she was starring, looked.

The woman's image, only two-dimensions, practically ushered my breath right out of my chest. She looked completely different, not the same woman at all. Suddenly, only momentarily, I was stricken with a sense of the unearthly, a loss of my bearings in a way, for who are we really behind these masks of skin? Exoticism. That's how I express this. Something about an unexpected introduction to being estranged from what we know, in this regard an old friend so artfully rendered by cosmetics that had so completely altered her appearance that suddenly I felt I did not know her at all.

"You look beautiful!"

"It's only for the theater," she replied.

"Who would have known—"

A smile on her face, she touched my shoulder and gave me a wink. On the surface of this gesture, everything was all right. I would have appreciated her wink and that brush upon my shoulder as a flirt, but I simply could not be certain about that. Need I return to those youthful benders when I shouted at the walls late at night, fit to disturb the neighbors, all of whom were sincerely trying to get the best sleep possible before waking the next morning and going to work?

What is it about drinking? Is it mere compulsion? What is it we are trying to reach when we drink so much we pass-out on the couch, the television still burbling and blinking before us, a strange bluish light crawling all over us as we are essentially knocked-out? This liquid, be it beer or wine or something much harder on our systems, goes into us, and then something changes. We become ebullient, snared in some kind of mute rapture, something deep within broadening outward until, relaxed, what had cloistered us to begin with seemingly disappears. But only for a while. Then down we dive into a deep irritability. The only medicine then is more.

I remember once going on a business trip with my partner, and we got ourselves a motel room that we meant to use to save ourselves a little capital expense. The motel room had twin beds, and when we turned on the television, my business partner immediately found The Playboy Channel. Vivid Videos presents...The young women, almost all blonde, were beautiful as they engaged in all sorts of acts I will leave to the imagination. My business partner? He was obsessed with this. He couldn't stop watching. As for me, well, I was interested for an hour or so, but then it got boring. Why was this?

Because this was television. Television is an odd magic, isn't it? There in two dimensions we see ideals, fantasies, all our aggressions and passions revealed, albeit almost pulled right out of us, and then the commercials.

Everything is so positive in TV land, isn't it? The people who shill autos, for example, are all clean, neat, well-groomed and often quite lovely in appearance, and because of the illusion, we drift into imagining we actually are those people. We identify with a two-dimensional ideal, and we suddenly wish to be those ideals. And positive. All is sunny. There is never really any darkness in our commercialism, is there? Sure there may be "the danger set-up," but that's all in order to sort of rescue us from some inner fear, the rescue being of course the product or service on sale.

So perhaps this is stand-up. I'm not a very good comedian, am I? I stand on a stage, peel onions and then cry. All for money. At least it seems this way.

In reality, I am an artisan. I work in a museum. I exhibit nothing. I mount paintings, expensive paintings, valuable works of art, lining them, one by one, beatific hallways a parade of nothing, actually, beyond paint, inks, various techniques, all of which are twice-removed displays of emotion or sensation, some of them honoring heroes, men (or women) who lived for something, and many who died for no reason. I paint the walls an ardent white beforehand, making certain the paint's complexion in no way detracts from or obstructs the closest approximations we can make of what the artist or sculptor intended. This is no easy work.

Yes, even here, as I am standing at the threshold of my house, cold wind is blowing against me, and once again, I tighten my coat. Then, standing on the doormat, I leave this house, looking for home, or expressions of home, knowing the horizon all around me is nothing, and that nothing is walled-in as some would believe.

INTRO TO *While We Sleep*

In Dawn's *While We Sleep*, the reader becomes aware that while humans dominate the planet, there is one domain they don't own: darkness. I love how the protagonist explains that either we play nice with the mysterious forces or we let them hurt us. Dawn delivers the tension and rawness you expect to hear from a war-weary soldier. That one terrible event that stains you for the rest of your life.

— ERNEST ORTIZ

While We Sleep

by Dawn Del Sontro

DON'T BE ALARMED. Really, there is no need. They won't hurt you, if you give them no cause. They know the house is yours. They know you are in charge. They love you, they do. They've always loved you. They won't hurt you, unless you give them good reason.

Don't give them a good reason. Please...

The only really horrid incident ever reported to our department happened a long time ago. It was bad—really bad. No one made it out alive. The carnage. My God, the carnage! I've been doing this job for a while now and I haven't seen anything like it since.

It was twenty years ago. I'm not old, but by industry standards, I'm a dinosaur. Thirty-eight, to be exact. This makes me the oldest in the company.

I am now the field squad commander. With age, belief fades, and with fading belief comes the inability to do field duties as they need to be done. Now, I am the field squad commander and I train the others. I might not have the belief, but I have the memories to successfully train the ones who come after me, the young ones. I help protect those who help protect you.

Those who make the mistakes like that night twenty years ago. Twenty years ago, it was the father who made the mistake and set the horror into motion.

We received the call at 4:17 in the morning. I was at my desk, drinking too much coffee for a girl of eighteen. I needed it though, since we work the nights. Night happens all over the world, never at the same time.

Back then, my team and I handled the entire Northern American section. In this line of work, the younger and less experienced you are, the higher rank you hold. It's backward and confusing, but it makes sense, and not a lot of things make sense with this job.

On that day, I was in charge. The young ones always are because of their continued strong connection to the hostiles. That day, I was the woman everyone looked to for answers.

As the youngest, I still held the most belief. It's the belief that gives you power. That's why I was the first one through the door.

I smelled it before I saw it: the metallic stench of drying blood sitting on my tongue, an unsavory weight. I gagged at that smell, the taste of it, before I could cover the lower part of my face with the standard issue mask. The silence in the house had its own weight. Not a tick of a clock, or a creak of the floor. Silence surrounded us. The main level of the house held no answers to why we were there. That's usually the case. Most of the incidents take place in bedrooms and playrooms.

Behind me, my team of four spread out, each following procedure. I was the only untested one. The others were veterans with several years under their belts. I was on point, weapon in my shaking hand. I'd only ever been to a scene this bad in scenarios. The live scenes I had been to had just been minor infractions which were easily cleaned up and explained away as yet another botched robbery or messy suicide.

I ascended the stairs of the modest home, slowly and cautiously. My heart pounded harder with each step I took. We'd been contacted by the neighbor's friendlies after they had sensed the commotion from next door. They are connected in a way we can't understand, but it helps us. Usually, they love and adore our kind, like pets, but sometimes, age or circumstance drive them to act out.

According to the friendlies, the hostile was still on the premises, hiding, most likely. We had to find it, set the scene, and get out before the local police were contacted.

It always gets worse when the "real" authorities get mixed up in these things. When we do things right, we can always explain everything away with just a few minor adjustments.

The hallway was bathed in the soft glow of several nightlights. I checked the first room; the lights were off, save a bedside lamp on the lowest setting. That low light let me see much more than I wanted to see.

Books were scattered across the floor, red drops decorated their pages like confetti. The stuffed animals pressed closely together, away from the carnage in the middle of the room. A little naked foot, the peek of a purple nightgown, a tiny hand clutching a blanket, the redness of blood.

Not the children...

Why...?

Why? They never hurt the children.

I swallowed hard and did my job. I checked the room's smallest spaces, carefully avoiding the pooling blood, knowing better than to leave any trace of my presence.

I exited the room, searching the hallway, and pulled the door shut behind me. It would keep the hostile from slipping past me and using the room for cover.

The bathroom was empty. So were the guest room and a powder blue room decorated with trains and cartoon toy cars. I pulled each door shut as we continued.

I found the little boy in the master bedroom with his parents. The father had started it. In his pale dead hand, he still held a scrap of gray and white cloth, white tufts clinging to his nails. Yes, he'd been the one to start it and it had led to the death of his entire family.

A scratching sound ahead and to the left had me back on guard. I yelled, "Peterson! Up here!" before turning to the sound and carefully stepping forward.

I scanned the room, searching for a sign of the hostile. I looked quickly, not wanting to commit the scene to memory, but failing. The blood bright red against cream walls and ceiling, a darkening pool on the bed, around the mother. A tiny body, broken.

The pounding feet on the steps behind me as Peterson approached brought me back to my task. The others would continue to search the rest of the house, in case our perp hadn't acted alone. It was rare for hostiles to work together, but it happens.

The sound was low, small and sad, as I knew it would be. I stuffed my weapon into my back pocket, hoping I would not have to use it. Once my hands were free, I raised them in front of me, trying to appear as friendly as possible. I'd have taken off the mask, but even through it, I was having a hard time not vomiting at the stench of blood that permeated the room.

It was difficult not to look away from where the hostile hid—not to focus on the mess on the walls, blood, and all the other gruesome details. Even now, after all these years, I still can't understand how something so tiny had done so much all by itself. It didn't make any sense then—and it still doesn't.

Then I saw the two black eyes peering unevenly at me from behind the laundry basket. Training and protocol required that I first try coaxing it out—try to convince it to come quietly. Still, after what it had done here, this day could only end with the hostile dead. Protocol, however, dictated that I try—so I did.

"Come on fella, I won't hurt you. I understand. I really do. You didn't mean it. It was their fault. It's always their fault."

I kept my voice as even as I could and my eyes off what remained of the family.

"I saw what the man did to you."

I shouldn't have said that last bit. Reminding it of the man was a mistake. I knew it as soon as the words left my mouth.

The shiny eyes blinked at me and then it rushed in, long arms flailing, head wobbling grotesquely as its little legs pumped furiously. Its tail stood straight up, like an exclamation point of its rage. It jumped at my face, leaping with an unexpected grace. It wrapped those arms around my head, trying to do to me what it had done to the others.

Its hands sunk into my hair as I grabbed it with both hands and pulled. It didn't budge any further than the length of my hair and that hurt enough to make my vision light up with bright dots of pain. Then Peterson was there. He pried as I pulled and together we wrestled the hostile to the floor. It screamed, high-pitched and furious as I found the hole made by the father and plunged my hand inside. Its stuffing puffed out of the wound like cotton candy. Its screams abruptly ceased and the weight of its pain filled the sudden silence. Its tail drooped and twitched. I'd done some nerve damage, but I plunged my hand back in and repeated the process, again and again.

When I'd done enough to incapacitate it, I picked it up and shoved it in the plastic bag that Peterson held open. He deftly tied it shut. You can't kill them like that. You have to burn them. It's the only way. We'd take the sack back to headquarters and toss it, with its contents, into the incinerator.

We searched the rest of the house and found nothing. Then, with our hostile safely bagged, we left the scene in the hands of the cleaners. They would ensure that the "real" world would be able to come to an acceptable explanation of what had happened here. I was sure that they would opt for a multiple murder/suicide, with the father as the one to blame. Which was, of course, only fair. He had started this whole thing in the first place.

Peterson looked at me as we rode back to headquarters.

"I didn't get a good look at it. What was it?"

I had been thinking in the darkness about how people forget. Like that father had done. How at night, the house that is yours, is not really yours. That the creatures who lurk in the shadows of the children's rooms, from behind display cases and the favored spot on the chair, are the owners. They own the darkness.

They will not hurt you – unless you give them a reason. But people forget.

I shook my head.

"What did you say?"

Peterson repeated his question.

I sighed. I felt so tired, suddenly much older than my eighteen years. I pulled some stray stuffing from the prong of my ring and flicked it away in the darkness. Without looking at my colleague, I said, "It was one of those stupid sock monkeys. Old as hell by the look of him, and crazy with it."

The rest of the journey we drove in silence.

INTRO TO *And So The Flies*

Sometimes, with so much emphasis on how love seems to roll-in its tidings where sea and sand meet, we forget the air above, that celestial thingness that, in terms of physicality, is matter as much as water is matter and sand is matter. Beyond even that stark science, contemporary research indicates that all matter is nothing but energy comported into different states, much as water is a liquid form of solid stone. Then, there is imagination, the realm of symbolic understandings bent to bypass language altogether due to nounish limitations. And this is exactly where Dan's poem takes us: a quotidian scene implacably bent by factors beyond the mere human relation into something both earthy and new. In afterglow, we fly, insectile or better otherwise.

— GORDON HILGER

~And So the Flies~

Dan Tompsett

Flies buzz kelp tossed aground
as brown eels monkey pool to pool
beneath the foam where broken creatures
churn and grind into mundane sand.

The cafe's dated tablecloth,
checkered white and blue,
is soiled from years of deep-fried fare,
sand from the shells you took
to your dry-land guy
with his basket of loot, sunny car,
and common sense.

I size-up the prevalent wind,
and from where I'm seated, your glass,
my glass, the spent bottle
and sourdough crumbs, still
as life becomes without you
suggest it's time to go.

The waitress brings the check. I pay,
deal out the tip,
as the surf below grumbles
and thunder-gray gulls
lift away like smoke.

INTRO TO *Soda Flies*

In the first volume of this series, we featured a poem by Dan Tompsett, and the story challenge that accompanied it. The whys and wherefores are spelled out on page one-hundred-fifty-eight of that book if you're interested in tracking the tradition, this being the second occurrence since its inauguration.

Dean always says that poetry is mostly incomprehensible to him, but he knows how it makes him feel, and Dan's poem when first discovered, brought a lot of feeling. So, he challenged the Black Hats Writers Group to write a story from the poem. Joan's response to that poem follows soon as you finish this intro...

The name Cynthia means moon. And like the moon, the main character in *Soda Flies* appears as a shade creeping through life as another's reflection.

But, if you've ever seen the bright creamy moon glowing full as it skirts slowly across the tree tops while the briny bay breeze fills your head with sweet summer jasmine, look behind you quickly... you may glimpse the primeval power that turns the tides.

— DEAN FEARCE

Soda Flies

by Joan Reginaldo

A HANDFUL OF PEOPLE WASHED up on this beach after their ship ran aground on the sandbar.

That was almost a hundred years ago, though; I don't think that's what Derek wants to talk about. Sand grinds beneath my loafers as I cross the parking lot to The Sea Witch Cafe. My long dark hair whips in my eyes, sticks to my lip gloss. I pull it all back into a low ponytail.

The gate to the cafe's patio dining area is open. From the parking lot I see Derek sitting at the table closest to the beach, staring towards the ocean, stoic, eyes the same wet-stone hue of the impending storm. Even now, especially now, the sight of him arrests me. I am so lucky.

"Derek," I say, smiling, expecting him to rise and give me a hug.

He stands but it's only to offer me his seat. He takes the chair beside me, putting the ocean to his right. His face is half in light, half in shadow from the patio awning.

"What is it?" I say. "What's wrong?"

"Let's eat first," he says.

"All right." I look around for a menu then gesture towards an approaching waitress, but realize the steaming plates in her hands are for our table.

It's Selena, with sun-brightened hair and new freckles, back from her vacation. I want to ask her how it was but she doesn't make eye contact as she sets the plates quickly onto the sticky blue and white check tablecloth of our tiny table.

"All right!" she says brightly. "Specialty mussels and sourdough rolls. Would you like another bottle of house white?"

"It smells divine," I say. "How was your —"

"We're fine," says Derek. "Thanks, Selena."

Selena nods at his chin. She glances at me. In the flash of eye contact, I read concern, but then she's gone, heading towards the front where another couple is waiting to be seated.

Derek pours wine into our glasses, fogging them with condensation from the steaming bowl of mussels. He butters a sourdough roll, takes a bite, nods to indicate his pleasure and to signal that I should also partake of the sourdough rolls.

I hate sourdough.

But I reach for the butter. I stop short, remembering, waiting, but Derek doesn't shield the butter bowl with his hand like he usually does. Cautiously, I dab the butter onto my roll, take a bite, and diligently chew as he parcels out the cafe's "specialty" mussels. We each get eight of equal size.

He doesn't pour the butter out of mine.

I should be...grateful. The specialty lemon-garlic-and-butter mussels is my favorite dish here and it's been so long since I've had the lemon-garlic-and-butter part of it.

But the heavy silence between us presses down on my stomach, shrinks my appetite. The briny air always makes me hungry but it annoys me now.

I want to put my hands over my ears to silence the shush of ocean and keening call of gulls. Something's about to happen, something bad, and I don't want to associate those beautiful sounds with the terrible thing that's coming.

Derek finishes his last mussel, tips the last trickle of wine down his throat, wipes a paper napkin over his lips.

Then says, "I want to see other people."

My lips go numb. I hold very still, like I can freeze this moment and he can't go, he won't leave. The waves can keep lapping and the sticky plastic tablecloth can flap, but if I stay very, very still—

"Say something," he says.

I don't know what to say.

And then suddenly, I have too much to say. "What do you mean? Are you leaving me? Is this...But you can't. I saved you, Derek. You were drowning in debt and I saved you. You'd be dead without me! You can't leave me, you can't, you can't just... just leave me like this. You owe me... I mean, you don't have to pay me back, I said I'd support you, but I thought that meant...I thought..."

He shrugs, taps his fork against his plate, pours himself another glass of wine.

"I can pay you back." His soft words are almost lost beneath the susurrus of the waves. His voice is as cold as the ocean. "Even though you said..."

"I know what I said, and I meant it when I said it but that was when I thought..."

"So you do expect me to pay you back?" His brows form two sharp accusing peaks. His voice echoes against the cafe wall behind me. The other diners glance our way.

"No," I say. "Of course not. But Derek—"

"It's done, Cynthia. I'm done." His gaze slides off me and finds the ocean.

"Is it the apartment?" I say. "It's my stuff, isn't it. I can put more of it in storage. I'm sorry about...about spreading all my scrapbooking stuff around the place. I can work in a smaller corner. Really, Derek, I can fix all my scrapbooking mess—"

"Dammit, Cynthia, you have to do things to scrapbook!"

"What do you mean?"

He throws back a swallow of wine. "Normal people don't scrap-book photos of food."

"But on Instagram—"

"Instant. Gram. People post a photo, then move on. You're not… you're not moving on."

"I can, Derek. I can!"

He leans back. I've leaned into his personal space, so I ease back into my seat.

"We can both move on," I say, voice quavering, "together."

"I'm trying to do this as gently as I can," he says. "But you're making it really difficult."

I nod. "All right. I'm sorry about that. What else do you want to say?"

He makes a slow chopping motion with his hand, severing the air between us. "That's it. Plain and simple, we're done."

I nod again, "Yeah, but you haven't said why. I need that much at least."

"That's enough, Cynthia."

I feel like he can't understand me for some reason. Like he's under a spell. Or I've been cursed.

"Tell me why!" I whisper. "I can try harder. I'll go… I'll see more doctors. I'll take more meds. I can try harder for you. For us."

"It's not working."

"Just give it a chance. Would you just give it a chance?"

"I've given it plenty of chances. You're not getting better. I'm not getting any younger."

"But I saved you," I say.

"And I'm sorry I can't return the favor…"

"Can you at least look at me and say it?"

He looks at me without seeing me. "It's done."

Then, for the first time ever, he pays for our meal.

Selena crouches by my table so we're eye level.

"We're closing, hon," she says.

I blink at the silver-gilt, blue velvet waves behind her. The rising moon beckons to me at the end of a glittering white path over the water. The briny scent has grown stronger.

"What time is it?" I say.

"Nearly six." Selena stacks the plates on my table. The butter on Derek's plate has congealed into a waxy mess.

"Can I have that to-go?" I say, nodding at the couple of sourdough rolls.

Selena flaps her hand. A cloud of flies rises then audaciously hovers, waiting for her hand to leave.

"You don't even like sourdough," she says.

"I like it when it's from here," I lie.

She wraps the bread in foil. I stick the rolls in my purse. Selena walks me through the empty cafe, toward the front door.

"Can I give you some advice, hon?" she says.

"Sure."

Selena grasps my shoulders firmly. I have to look up to meet her limpid gaze, but she doesn't speak until I do.

"You can do better," she says, nodding.

I'm taken aback that she'd speak about my personal life. I've eaten here often enough to feel obliged about giving her a Starbucks gift card every Christmas and a bouquet of carnations every Mother's Day and on her birthday, but we've never spoken more than pleasantries.

I say, "But he's so…" handsome and smart and charismatic and ambitious and…and…

"Go home," says Selena. "Get out your biggest tub of ice cream. Turn on Netflix. And you cry, cry every part of him out of every single one of your cells. Call in sick to work. Then you cry some more. Then you start to heal. Then you get over him. Then you move on."

"I can't."

"You can. Guys like him… They prey on girls like… Well, on girls like you."

"What?" I yell, shrugging her off. "What do you mean, girls like me?"

She stares at me a moment. Her face softens as she sighs. "Girls who still believe in happily ever after."

"You don't know anything about us. I saved him once. I can save him again. We're meant to be together. I'm not giving up on him."

Selena retreats. Grim-faced, she opens the door.

Once I get home, I do exactly what she prescribed and it helps just enough to keep my head above water.

My psychiatrist calls because I miss my weekly appointment.

After I explain what's going on, she calls new prescriptions in to my pharmacy.

I can't tell if the new pills help, but I do have to go to my next appointment or risk my psychiatrist cutting me off from my next refill. I almost appreciate the irony in that threat.

"So what's going on…?" Dr. Desmond glances down at her notepad, "Cynthia?"

"Derek and I are on a break," I say.

"That's not what you said over the phone."

"I know. I was confused."

"Are you confused now?"

There's a lot I want to say, but it feels like she's waiting for me to say certain key words that'll trigger something she's learned in school, like I'm some kind of equation, holding out on variables that'll help her solve me and move on to the next patient.

I want to keep quiet and not risk being disappointed again, but I take a chance.

"I feel like I'm cursed or something," I say, shrugging. "Like I can't... There's all these things I try to say but it's like no one understands me. Like no one hears me or something. Like, sounds come out, but..."

We stare at each other over a neutral expanse of carpet the color of wet sand.

"How has work been going?" she says. "Last time we talked —"

I mentally close the door on hope and take this opening instead. "I'm on vacation right now. I mean, I called in sick for a few days. Then it just seemed like a good idea to not go back to work quite yet."

Dr. Desmond glances at her notepad again.

"Cynthia, didn't we talk about the importance of maintaining a routine?"

"Yeah, but —"

"Work was helpful, wasn't it? The routine kept you from dipping too low?"

"Yeah, but —"

"What's filling your time away from work?"

I tell her about my scrapbooking.

"Cynthia, scrapbooking is more about keeping mementos of activities and people and activities you do with people, not so much… keeping photos of cookies and cupcakes."

"Yeah, but I baked them myself."

Dr. Desmond tells me that no one even scrapbooks anymore, in this digital age, but maybe I could find a scrapbooking club or something. She lectures me on the importance of getting out, connecting with real people, going back to routine.

"I have some books I'd like you to read for next session," she says.

I can't believe she's giving me homework. She went to med school to learn the secret language of the heart and how to mend the shreds of a tattered soul and she's giving me…homework.

She takes some paperbacks off her desk and gives them to me one by one as she tells me the titles and what they're supposed to help me with. Finding Your Voice, and Using It. Walk, Run, Dance: Healing in Baby Steps. Silence your Ocean of Emotion. I thank her, leave her office, and dump the books in the trash can next to the receptionist's desk.

Back home, I turn on my laptop and, in the dark, do something I rarely do because it exacerbates my condition. All those announcements—birth announcements, graduations, raises, engagements—when I was with Derek, they'd made me feel like I was waiting on him to start my own life. Being with him had made the waiting bearable. But after Derek, looking at that stuff just makes me feel…disappointed with myself. Like somehow, my life is worth less than everyone else's.

But I have to do it because I have to know. I Facebook-stalk Derek, who, out of pity but more likely just forgot about me, hasn't unfriended me.

I don't know how long it's been since we last talked. A month maybe? I scroll down to the date of when our "break" started, not really knowing what to expect. It'd be nice if he didn't post anything. Or better, if he posted a selfie of himself crying. Or one of those cry-for-attention posts like "Everything hurts, but no one would understand."

Instead, there's a photo of the ocean from that overcast afternoon. He'd been fortunate enough to catch a sunbreak's golden beams shining down on a pod of dolphins.

His caption reads: "A good omen for a fresh start. Graduating in three months!"

And there's over a hundred comments and twice as many likes. I didn't know he had that many friends!

I slump over the keyboard, suddenly weak and overcome by the beauty of the image, by envy of his life, by the unfairness of everything. Numbness is preferable to this deeply penetrating pain that has no physical source.

Knowing better but unable to stop myself, I look at the picture again to make sure it's from the day we last met. Maybe, just maybe, I have some presence in the photo. I'd settle for my shadow crossing the table in front of him, or a blur of my hair. Any indication that I have something to do with this "good omen" for his future.

But I am completely absent.

And there's another photo a bit after that. I can see the bottom edge on the screen.

I rest my fingers on the touchpad to scroll up. I shouldn't…but I can't help myself; I have to see.

I scroll up.

It's a night-photo of Derek and another woman, dark-haired like me, but with pink cheeks and a wide white smile. He's hugging her from behind as she holds the handle of the selfie stick.

The caption: "Me and my girl going out to a celebratory dinner!"

And the date the photo was posted was the same day he broke up with me, hours after our late lunch.

In the comments below, not one of his friends asks, "What happened to Cynthia?"

They hadn't known about me. Or they knew and didn't care. The story of my life.

The pain turns to anger. Longing for numbness turns into longing for revenge.

As much as I gave him, I could take away.

I could reveal everything.

He'd used me for money. He'd been drowning in debt, about to get kicked out of school, and I'd paid for his tuition and books. I worked three jobs to make sure we had three squares, a roof over our heads, his laptop and smartphone and pens and papers and textbooks and car and parking fees.

I was drowning as I'd saved him.

Once saved, he abandoned me.

He's forgotten that I can still kill him.

These days, physical death isn't the worst thing that can happen to someone.

Death by social humiliation can last a bitterly long time, and the best part is, the person is alive to experience the shunning, the public shaming, the bone-cold desperation of being penniless and unhireable.

First thing I do is Friend-Request his new…I don't want to say it but relationship statuses don't lie—she's his new girlfriend. Helen Chang. She works in finance and already has about five hundred friends so I'm betting she gets a lot of requests from colleagues. She wouldn't notice my name in the mix if she batch-approves or auto-approves.

Next thing I do, while I wait, is open up a blank document and pour my heart out:

"Open letter to Helen Chang,

You don't know me, but…"

To establish credibility, I describe Derek in ways only a girl-friend would know. To establish trust, I give her a little bit of myself. Tidbits of truth she could look up if she wants to, like my matricu-lation at Berkeley and my parents' names.

In the body of the letter, I tell her about how I met Derek during my last year at Berkeley, his dream of going to med school, which became part of our dream en route to white picket fences and children and puppies. Which led to that stupid, stupid pact we made in which we would take turns supporting each other through grad school.

Had he known then what he would do? Was it his master plan all along, to find some chump to foot the bills?

I don't know, and it doesn't matter. What matters is that I kept years and years of receipts, because I'd meant to put some in a scrap-book of our dating relationship and present it to him as a wedding present.

The most major receipts—for his tuition, textbooks, car insurance and car payments, adult braces and gym memberships—I scan or screen-cap and paste into the letter as proof. Good proof, too, since they have both his name as the student or owner and mine as the payee.

By the time I'm done, Helen has approved my friend-request and given me full access to her timeline.

Lots of little black dresses and slingback heels, tastefully gaudy cocktail rings and pink drinks in martini glasses. When she's not out drinking with friends, she's at baseball games with her brother, apple-picking with mom and dad, baby showers and bridal showers and engagement parties and weddings.

It's a life as beyond my reach as the moon.

And then Derek comes along.

He fits into her life seamlessly.

They both look…happy.

It's a feeling I barely remember but I know that once I have it, I'd recognize it, like the scent of an old teddy bear. Now, though, I'm like an archeologist examining her life, which has become their life, perpetually an outsider trying to make sense of something beyond my ken. The colors in their world only make my life drearier. The depth and expanse of their world makes mine feel like it's trapped in glass.

I am an onlooker to their merry parade of "life moments."

That alien, unreachable, unattainable happiness, I could not destroy; I had built half of it.

I shut my laptop but the feeling to do something doesn't leave me. Since it's been a long time since I've felt that urge, part fight, mostly flight, I hang on to it.

Scooping a few things into my purse, including my laptop, I put my apartment in order. Then I head for the last place I'd glimpsed my own happiness.

—————— ∞∞∞ ——————

In the amber glow of The Sea Witch Cafe's security lamps, Selena is hunched over the cafe doorknob, trying to lock it. She whirls around, squints into my headlights.

"It's me," I say. I open my door and turn off my lights and engine.

The startled look on her face is replaced by wariness, then concern.

"You look like you haven't slept for days," she says.

"Thanks," I say. "Can we go inside?"

She keeps staring at me, her right hand on the knob, left hand clutching the cafe key.

"Ten minutes on the rear patio," I say. The gate to the rear patio would already be latched from the inside, otherwise, I wouldn't have bothered her.

"All right," she says. "Ten minutes."

She opens the door, locks it behind us. Inside, the cafe smells like Pine Sol with a hint of fishy grease. The floor tiles and counter-tops gleam de-oxygenized-blood red in the dim security lights.

"Go on out back," she says. "I'll get us some soda."

"Ginger ale," I say. "Thank you."

I unlatch the rear cafe door and step outside to a calm, balmy, briny spring night. I sense my happiness hovering like a ghost at the table where we last sat.

Beyond the patio, moonlight infusing the ocean spray gives the beach an ethereal glow like the line between heaven and earth is blurring. Because beyond the beach, the ocean is an unfathomable darkness unconfined by silver-tinged, eternally shattering chains riding the waves.

I open my laptop and ready it for Selena. She comes out a second later with two bottles of ginger ale.

"Should I post this open letter to his new girlfriend's account?" I say, turning the laptop.

Selena scans it as she sits down beside me. She gives me a wry smile.

"I think it's a good start if you want to ruin his life," she says. "I'd be glad to help you think of more ways."

It's not what I want to hear, which is a good indication that I'd already made up my mind and had come here for affirmation.

But the curse continues.

No one understands me.

"How about some sourdough to go with these drinks?" I say.

Her lips tighten in annoyance.

"Then I'll leave you alone and you can go home," I add.

She puts on her fake waitress smile. "Coming right up!"

As soon as she leaves, I send the letter to Derek's new girlfriend as a private message. She'll have it, in case he does to her what he did to me. Or at the very least, she'll have a better idea of what she's getting into.

From my purse, I take out all the bottles of pills I've been prescribed. I pour them into my mouth, swallow them down with ginger ale. Then I open the gate.

While I walk through the rising mist, I use my teeth to loop my leather purse strap around my wrists. Over and over and over, scrambling it in knots.

Cold kelp caress my feet. Cold waves snap at my ankles. Then I'm on the silver path, heading toward the moon, sinking and weightless at the same time.

INTRO TO *Glamazons vs. Red Plaids*

In another departure from his usual plot-driven thrillers, Dean presents a poignant character-driven love story. I think the title itself is interesting. Rather than using the full word *versus*, Dean uses the abbreviation, perhaps signaling that other things in the story to come are truncated or altered in some way.

In that cleft between words, in that no-man's land between the Glamazons and the Red Plaids, in the valley made by fate or science, two people hide a love that promises both freedom…and destruction.

This is one of my favorite stories he's written, and I'm happy to announce it's a glimpse into the world of a story he's releasing later this year.

— JOAN REGINALDO

Glamazons vs. Red Plaids

by Dean Fearce

———∿∿∾———

THE DRIVEWAY AT WORK HADN'T been plowed yet, and in fact, that's why Alex had stayed late past his shift when he could have been at the Plug Nickel swilling beer with his buds. Not because of too much snow in the driveway, but because of the snow plow driver. Everyone called her PlowGirl.

It went like this. When his boss, Mick, had shown up unexpectedly at the treatment plant, Alex had turned on the signal light to warn her away from their usual secret meeting.

Idiot Mick ran into the pack of coydogs that had been coming around the plant at night. They'd chased him to the side door where Mick came bumbling through, but now Alex couldn't help wondering what would have happened if he'd left Alex out there to the coydogs, especially after Mick had given him shit about smelling beer.

Alex got pissed about that. His shift was over. He could smell as beery as he wanted, and anyway, it had been a shitty day and a crappy night. And, now he had to drive into town instead of meeting PlowGirl at the plant for their rendezvous because she probably saw the signal light in the window and skipped the plowing. It had all become a confusing cluster fuck!

Seems like it would have solved a lot of problems for Alex if the coydogs had eaten his boss at the sewage treatment plant, frigging OCD anal-retentive breeder that he was, with all that curly chest hair oozing out of his shirt. That alone was enough to hate the fucker.

Alex drove his old Ford pickup through the snow, swerved out of the plant driveway, tires spun and the backend fishtailed toward a stand of pines while empties tumbled across the floor. He steered into the slide, spun the truck back the other way. The tires bit down and gained some traction.

He righted the ship, plowed a wake through the snow—winter driving reactions are instinctual to upstate New Yorkers—and headed to the backup meeting place at the marina. Now that he was headed into town, he hoped PlowGirl had gotten the signal. They could meet. She could clear the drive at work later, and he could stop at the Plug Nickel for a few beers, catch up on the gossip with his Red Plaids.

The marina was downtown, and both marina and downtown were deserted as expected. It was the middle of night in the limbo time before the lake froze over and the ice fishermen came to build tiny shanty towns.

But, the ice sheet on Lake Champlain grew as the temperatures plummeted and Alex looked forward to putting a shanty up and catching his share of fish. Nothing better than a fried lake perch sandwich. Throw in all the extras and a cold one and it was a feast.

He drove down the hill toward the lake, past the marina, the restaurant, the boat storage, all locked up tight for the season, and continued past the boat launch to the auxiliary pumping station in a dead end near the lake's edge. It wouldn't be as suspicious if he was seen at the sewage pumping station, him being a county employee working for the Water and Sewer Department, though his boss would be curious about what he was doing there this time of night. Alex didn't give a crap about that. He was stargazing at water's edge with a six-pack. That wasn't a crime. Being a dreamer. Enjoying a beer.

The truck's interior light didn't work when Alex opened the door. It had been disabled some time ago. He stepped onto crunchy, squeaky snow. The night was clear, the cold wind sharp as broken glass. It slashed his face as he surveyed the sky over the lake. The stars were bright, seemed close enough to touch, like he could reach out and pull one down, maybe give it to PlowGirl. She'd laugh at his display of mushiness.

He walked back to the marina, alert to traffic on the road, but the townies were packed up warm and cozy in their homes, their beds, their dreams. He felt the regret of an outsider, of one missing a life of normalcy which included cuddling up in bed with your sweetie on these cold-ass nights instead of stopping to an unheated storage unit full of rusting snow plows and busted leaf blowers. It sucked as a secret rendezvous spot. The plant was better: warm, secluded, and plenty of cuddle places.

He wished they had a place like the party shack behind the Plug Nickel. There was beer and a couch, a wood stove, a cozy place for guys and gals to hook up. But, meeting there in the Red Plaids not-so-secret place, or his trailer, or even her place out in bum-fuck Glam Nation, would be bad for their health and cause a terminal case of dead because Glamazons and Red Plaids were mortal enemies. To the death. Always were and always would be.

He and PlowGirl had met on the job and, unlikely as it was, had fallen in love. So, what else could they do?

"Run away to Barbados," she'd said.

"And do what?" he'd said.

"Anything we want," she'd said.

"With what money?" he'd said.

"You're about the closest thing to a real man I know," she said, "but, you're kind of a pussy."

That ended that conversation and it hurt Alex bad, too. He didn't talk to her for weeks which only made him look more like a pussy. In the end, he gave in because she wasn't going to back down or apologize. Too proud, and he respected that. He needed her more than she needed him, so he crawled back and apologized for being an asshole and said he had started a savings account.

"For Barbados," he'd said when he showed her the passbook. "Two-hundred forty-seven clams. It's a start." The sex after was nearly epic. It still brought a smile.

He turned the corner at the marina building toward her storage unit, and something hard hit him in the face, left it wet and stinging with the burn of cold.

She laughed.

"What the hell?" He scooped a handful of snow but it was too powdery to stick. She must have been packing that missile while waiting for her target to arrive.

"Got your signal," she said, and wrapped her strong arms around him. Girl had some guns.

"Let's go inside."

"So pretty out here, so quiet."

"It's colder than shit."

She pushed him away. He stumbled backward.

"Look, you can see the Milky Way." She pointed up to the smoky cluster that looked like diamond soup had spilled across the night time sky.

Alex looked up, said, "Whoa, that is really something...but, who gives a damn?"

"Cynical bastard," she said. "The Milky Way is one of millions of galaxies, and it's all so much bigger than us. I hope that's where we go when we're dead. Up there, in the stars of the Milky Way."

That was a thing about PlowGirl; she could say stuff that had deeper meaning because she noticed stuff others missed. And she was positive when he felt negative. Cheerful when he was cranky. Strong when he felt weak.

"Because we're bipolar," she would say.

"Just tell it like it is," he would say, "we're fucking nuts with a death wish."

Nuts with a death wish barely scratched the surface with PlowGirl. Glams were naturally insane bitches and she was a Glam stoked on black market 'mones and 'roids; Alex wondered how she didn't explode from the pressure.

"Listen, Girl," Alex said, "I love you, but it's cold out here and we don't need to be seen, so let's take it inside."

"It's not any warmer in the shed."

"We can warm the place up with some friction."

PlowGirl started to say something, changed her mind, lead Alex into the shed where she lit a kerosene lantern. She was in a mood. He could tell. Something had upset her. Alex tried to think of what he had done or said that would have pissed her off. Sometimes, she was like an unexploded bomb. It was hard to guess what might set her off. It didn't occur to him that she might be upset at something other than him.

The lantern didn't throw off much light but Alex could see the storage shed was long and narrow. He'd not been here before. Didn't have a reason to before tonight. Garden equipment hung on planks nailed to the bare wall studs. There was no insulation or heat source. A truck was parked plow to the bumper of another vehicle that looked like something special wrapped snug under a cover.

In the winter, PlowGirl plowed the snow. In the summer, she mowed the grass. PlowGirl owned at least four trucks Alex knew about, and usually had a half dozen workers on payroll. Maybe more. He didn't try to keep track of her business, although somebody in the Red Plaids did. They had a file on the Glams, and most of the Squares, too.

Alex didn't like that about the Plaids. It made him uncomfortable even before his illicit Glamazon love affair. Felt like they were keeping a list of their enemies, like they were planning retribution. He didn't consider himself a freedom fighter, what the Squares called terrorists. He was just a man nostalgic for a past that had promised a different future than what he'd gotten, shrunken testicles and man-boobs. That was just for starters. Fucking hormone disruptors. When you're a boy thinking you'll grow into a man but it doesn't work out like that, it really torques your Oedipal complex.

"I heard you found a body in one of the sludge tanks. What's that all about? Was it a murder? Do they know who it was?"

"Where'd you hear that?"

She grinned a lopsided, wide-lipped grin that Alex lived for, but there was something unsmiling in her eyes. "Small town, Bub, no secrets here."

"We got a secret," Alex said, reaching for her. She swatted him off. PlowGirl was always horny, so that made everything serious now.

"You got any beer?"

"In the cab."

Alex opened the driver-side door, found the six-pack behind the seat. "Shit, it's nearly froze." He handed her a beer, popped the top on his, lapped at the beer spray. "Mostly ice."

"What happened out there, Alex?"

"Shit, Girl, I don't know. I went to the Nickel after my shift, heading to home when the beeper went off. Something got caught in the scummer, set off the alarm. Looked like a body so I called

Mick. He called the Sheriff. We had to pump the shit out and filter it, see if there was a weapon or some frigging evidence."

"Did you see the body?"

"That's what I said, it was in the tank."

"I mean, did you see who it was?"

"The face was mangled when they pulled it out. Looked like a pulled pork sandwich. Might have been the scummer shredded it. Maybe it was chewed off. Either way, it was nasty."

"How could a body find its way into the sludge tank?"

"I heard'a alligators growing up in the sewers, living on giant rats. Maybe it was an aborted sewer baby raised by them 'gators."

"That's disgusting and ridiculous." She shoved him, caught him off balance. He bounced off the truck's mirror and dropped his beer. It hit the concrete with a slushy aluminum thud.

Alex laughed, picked up the beer, sipped it. "What's so interesting about a dead body in the sludge tank, anyways?"

"Seems strange, don't you think?" She took a beer from the cab, aimed it at Alex, and opened it, but the spray barely reached him. "It's not like someone would go out there for any reason, in the dead of night, right? So, stands to reason they were dumped there. The question is, who dumped them and why?"

"No, that's not the question. The question is, why do you even give a crap about this?"

"Because it's a mystery," PlowGirl said. "And I love a mystery. Don't you?"

"The only mystery here is what you have under that car cover," Alex said. "You gonna show me?"

PlowGirl smiled the crooked smiled. She put her beer down and pulled the cover off the vehicle to reveal a lavender-colored vintage GTO. It looked pure stock, and all muscle.

"Holy shit, Girl. Is this your ride?"

"Sixty-five Pontiac Le Mans GTO. I call her Irish Mist. She's all stock." PlowGirl opened the hood. "Four-speed, three deuces, a three eighty-nine. Fast as hell."

"She's a beast," Alex said, "a big, bad, beautiful beast."

PlowGirl opened the two-door coupe, pulled Alex into the back seat on top of her. "C'mon, Honey, let's pop her cherry."

She nuzzled him, put her hands inside his shirt, felt the scars where his breasts had been.

He flinched and squawked. "Holy shit, your hands are freezing."

"Don't be a wuss," she said.

"Let's see how you like it." Alex opened PlowGirl's dungarees, flattened cold hands on her warm flat stomach.

"Your hands are so cold, brrrrrrr, but it feels so good...put 'em on my titties."

Alex reached his hands up under her top and cupped her breasts. They were hot and round as grapefruits.

"I'm your first in this GTO? For reals?"

She pushed his head down. "For reals, my Mooseyman, for reals," she said, a moan building deep inside her belly. "Now, shut up."

Alex drove to the Plug Nickel after work the next night, but couldn't find a parking spot. Place was packed full, like every Red Plaid in the county was there. Anxious to get inside, get a beer and be part of the conversation, he risked a ticket by parking on the roadside, his truck tucked into a giant snowbank. Temperatures were in the teens. A warming trend. His breath frosted as he walked to the bar, a light snow falling.

Inside, the familiar smells of stale beer, wet wool, worn leather, and diesel fuel released dopamine in his brain. He felt better fast like the old-time aspirin commercials when the hammers stop pounding inside the skull. The knotty pine walls, the green and orange glowing signs, the drop-kick-me-Jesus country music his balm. And his tribe, the Red Plaids, damn near every one of them, were all stuffed into the bar. They all seemed happy to see him.

It was the murder at the treatment plant. Alex had intel that would remove doubt. Of course, Max Germaine had made book on the outcome, and folks bet their money on murder, accident, suicide, or act of God. The stakes made it a matter of principle that his intel would be challenged. And most folks probably bet on murder. It was the best choice, the most exciting.

"All the evidence ain't been sussed out," Max Germaine said. He had to yell over all the voices. "Let's hear what Alex has to say. He's our inside man, our expert eyewitness."

Alex beamed. He liked being an expert in something, liked the attention and free beers already lined up on the bar from his brothers in arms. The beers wouldn't influence his opinion because the evidence uncovered at the treatment plant was huge. That's what Deputy Polly had said to Sheriff Tator. Alex heard it with his own ears, that the alleged crime scene had looked like irrefutable evidence of foul play.

Max shouted out above the noise, "Quiet! Let's get the update from Alex." He banged the bar with a baseball bat. It helped some to lower the noise level to a growl instead of a roar.

Alex stood tall on the foot rest under the bar, took a swig of beer to lubricate his throat. "So, when I found the body floating in the tank, what was it? Three nights ago? Seems longer. Anyways, I had a bad feeling about it then. I mean, it's a dead person. Of course, you're gonna feel bad. But, this was worse, because I figured in my gut it was murder.

"Well, yesterday, the Sheriff's department came back to the treatment plant. They covered every inch of the grounds. Even inside the buildings. They were looking for concrete evidence."

Alex took another swig of beer, let the tension build a little. "So, what they said, what Deputy Polly said to Sheriff Tator was that there was irrefutable evidence of foul play in the death of the victim."

The shouting and commotion commenced, so Alex stepped down for the backslaps and fist bumps. Yep, it would be good times all night, except for the evil looks Max gave him as he tried to regain the floor.

Max Germaine might take a huge bath if it was a murder. Max owned a lumber yard and a contracting company, was part owner of the Plug Nickel, and the de facto leader of the Adirondack Chapter of the Red Plaids. He was known to tell folks I can do whatever I want, whenever I want. It often seemed true. Property owners sold out cheap to him. Elected officials favored his economic and political agendas. Folks feared him.

Alex didn't want to be on Max's bad side, but facts was facts. The truth of the matter would come out anyways. It always did, and he was just the messenger. He ignored the nasty looks and kept his distance.

"Quiet," Max boomed. He pounded the bat on the bar. "We have another report from a trusted source. Puts a different light on the subject of the body found in the tank."

Max beckoned into the crowd. It parted, reluctantly, as a fellow stepped into Alex's line of sight. He looked vaguely familiar, but Alex could be mistaken. The guy wasn't much to look at, skinny dude, girly-looking with artificial turf for facial hair. He dressed like everyone else in the room, bomber hat and a heavy wool plaid shirt, work boots. Basic lumberjack, the outfit of the Red Plaids.

"This here is Robert. He's a special agent from downstate. I guess that's all you need to know about him. Whatever he asks of the Red Plaids, we expect you'll help him out," Max said, "and save yourself from any conflict of interest."

"Guy's a spook," someone whispered behind Alex, stating the obvious. "You know they don't cut their tits off."

Max pounded the bar again to hush the crowd. The bat's dull thunk made the bottles on the bar clink against each other. "Okay, this ain't personal, but if any of y'all's Double X is here tonight…"

Someone yelled from the back, "If she ain't a Double X, you got some 'splaining to do."

It got a good laugh. Even Max snorted and smiled. "Yeah, what he said. It ain't that I don't trust the ladies, but, well, I don't trust 'em enough to hear what Robert's got to say. So, they gotta leave."

Everyone always agreed that was some bullshit, but the Red Plaids was a men's club, and men's business wasn't none of theirs.

Someone yelled from the doorway, "What about our money? A lot of us had murder with decent odds."

"It ain't official yet until it's proven official," Max said.

He squeezed the bat, made the tattoos on his forearms dance. Some guys take to the steroids like Max did. It gave an advantage, and they usually became the alpha in the pack. They bulked up, grew a decent beard, which they needed because the 'roids ravaged the skin.

"Anyone got issue with that can take it up with me right here, right now."

The place got quiet, quiet enough to hear the jukebox before someone pulled the plug. The party-like mood felt more dangerous.

Alex noticed guys slipping out the back. Some were dragged out by their ladies. He took a big gulp of his longneck. The promise of tonight's magic had disappeared.

Alex wanted to leave, too. This could get unhinged, what with the spook, and Max's pounding with the bat. But, he didn't want to be a pussy, so he hung in there with the thinned-out herd of hard cores.

"Now that we got rid of the riff-raff," Max said. He pointed the bat at Robert. "Tell 'em what you learned."

Robert cleared his throat. He scanned the crowd, making eye contact with most everyone there. He said, "We got verified information from the Sheriff's office. They issued an arrest warrant on a suspect for the killing at the treatment plant."

The guy had seemed a little nervous at first, like a rodent, but Alex decided Robert was more like a weasel than a rat after he started talking. Rats are disgusting, for sure, but weasels are dangerous and unpredictable.

"Tell them about the terrorist act," Max said. "These are the guys need to know what's going on around here."

"We're fairly certain the killing was an act of terrorism," Robert said. "And—"

"Not a murder," Max said. "It was a terrorist act, the two ain't the same." He hit the bar, knocked over a beer that crashed to the black and white tile floor. "Continue."

"Right, yeah, we believe the killing was part of a terrorist plot, rad-fems collaborating with this suspect. The one we're looking for has lived here her whole life, among you. And now, she's betrayed you. The Sheriff's moving slow on this, because, that's what they do, so we got a small head start. We've identified where she lives, and places she might be holed up. We got enough guys to find her first. And, we're serious about getting her, even if we have to go through the Sheriff."

Robert made a gun hand, shot an invisible round into the ceiling with a silent bang. It might have been more dramatic if he had bigger caliber hands.

"So, we're forming an official posse right here, right now," Max said. "And we're going to catch this terrorist. And, this plastic gash is gonna get as good as she gave."

The bar room erupted into hoots and cheers, a blood lust blooming in the boozy atmosphere. The Red Plaids were being primed to hunt and kill their enemies if needed.

Shit was going to hell too fast for Alex's taste. People were going to die tonight. Nobody even cared about the body in the tank. It was like the early days of the Chromo Wars, everyone going crazy and killing.

Alex spoke up, "Who was in the tank?" After four fast beers, he got bored of this stupid shit.

"That's classified," Robert said. "On a need to know basis. And, you don't need to know."

A beer bottle came out of nowhere, crashed at Alex's feet. "What the hell is that? You got something to say to me, come up here to my face, you little bitch."

Nobody came to challenge Alex, so Max said, "Any more questions?"

No questions came.

"We got a mission," Max said. "We gotta catch a terrorist, an enemy of the Red Plaids. If I call your name, you'll be a squad leader. Come get your orders. I'll leave you to it to pick your crew."

Max hammered the bat on the bar for attention. "And remember, the terrorist must be taken alive."

While Max delegated orders to the squad leaders, Alex asked Robert "So, who we looking for?"

Robert looked him over, said, "I'm curious about what the Sheriff said at the plant. You got any more detail on that?"

So, it was like that. Alex had to give something first. And maybe get something in return, but he wasn't that interested, except this whole situation felt off. It was common knowledge, Max would do anything to avoid taking a bath on a shitty book. Maybe it was better not knowing who it was, keep his head down, avoid the blood shed that would come.

Alex took a fresh beer from the bar, wiped down the condensation, had a drink, decided to see where this would go. "The deputies walked a grid. They found a tree in the woods with a broken limb, foot prints everywhere under the fresh snow. Wasn't anything like solid evidence, but it was clear there was some kind of party. It looked like what they used to call a neck-tying party. You know, a lynching."

"Like the victim might have been hung first, then tossed in the sludge tank?"

"Maybe," Alex said.

Robert nodded. "Anything else?"

"They might have found something in the utility shed, but I didn't get in there. Sheriff went back in with a couple deputies carrying cases."

"Evidence kits."

Alex nodded, took a long drink from his beer. "That's all I got," he said.

Robert said, "The terrorist's name is Jean Bonhomme. We been tracking the Sheriff's radio frequency. They issued an arrest warrant for her, and anyone she's associated with for suspicion of murder and terrorist activity."

Robert thought of something, turned to Max, "Hey, did you tell the men who they're looking for?" He said it with attitude, like what kind of rinky-dink outfit you running here? At least that's how Alex took it.

"Ah, shit, guess that would help. Everyone, listen up. Robert says the terrorist we're looking for is a Glam named Jean Bonhomme."

Once again, the small crowd of soldiers were quieted.

"You all know her as PlowGirl."

Alex dropped his beer. It crashed into foamy shards on the floor.

Max said, "PlowGirl's an ultra Glam. She got lotsa friends, and they got resources. And I don't have to tell you fellows, they're all crazy bitches stoked to the tits, so be careful out there in Glam territory."

Alex went to the bathroom. He had to piss and wanted to avoid getting pulled into a squad. This was the most messed up thing ever. He smashed his fist, left a dent in the drywall, his hand bloodied. He was so mad now he had tears in his eyes. He tried to think of a plan, but his brain was like the pinball machine in the bar when you nailed the bonus-round bumper.

Bing! Bing! Bing! Bing! Bing! Bing!

He finished up, snuck out through the back, and stumbled toward his truck. The parking lot growled with diesels. Alex was oblivious as they grumbled past him. The trucks bounced in the pot holes of the parking lot, their big tires screeching when they reached the macadam.

A truck pulled up and stopped. The window came down. Alex ignored it.

"Alex! Hey, Alex, ride along with us, brother. We got enough fire power to take out Albany. Shit, maybe we will," the driver said.

Alex didn't look to see who it was, didn't even care. He waved them off. Got in his truck.

"Come on, Alex," the driver yelled. It was Jake. "Let's go. That's an order, you pussy."

Two soldiers got out of the truck. Chester and Sam. Alex knew these guys his whole life. They ushered him into the back seat of the four-door.

"What the fuck, dude? We gone be rockin' sumbitches," Sammy said. "Who wants a beer?"

Alex took the beer and nearly drained it in one gulp.

"That's right, pussy boy, drink up. Huntin' she-man whores is thirsty work. Check this out." Chester was in the back with Alex. He unholstered his side arm, stuck it in Alex's ribs, who ignored it, at first. "This here's Little Chester."

Alex grabbed the barrel and twisted it out of his hand. "You stick this cannon in my side again, I'm gonna..."

Miffed, Chester took his pistol, spun the cylinder. "Yer gonna do what, you fucking pussy."

Between the three of them, Chester was the bad ass. All the testosterone made him mean, too. Jake and Sam just didn't have the weight or the rep to pull it off, and they looked a little light in the Y of the XY.

"All right, you two, quit trying to corn hole each other and pay attention. This is a critical mission into the enemy's stronghold."

"Where we going?" Alex said.

"Deep in the heart of ass-fucked bitches," Sammy said. "We're going to the Glam Nation."

"This is messed up," Alex said. "Someone's gonna get killed."

"That's the idea." It was Chester, waving Little Chester like he was popping off shots out the window.

"Three squadrons heading in," Jake said. "We're going in three different ways so it don't look like an invasion. We'll meet up at the target."

"Damn," Chester said, "I hope we catch that bitch."

"What'd she ever do to you anyways?" Alex said.

"That ain't the point. It's what she done to the Red Plaids."

"What's she done?"

"She's a terrorist, like the man said."

"That ain't been proven."

"Well, she done something to bring that spook up here from Albany. That's good enough for me." Chester crushed his beer can, said in a falsetto, "Another cold one, pretty please."

Sam turned from the shotgun seat and handed Chester a beer.

"I heard the body they pulled from the sludge was an XY super breeder," Chester said, "so the rad-fems hired Glam mercs to take him out. Ain't that right, Sam?"

"That's a stinking load of crap," Alex said. "Glams don't give a fuck about that Chromo War shit."

"Just 'cuz they got tits don't make them women," Chester said.

"It don't make them rad-fem terrorists neither," Alex said, "and what the fuck's that even mean?"

"I didn't say that. I said they was mercs. Whose side you on, anyways?"

Sam turned back to navigating from a map as Jake drove them to Glam Nation. Alex sipped his beer, watched the route they were taking to Glamazon territory, tried to think a way out of this night where no one got hurt, but all he got was random unlikely acts of God. And he'd lost his faith a long time ago.

Jake turned off onto a smooth blanket of snow over a road that had been plowed cleaner than the main highway. Of course PlowGirl would keep her road clean. She may have been born Jean Bonhomme, but she was PlowGirl. And that's what she did.

Alex was certain PlowGirl had no personal enemies, and she sure as shit wasn't a terrorist. Alex was sure of that, but there was no use arguing with these backwoods bum fuckers. Even so, there was a niggling bit of doubt in his mind about her, mostly due to the fact that Glams had worked as mercenaries in the on-again, off-again Chromosome Wars.

Glams were fearless and had mad skills for tactical warfare. They made great spies on account of their dual nature. Hell, it wasn't even right to call them mercs. Most of them would do it for the adventure. They were crazy-ass thrill seekers.

Jake pulled over, put the truck in park. "This must be the place. That's her mailbox back there."

Chester said, "Let's get her."

"We're 'sposed to wait for the other squads. Let's follow the orders."

"To hell with that," Chester said. "Them boys coulda got lost in these backroads."

"Don't see the point of waiting," Sam said. "There's four of us, one a her, and we got lotsa guns."

"Our orders were to reconvene and take her alive," Jake said.

Chester said, "You getting all pussy-fied on us, like Alex here?"

"Let's take a vote," Alex said.

"Me and Little Chester says let's get her. That's two votes for."

"I vote with the Chesters," Sam said. He turned to look at Alex in the back seat.

"Yeah," Alex said, "let's go get her."

Chester and Sam cheered.

Jake had expected a tie vote. He stared at Alex in the rearview mirror. "You sure?"

"Yep, I'm sure."

Jake cut the engine. "Okay, then, we're going in."

Sam said, "Alex, what are you packing?"

Alex unsnapped his ankle holster, ".38 Special."

"Shit," Chester said, "you ain't gonna take nothing down with that pop gun."

"How about I take you down."

"Cut the chatter. That's an order. Let's do this by the book. Alex, you're point through the front. Chester, you go in the back door. Me and Sam will cover."

"Aright, let's have some god-damn fun," Chester said.

Alex jumped out of the truck, took the lead, wanted to get inside first, wasn't sure what he'd do if she was in there, hoped something would come to him, maybe get her out to the woods so she had a fighting chance.

PlowGirl's place was on a deep lot. Alex stayed to the edge of the drive, unwilling to risk the deeper snow under the tall trees. He could hear Chester's harsh breathing behind him, and quickened his pace. The outline of her place looked like a tiny cabin, bigger building behind it. Probably a garage for her plow trucks. Looked like a nice place, nicer than his old double wide in the ghetto trailer park of cars on cinder blocks where he stayed.

It was quiet here, peaceful under the hush of falling snow backlit by starlight. No lights on inside the log cabin. Up on the front porch, he reached the door, saw a shadow. It was Chester headed toward the back door. He pressed the old-time latch. The front door opened, unlocked.

Alex felt a prickle up the back of his neck as he stepped through the door. His heart pounded in his chest. It was hard to breathe, heavy, like being smothered. Thought he saw movement in the shadows. Maybe not.

"Hey, Girl, it's me, Alex," he whispered. "You in here? We got trouble."

He moved through the cabin, short quiet steps. It was dark, hard to see, but the floor plan was familiar. Bedroom to the left, a bathroom behind it, the kitchen along the back, a spiral staircase to a loft that looked out to the great room with its high ceiling above him.

Something rattled. Chester at the back door. Must be locked.

He moved to the bedroom, opened the door, crashed into a bed. "You here, Girl?" He felt across the bed, the sheets and comforter pulled up to the pillows. Warm. With body heat. "Where are you, Girl?"

Behind him, a floorboard creaked. The back of his head exploded into pain-sparked fireworks behind his eyeballs. His knees crumpled and he fell to the bed, the only place he had ever wanted to be.

Consciousness came slower, much slower than it had fled. He couldn't remember where he was. He opened his eyes. Everything swam like he was under water in the dark. He felt wet on his hand when he touched his head, the pain so sharp and intense, it made him go blind.

Upstairs, he heard a scuffle. He tried to get up. His head screamed, *No, don't move!*

Something landed hard on the floor overhead. The weight of it reverberated through the ceiling. Alex pushed off the bed, his teeth gritted. He got sick, vomited sour beer. It worsened the pulsing throbs in the back of his bloodied head.

He made it to the metal stairs, barely able to see, and began to climb the dizzying staircase. He pulled himself up to the landing and tried to make sense of the dark shadows, grunts of pain, maybe pleasure, not knowing if the pounding came from inside his head, or outside, or both.

Eyes wouldn't focus; they barely adjusted to the faint silvery light from outside. The gleam of nickel plate, a flash of white skin on the floor. Something human and flabby-looking bounced in the meager light. Someone underneath it struggled, kicked, fought to get up, got pistol whipped.

Anger erupted in the pit of Alex's belly. It rose up and burst inside his skull like Fourth of July as the dark tableau became clearer. He pulled his revolver, shuffled close, and put it in Chester's ear.

"Motherfucker," he said. Pulled the trigger. Sensory overload. The room spun. Senseless, he fell, and blacked out when his head bounced on the floor.

Alex came to in the cold air outside. Jake and Sam had him by the arms. They walked-dragged him toward the truck.

"PlowGirl," he mumbled. "Where's PlowGirl?"

"We got her, Alex. We got her. What the fuck happened in there? She almost took you both out."

Alex couldn't tell who talked. Didn't matter. Every step sent a flash of lightning that seared through his head with white hot pain. "Where's she at, where's PlowGirl?"

"We got her in the truck. She's secure," Jake said.

Sam said, "Bitch got Chester, almost got you, too. Dang! That's fucked up."

"No, not Chester," Alex said, agitated, "No man, she didn't."

"Dude, she got him, almost killed you, but we got the drop on her. Chester had his fucking pants off. What the fuck?" That was Sam. He talked fast, agitated, adrenaline pumped.

Jake said, "We shoulda waited for the others."

"His head is fucked up," Sam said. "I think that's his brains sticking out."

Alex lurched, fell to his knees, gagged and puked, but nothing came out.

"We gotta get outta here." Jake tried to pull Alex back up, stopped, said, "Aw, we're screwed now."

It hurt to move, but Alex looked up. Oncoming headlights, red and blue flashers, multiple vehicles. Tires skidded to a stop in the snowy drive.

A bull horn crackled then screeched, "Drop your weapons and put your hands in the air." The Sheriff had arrived with a SWAT team backup.

Alex rested his face in the cool snow, wishing he could melt himself into it.

———— ∞∞∞ ————

"An open fracture," Dr. Andrews said, pointing to the x-ray of Alex's skull, "is when the bone sticks out from the wound like this."

Alex wasn't that interested in the medical history of his recent surgery to repair the head wound.

"So I'm good to go now?" he said, and lifted his arm, rattled the handcuff that kept him tethered to the hospital bed. It really sucked when he had to use the bathroom. He had two choices: call for the nurse to help him to the head, or use the bed pan, which he refused to do, all under the watchful gaze of the Deputy they'd posted to keep an eye on him.

"Sorry, Alex, we can't help you with that," the doc said. She was attractive with her stylish haircut and trim figure under the white lab coat. You could tell from the way the light cast shadow on her face that she was all X, and probably older than she looked with her confident middle-age smile.

"You're recovering nicely. The wound is already healing. You're not displaying any obvious symptoms, but there's likely to be memory loss, especially of recent events." She made a few more scribbles on Alex's chart then put it back into the holder. "We can release you after your CAT scan results come back with an okay."

"And when you say release, you mean into the Sheriff's custody."

"Alex, we can repair your broken bones, but we can't do anything for your broken personal life. You'll have to fix that." Then she left the room.

"Shit." Alex banged the bed rail, annoyed.

He'd hoped to get more answers from her about what the hell had happened, current events, what have you, but had veered down his own bad luck. He'd try to avoid that next time.

Funny thing was, being under watch make him feel sort of important. But, he needed more info. He didn't have a clue what happened to PlowGirl. It made him crazy not knowing.

Now, he wanted to piss. He buzzed for the nurse, hoped a chatty one would come help him take a leak, maybe shake it off for him while the deputy watched. He smiled at the thought of it, liking the way the image looked in his head.

There was a knock at the door. Someone was here but not a nurse. They never knocked. Neither did the deputy.

Whoever it was, they waited for him to say, "Come on in."

A suit walked in, said, "Hi Alex."

Alex didn't recognize him at first, dressed up like a lawyer.

"Bruce, what happened, you chase the wrong ambulance to the hospital?"

Bruce nodded with a wry smile. "It's been a while, Alex."

"Yeah, maybe."

"You know, one of the perks of the Red Plaids is legal representation."

"So, you wanna be my mouth piece."

Bruce sat down in the visitor chair and parked his briefcase by his feet. "So, how you feel—"

And the nurse bustled in responding to Alex's call. "What do you need?"

"I gotta piss. And an aspirin would be nice. Feels like I got permanent brain freeze."

"Let me find the deputy," she said, with no attempt to mask her wearied annoyance. "She's wandered off somewheres..."

Bruce followed the nurse out. Alex heard them talking. Everyone knew Max Germaine was the muscle of the Red Plaids, and that Bruce was the brains.

When Bruce came back in, Alex said, "You know, right now, I'd like to know what the hell's going on, man."

"I'll get right to it, then, if we're done with the small talk. You're being charged with multiple crimes, most of them felonies including attempted murder. Good news is, we're confident we can get most of them tossed. Lot depends on how they interpret the testimony of the defendant, and her own legal troubles."

"Is that PlowGirl?"

"Yep."

"She okay?"

"She took a beating. Said she was raped. But, she's not what you'd call a trusted witness. District Attorney likes her for the treatment plant murder, and now Chester Long's murder. And he's sympathetic to our cause. Likes the pro-active approach you fellows took with your citizen's arrest."

"Is that what we did?"

"Damn right, Alex."

"What about Chester?"

"You don't remember?"

"It's blurry."

Bruce pulled out a yellow legal pad from his case. "Tell me everything you remember from the other night."

"Everything?"

"Everything you got, Alex. We don't need any surprises down the road."

"Yeah, right. Who would." Alex stared out the window, tried to put the jumble in his brain back together. "It started at the Plug Nickel with this guy, Robert, and Max Germaine using him to squeak out of paying on his bets."

"Listen, Alex, some advice from your lawyer, okay? Anything about what took place at the Plug Nickel prior to when the four of you decided to run off to Glam Nation is going to be met with a lot of testimony to the contrary."

Alex stared at Bruce in obvious disbelief. Finally, he said, "Those fuckers. You know, I didn't want any part of this shit from the get go. Just to hang out and have a few beers. Sons a bitches."

"Okay, let's focus on the four of you in the truck, after you decided to go get the suspect, goes by the name PlowGirl."

"What difference does it make what we say? You all are gonna whitewash it to cover your asses."

"None of that's even relevant, Alex. Only thing that's relevant is what took place at PlowGirl's cabin. My advice to you is just let it go. It's better for everyone."

"Fuck you and the horse you fucking rode in here on." Alex jammed the call button. "Where's the god-damn nurse?"

Bruce got up from the chair and walked to the window. "Snowing again," he said.

Alex realized the nurse wouldn't be back until after this meeting was over.

"Things went south, Alex, but we can fix it, as long as we get you four on the same page. Make no mistake. The enemy is real. They have tentacles into every aspect of our government. Their strategy is to divide and conquer. They want to take you and your brothers down. Do not doubt that."

"Okay, fine. Whatever."

"Max said you're a good soldier, that you'd be loyal to the Red Plaids."

"Just tell me what's the story, and we can all get on with our day."

Bruce sat down in the chair. He rested the legal pad on his knee. "Dr. Andrews said you had a fractured skull and severe concussion, and you suffered memory lapses."

Alex nodded.

"What do you remember?"

"I remember going into the cabin through the front door. Chester went around to the back. Door was unlocked so I went into the bedroom to find PlowGirl. That's when my head exploded. Next thing I know, Jake and Sam dragged me out of the cabin and planted my face in the snow."

"So, you don't remember PlowGirl taking your .38?"

"No, I don't recall that at all."

"You weren't upstairs when she shot Chester in the head, point blank?"

"That don't sound right." Alex thought about it, tried to bring memories of the night back. All he got was more headache. "Shit, I don't remember anything but what I told you already."

Bruce got up, put the legal pad into his case, said, "Okay, Alex, that's enough for now." He put a card on the side table. "You contact me if you remember anything else. I need you to promise me that."

"Yeah."

"You have a right to an attorney during questioning. Remember, don't say anything until I get there."

"Yeah, yeah."

Bruce went to the door. "Let me get the deputy in here so you get your bathroom break already."

"Yeah," Alex said. "At least that'll be a relief."

———— ∞∞∞ ————

Bruce, the Red Plaids lawyer, got Jake and Sam released and they took the handcuffs off Alex, and sent the deputy home. They still had to answer for the unlawful entry charge. It didn't matter. The citizen's arrest of a murderer would tank any of the lesser offenses against the vigilantes.

For Alex, hardly any of it mattered now.

He was recovering from the head wound and the surgery and they needed the bed, so they released him from the hospital. It didn't matter.

Mick, his boss, gave him paid time off for the days of work missed. It didn't matter.

One of their own had been killed in their mission into Glam Nation. It didn't matter. He never liked Chester anyways.

Their squad had captured PlowGirl, though the Sheriff had arrived and spoiled their plans to avenge the death of an unknown victim found dead in a sludge tank.

None of that mattered.

He'd heard the Glamazons threatened to deliver a heavy toll of retribution to the Red Plaids for their actions. It didn't matter.

There was unrest in the world. Violence threatened. Many spoke like the Chromo Wars would be resurrected. It didn't matter.

PlowGirl was innocent of the John Doe murder. He had been with her that night. They'd been in the utility shed at work while the John Doe was being tortured and murdered. But that didn't matter now.

It would be suicide to out their relationship. They'd both be put to death by the Glams, or the Red Plaids. A spook or a merc would sneak into their houses late at night and double tap them. Did it matter which side did it? Nope, didn't matter.

When Alex woke night after night at three in the morning in a cold sweat, reliving the vivid images of Chester's head exploding, it didn't matter.

But the persistent crystalline outline of the nightmare crept into Alex's psyche to erode his indifference. Maybe it did matter.

Made it seem more likely that he, and not PlowGirl, had killed Chester Long. But, it was a contrary story that wouldn't change anything, so it didn't matter. But, Alex was mad enough to kill him again. Right now, maybe there was something that did matter.

The truth, he decided. He had to get to the truth. Jake and Sam were no help. According to them, Alex had been ambushed with an axe handle, then PlowGirl took his revolver and executed Chester, but Jake and Sam got the drop on her. After a reasonable beating, they'd hog tied her and handed her over to the Sheriff's Department. They told it like they were trying to protect him, and Alex had serious doubts about their story because that didn't matter.

There was only one place where he could get the answer that mattered. It was a huge risk to visit PlowGirl in jail. It might be the last time he ever saw her. But now, it mattered too much not to know the truth.

Jean Bonhomme, a.k.a. PlowGirl, was being held in solitary confinement at the county jail. She waited for her trial and was in good spirits even when everything had been stacked up against her, including the media exposure that pummeled her reputation and referenced irrefutable evidence of her guilt. For whatever reason, she didn't seem to care her life was in the balance and bad forces were aligned against her. Total Glamazon attitude toward life.

Alex figured he could disguise himself enough to avoid being recognized from a distance. Up close would be sketchy. He was a county employee even if he didn't work in the same building as workers at the county seat. He knew people, they knew him. It was a small town. Red Plaids worked in the county that knew him, and word would get out if they saw him.

If he was seen visiting PlowGirl, it would get ugly, considering he was a witness for the prosecution in the case against her, not to mention consorting with the enemy was punishable by death in the unwritten Code of the Red Plaids.

He'd removed all facial hair and got ahold of a fake ID that might work. He even took a cab to the jailhouse to keep his old truck from being spotted. He made it through the security check-point and was told to wait with others. They were here to visit PlowGirl. Her dance card was full, mostly with Glamazons. They took little notice of him, probably thought he was a lawyer or her accountant dressed as square as he was.

It was first come, first served, and he'd been one of the last to check in, so when they finally called his name and led him to the visitor room, he'd had time to think about options and outcomes. He had a plan. It helped to have a plan, even if it was a shitty one.

PlowGirl recognized him soon as he walked into the room. Her eyes lit up but she didn't blow his cover. At first he thought the bailiff was going to stay. That would have been awkward, but then she left him alone in the room.

"Hey, Girl, been awhile. You look good in orange."

"Mooseyman, you look like shit on a shingle."

Alex laughed, "That's what I feel like."

"What happened to your beard?"

"I'm in disguise."

"That explains the make-up."

"That's to cover up the bruises from when you cold-cocked me with the ax handle."

"Yeah, sorry 'bout that. Seemed like a good idea at the time. Didn't know it was you."

"Water under the bridge. Anyway, we don't have much time, so I'll get to it. I know you didn't kill the John Doe and throw him in the sludge tank because you were with me."

"Yeah, you're my alibi but I ain't gonna hold you to it."

"You're at the plant all the time, Girl. Your work takes you there. Just tell the truth about that."

"They'll still come for you if you testify for me."

"That's my problem, not yours."

"We don't both have to get thrown under the train."

Alex shrugged. "You ain't a killer, Girl. We both know that. You didn't do Chester. You were out cold on the floor after he pistol-whipped you. I stuck the .38 in his ear and splattered his ugly melon. We both know it."

PlowGirl laughed, "So, what the fuck you gonna do about it? If I take the fall, you get to live."

"I know, Girl. But, I can't live like that."

"If you give it up, we're both dead."

"Yep, that's exactly right."

The bailiff knocked on the window and twirled her finger. Time to wrap it up.

"I love you, Girl. I love you with everything I got."

"Why you gotta do this?"

"I don't know. Just feels right, you know, to man up."

Alex stepped around the table, got his arms around her in a tight hug, kissed her hard until the bailiff pulled him off and dragged him out the door.

"See you in the Milky Way, Girl."

PlowGirl smiled, wiped her face. "Ah, Mooseyman, you dumb fuck."

INTRO TO *Twitch*

A long time ago, I worked in a cubical with the soul-sucking fluorescent lights, the guy who reheated fish in the microwave, and the girl who called her boyfriend every 30 minutes to describe her day…in detail. I hated that job with a passion so intense that when I had the opportunity to leave, I never looked back.

We've all been there. That crappy job with okay pay you wish you could leave, but stay at for various and reasonable reasons. That job that pays the bills and helps you get your foot in the door of your future.

Twitch, by Ernest Ortiz, is a story that will make you happy that all you ever had to deal with was a few headaches and a constant wish for a new job. Alex is an average Joe, with an average job, plugging away and collecting his check. When things get stressful, Alex rolls with it (you'll see what I did there) when the rest of us would be, well, screaming forever, and ever, until death.

Alex is a good worker, just trying to get ahead. Maybe, he should have taken a vacation. At least part of him thinks it's a good idea to leave the stress of the job behind.

— DAWN DEL SONTRO

Twitch

Ernest Ortiz

ALEX STEPPED OUT OF THE conference room and went back to his cubicle. That boss of his, Reina, was a slave driver, not to mention an all-time bitch. Now he was stuck inputting data on the company's customer database system. He could complain if he wanted to, but there was no point. The paycheck and experience were all he cared about. He was working when Robert, his co-worker the next cubicle over, knocked and stuck his head in.

"Hey, Alex, you got a few minutes?"

Alex turned in his chair and said, "Sure, I could use a break."

Robert stepped in with his hands in his pockets. His wrinkled button-down shirt and trousers were always one size too large for his body.

"So, what's up with Reina?" asked Robert.

Alex scoffed. "Ever since she became manager she always acts like she has a stick up her ass."

"I know what else she can stick up there." Robert winked.

Alex chuckled, "I'll leave the honor to you. Maybe she'll be nicer to everyone." Alex's right eye twitched and he rubbed it.

"What's wrong with your eye?"

"I don't know. I've had this twitch since Reina became boss."

Robert crossed his arms. "Could be stress. Wish I could help with the workload, but I don't know anything about database systems. You should get it checked just in case."

"I will. Thanks, buddy."

Robert nodded and left. Alex continued adding customer information into the database. Throughout the day, his eye kept twitching randomly. Closing his eye helped somewhat, but it was hard to stare at the computer screen with one eye. Despite the added challenge, he finished his work and emailed Reina before leaving for the day.

At home, the spasms continued and he felt some mild pressure around his eye. The sensation was strange but at least it didn't hurt. He called his optometrist, Dr. Haley, and scheduled an appointment with him for the next day. The doctor told Alex to minimize looking at bright monitors, so Alex read a paperback mystery for about an hour before he went to bed. He managed to sleep through the night in spite of the twitching eye.

The next day during lunch break, Alex went to see Dr. Haley. After the cute nurse took his blood pressure and told him she had a boyfriend, a large stocky bald man in his sixties entered the examination room and greeted Alex.

"I see that your right eye has been twitching."

"Good one."

Dr. Haley was at first unaware of the pun, then the doctor chuckled. "Sorry about that. Now, let's see if there's anything wrong with it."

Dr. Haley shone a light at Alex's eyes and told him to follow it. Then, Dr. Haley placed Alex on a tonometer. Alex almost freaked out when the air nozzle puffed on his eyes. It was worse than the twitching. Finally, Dr. Haley dilated Alex's pupils and examined the retinas through a microscope. Alex sighed in relief when it was over.

Dr. Haley wrote on his chart. "I don't see anything wrong with your eyes. You don't have glaucoma, and your retinas are fine. Your blood pressure is a little high though. And from your sheet, your family doesn't have a history of high blood pressure, hypertension, or diabetes."

"So, it's stress then?" said Alex.

"Pretty much. Just make sure you exercise, eat right, and try to meditate whenever you can. Oh, and make sure you don't rub your eyes and don't stare at bright monitors for long periods of time. Let me know if the twitching doesn't stop after a week or so."

Alex thanked the doctor and went back to work. However, his dilated eyes prevented him from looking at his computer screen or any paperwork. A few minutes later, Reina stepped into his cubicle with a large pile of folders.

"Alex, I need you to finish these before you leave."

He continued looking at the screen. "I still need to finish the first load you gave me and I just got back from the optometrist."

Reina said, "Yeah, and after you're finished with that you need to input the second load, and you can't leave until you do."

"Fine, just leave them on the desk."

Reina dropped the folders on his desk, then left. He watched as the tiny woman walked away.

"Bitch," he whispered to himself. His eye shook again.

Two hours of overtime later, Alex finished the second load and went to his car. During the drive, on several occasions, he felt some pressure around his eye and his head was pulled toward the windshield. He didn't know what was causing it. It was as if some unknown force grabbed and attempted to drag him by the eye. The sensation stopped when he finally got home. He plopped his ass on the couch and surfed through Netflix to find something to watch. The pulling happened again and it was more painful. He ran to a mirror beside his front door and saw his eye and optic nerve stretching out of his socket. He tried pushing it back in, but the added pressure caused even more pain.

Snap!

The eye was free from Alex and it rolled away from him quickly.

The eye went under the couch, collecting dust and other crap he never bothered to vacuum. He lifted the couch and the eye sped away into the dining room. This time, it jumped onto the table and climbed into a fruit bowl. He threw out all the apples, oranges, and bananas until just the grapes were left. He then picked off all the grapes, one by one, until only the eye was left. It jumped the stem, hit Alex's forehead, and dropped into the kitchen where it rolled onto the counter, past the sink, and stopped at a rack of kitchen knives.

"Not the knives, not the knives!" he yelled.

The eye must have agreed because it jumped off the counter and rolled behind the trashcan and refrigerator. Alex growled and dragged away the heavy fridge. The eye rolled between his legs, then climbed up the wall and onto the ceiling.

"You've got to be fucking kidding me," said Alex.

It went to Alex's bedroom and dropped to the middle of his bed. He stopped and stared at his eye. It stared back at him. He squatted and said, "I got you now."

His lint- and Doritos-crusted eye turned sideways as if it said no. Alex pounced, but the eye jumped higher, bounced on his head, and rolled back toward the bathroom. Alex ran to the bathroom only to receive a door slam to his face. The door was locked. He kicked it open and saw the eye trying to go down the sink drain, but it got stuck.

"The sink has a stopper and you can't remove it." He rushed to the sink but the eye got out in time and landed on the toilet handle.

"Don't you dare flush yourself!" yelled Alex.

His eye jumped from the flush handle to the sink counter and rolled toward him. As Alex walked slowly toward his eye, it jumped back, pressed the handle, and whirled down the toilet drain. He stuffed his hand into the toilet as far as it would go but it was too late.

"Why?" That was all he could say. He whimpered and curled around the toilet.

Half an hour later, Alex drove to the emergency room. There was still pain, but the reality of losing his eye due to some freak of nature numbed him. He couldn't understand how and why his right eye would divorce from his body. There was no reasonable or logical explanation for this phenomenon. Once he arrived, he was thankful to see that Dr. Haley was on call.

They both went to the examination room and the doctor examined Alex's eye socket. "How did you lose your eye?" asked Dr. Haley.

What could Alex say? That his eye didn't want to be with him anymore? So he said, "Uhh, it fell out."

Dr. Haley raised his eyebrows. "It fell out?"

"Yeah, it fell out."

"I see. And where's your eye now?"

Alex decided the half-truth approach was best. "It went down the drain."

"The drain?"

"Yes, the drain. Are you going to repeat everything I say?"

"Is there something you're not telling me?"

Alex yelled, "Like what? I just lost my eye. The same eye that you said twitched constantly due to stress."

"Alex, there's tearing at the optic nerve. The only way your eye could have detached is if someone forcefully pulled it out."

"Doctor, I did not pull or cut out my eye. It just fell out and it went down the drain. Even if I could fish it out, it's probably damaged beyond repair. Now, what are you going to do about it?"

Dr. Haley sighed and said, "I'll have a nurse clean your socket and give you a conformer to protect it. I'll also set you up with an ocularist so you can schedule an appointment for a prosthetic."

"Thanks, doctor," said Alex.

Dr. Haley grunted and left the exam room. A different nurse, not the cute nurse unfortunately, came in, cleaned his eye socket, showed him how to apply the conformer, and gave him a couple of eye drops. Alex got home and checked himself in the bathroom mirror. He didn't like how the clear plastic looked but he was too tired to deal with it, so he went to sleep.

The next morning, Alex almost didn't go to work but decided to go at the last minute. Maybe working on some more database inputs would keep his mind busy. He put on some sunglasses and went to his cubicle. Robert knocked a few minutes later.

"Come in, Robert," said Alex.

Robert looked at him and said, "Nice sunglasses."

"Yeah, I had to go to the emergency room last night."

"Why? Are you okay?"

"I lost my eye. So much for workplace stress."

"What happened?"

"I don't want to talk about it."

"Alex, what's wrong? You just lost an eye, came to work anyway, and you don't want to talk about it?"

"Okay, fine. My eye popped out, and I chased it around my house before it ended up flushing itself down the toilet."

Robert laughed and slapped Alex's shoulder. "That's a good one. Come on."

Alex sighed. "The truth is it was a freak accident. I still don't know how it could happen and I'm still trying to process it."

Robert nodded. "Fair enough. A least you don't have to worry about the twitching anymore."

Alex's body itched all over and he scratched like crazy. "Yeah, I guess."

"What's wrong with your skin?"

"I don't know, it just started happening." He checked his arms, legs, and chest. There were no blisters but his skin was red.

"Look, Alex, I'm worried about you. Maybe you should take a week off and try to relax."

"That's a good idea. I don't feel so well anyway."

"Take your sick leave, watch movies, and order take out. Make sure you don't leave the house. HR likes to hire PIs to make sure we don't abuse the system."

"I know how it works, Robert. Thanks."

Alex emailed Reina he wasn't feeling well, bought some items at the pharmacy, and went home. He took a thirty-minute oatmeal bath, applied the moisturizer, and took the antihistamine. The itching stopped. Afterwards, he watched comedies on Netflix and ordered a large combo pizza. Other than losing his favorite eye, life was getting better. Four slices and a couple of movies later, Alex went to bed.

❦

Sunlight pierced through Alex's bedroom window. However, his entire body was cold and his bed was wet. He rubbed his eye, but his hands and face were wet as well. His blanket was stained with blood and he tossed it aside.

Alex screamed. His skin was gone. He searched the nightstand for his phone. He knocked off his alarm clock and Bluetooth speaker. The phone wasn't there. He got up and looked at himself in the mirror. He looked like one of those anatomy posters of the human muscular system. A car horn honked outside his house and he ran to the living room window. His feet slopped on the wood floor. Outside, his skin entered an Uber car with Alex's phone in his—its—hand. He ran outside but the car sped away.

"You son of a bitch," said Alex before he collapsed to the ground.

The next day, Robert and Reina stepped into Alex's cubicle and they both screamed.

Alex turned in his chair, crossed his leg, and said, "What? You've never seen a guy working without his skin and right eye before?"

Robert ran and barfed into a nearby trashcan. Reina fainted with folders dropping beside her. Alex laughed and went back to work.

INTRO TO *A Mile in My Shoes*

In Joan's *A Mile in My Shoes* I can relate to Anne the most and her constant feeling of always being a fish-out-of-water (or universe, for that matter). The struggle that no matter how hard you try, it's never good enough in a parent's eyes. Joan does a great job in capturing that vulnerability, sense of ineptitude, and the pressure of getting that one task just right. I can't wait for the next short story of this series.

— ERNEST ORTIZ

A Mile in My Shoes
Take Your Daughter to Work Day 2
Joan Reginaldo

FROM MY PERCH ON THE bannister separating the upstairs sleeping loft from the kitchen and living room below, I watch Kyle check and recheck his supplies. The mission should be easy; they'd done reconnaissance yesterday and this universe was halfway between backwater and astral-tech. To Kyle and Jess, both from astral, universes where traveling from solar system to solar system was akin to how people in my universe traveled from San Francisco to Tokyo, security for the Chinese Ancient History Museum will be a piece of cake to bypass, break through, or avoid.

Kyle closes the flap of his canvas satchel and turns to check his reflection in the panoramic mirror over the sideboard in the eating area of this strange, small house. A house Jess owns, apparently. She "bought" it last time she was in this universe. By bought, I mean, she got into the local banking system and put the house under her name. Something she does every few jumps, just in case.

I dusted and swept the loft/sleeping area, made it livable while they were out scouting and buying or stealing supplies and clothes.

Back in my world, we'd had minimalist fashion, but I'd call what they wear here "minimalist-pajama chic." Kyle adjusts his sleeves and straightens their seams. The fog-blue cloth looks soft, and the shirt seems designed and constructed to be close to the skin. No buttons or zippers, no fastening devices, no embellishments except for a stiff collar about an inch high with a small V-opening that reveals the dip between his collarbones.

The room has turned orange from the sunset. In the mirror, Kyle's dark hazel eyes meet mine and he winks.

"Do I look okay?" he asks, tugging the too-short shirt into place around his long torso. He's got a good figure but a little thin for my taste. It's why I never went out with fellow dancers; I like my guys a little on the paunchy side.

"That color makes you look deathly pale," I say.

He frowns.

"Sorry," I say, mentally kicking myself for saying something so morbid before a mission.

A commotion at the front door puts us on alert. I whirl, swinging my legs over the bannister, and hide beyond line of sight to the door. Then I creep down the steps, peering around the rail to see Kyle. He's got his back to the wall and he's strafing towards the door with Excalibur in his right hand. The sword's shadowy, wavering edge distorts Kyle's form. He must be wearing the Asset patch with King Arthur's blood, which is diffusing chemicals into his body, setting off an enzyme cascade to release light-bending pheromones.

I clench my right fist, disappointed in my lack of preparedness. My own sword, Urduja's Blade, is in the kitchen, on the counter, where I'd been using it to hack open oysters and coconuts. Running in to get it would put me in the open.

Kyle must've realized. He glances at the kitchen, raises his sword hand a bit, and nods for me to run through, he'll cover. I nod back and push off the stairs.

Just as I'm halfway towards my sword, the front door bursts open. *Whrush!*

It's the whistley-vibrating sound Excalibur makes when slicing air. But the sound of impact never comes.

I keep going, don't look back until I've got my sword in hand. Only seconds.

Then I turn. And see it's only Jess.

Kyle had swung and stopped short of decapitating her.

Jess looks unperturbed, even haughty as she looks down her long nose, first at Kyle, then at me. Her dark eyes are beady and calculating.

"Change of plans," she says.

"What?" says Kyle, sheathing Excalibur. "Why? What's going on?"

Jess tosses a wad of cloth at me. I catch it awkwardly, in my offhand.

"Anne is going," she says. "Not you."

"Why?" Kyle and I say at the same time.

Jess's expression is inscrutable, as always. "Get dressed, get supplies. We go in fifteen." Then she leaves, closing the front door behind her.

"What was that about?" I say.

"I have no idea," says Kyle. "You'd better get ready."

I head up the stairs with my cloth bundle and sword as Kyle takes off his shirt. He balls it up and hurls it in the corner.

In the loft, I get out of my jeans and tank top quickly then shake open the wad Jess had thrown at me. It's an outfit like the one Kyle had on but dove-breast-gray, a color more suited for Kyle's pale skin. When I put it on, it makes my dark skin look jaundiced. But it's a strange fabric that reminds me of linen but a bit thicker, a bit stiffer.

"Ramie," says Kyle. He's standing in the doorway, back in his normal clothes of threadbare plaid shirt and khakis so worn they're shredded at the knees.

"Seriously?" I say.

"Didn't have it in your universe?"

"We did, I think. At least, I saw a preserved ancient Filipino *Barong Tagalog*, a formal shirt, in a museum."

"Remarkable cloth," he says. "Incredibly strong, and stronger when wet, which might be why they like it in this...very watery universe." He hands me his satchel. "Faster than if you have to pack your own. All the supplies you need should be in there."

I know. We'd created the list together and I'd watched him pack and repack, check and recheck, more a soothing habit for him than an act of hyper-caution.

"Why do you think she changed her mind?" I say.

Kyle shrugs. "She's your mom. You have no insight?"

I turn away, frowning.

"Sorry," he says. "I meant... In your world, she was your mom and you were her... Bollocks."

Despite my sadness and annoyance, my mood lightens a little. It's always amusing when Kyle is frustrated to the point of using slang from his universe. Any slang, really.

"My mom is dead," I murmur. "And Jess's daughter is dead. We might look the same as the people we lost, but we're strangers to each other. At this point, you'd know her better than I do. She's never changed things this close to a mission before. Why now?"

Kyle shrugs again. "Only reason I can see is... Coming here was your idea. Maybe..."

"Maybe what."

He breaks eye contact.

"Just say it," I say.

Without looking at me, he says, "She has her own plans and her own personal mission. And you, you were so keen to get back home.

I think to her, this detour to a universe that has or had no powerful legendary heroes for us to get DNA from is a…"

"It's not a waste of time," I say. "There is a hero here. Was, I mean. Maybe not your type of a hero, but a hero nonetheless."

Kyle's face grows pink. "Cinderella could hardly be counted as a hero in anyone's book."

I raise a brow at the insult and say, "Her name was Yeh-Shen. The name Cinderella came much, much later."

"What did she do?" Kyle's face gets redder. "Who did she save? What was so important about her?"

"You know what? I'm glad I'm going. I need a break from you."

I try to push past him but he grabs my arm, not ungently but firm enough that I can't shake him loose.

"What Assets are you wearing?" he says, looking at my chest like he can see through my shirt.

"None," I say.

"You need something at least."

I don't like this part of Jess and barely tolerate it in Kyle: the need for an Asset patch to give them Strength or Agility. But there's always a Downside.

Downside… Such a soft name for such treacherous consequences.

Hercules' strength comes with psychosis. Murderous madness.

The Pied Piper's charisma has the terribly ironic Downside of causing paralyzing agoraphobia.

Mercy Brown's ability to stay alive with less oxygen requires eating freshly-dead corpses. That one I'd learned the hard way.

So for all the good qualities the Assets could give me, the side effects are rarely a price I want to pay.

For Jess, acquiring and wearing Strength-based Assets is almost an obsession.

For Kyle, as practical and soothing as packing and repacking his bag before a mission.

For me, an unnecessary risk. I scoff at most of their patches.

But deep down, I fear them.

Kyle must see it in my face because he lets me go.

I leave him and find Jess, who's sitting on the steps outside.

The setting sun gives her hair an auburn tint. I can't see her face because her back is to me, but from the height of her shoulders and rigidity in her posture, I can tell she's angry about something.

To be fair, she's angry a lot. Usually at me. Or about me. Something I did or said, maybe even just how I disturb the air by moving. So mostly, I avoid her. An easy and difficult thing to do because she looks exactly like my mom, who was killed just a few…

Wow, has it been months already?

And I realize something and wonder if the last time Jess was here, her family had been with her. It would explain why it seems like she can barely set foot inside.

"Ready?" says Jess without looking at me.

Her voice, hard with authority and impatience, is the biggest difference between her and my mom.

"Ye-yes," I say.

She starts walking down the narrow path to the road. I hustle to catch up to her. Since her mood is so bad, and since it's rare for her to allow me to explore any of the universes we've been to so far, I turn my attention to this world.

It had seemed…more technologically advanced, according to Jess's notes from the previous time she'd come here on a fruitless search for artifacts or weapons from powerful heroes. She'd noted the people here have planet-to-planet travel, a prevailing use of implants for nonverbal communication, no dependency on fossil fuels at all.

But looking around now, at the narrow footpaths meandering like rivulets through dark, almost black soil, at the absence of motorized transportation, it seems like one of the backwater worlds we'd narrowly escaped. It had taken nearly a month for us to practically invent electricity, build a battery, and charge it with enough juice to power Kyle's transport pad. We'd had to leave behind some of our friends—a couple of the "timid" people we'd rescued from a universe several jumps prior. Though they'd said they were sad to see us go, they seemed to wave us off with some relief.

This world reminds me of that one because of the small, round, one-story houses. In the gloaming, lights are turning on like stars blinking into existence. And everywhere like white noise, the gurgle and bubbling of hidden streams.

I walk a few paces behind Jess so she can't see me rubbernecking like a goddamn tourist, which she's yelled at me about. Several times. I can't help it. The city seems to be transforming before my eyes.

As it gets darker, the round houses get brighter. I can't figure out how it's happening. Maybe they're coated in glow-in-the-dark paint. But the light they're emitting doesn't reach far enough to illuminate anything usefully. In fact, Jess and I are walking in near-darkness. She must be using an Asset to see clearly enough to keep such a brisk pace.

In a few minutes it's true night, and in the moonless dark, the houses look like pearls.

And we're heading to a giant pearl ten times bigger than the rest.

"That's it?" I say.

"That's it," says Jess.

Our footpath merges with several other paths but we're still the only ones outdoors. Granted, this place doesn't seem to have much of a nightlife.

"Jess," I say. "Can we stop a moment? I have some questions."

She glances at her watch, shakes her head. "We have to be inside before they start denying entry. It's getting too close to their closing time. Come on."

She runs off before I can ask why she brought me instead of Kyle.

Whatever the reason, I won't let her down, which shouldn't be too difficult; she already has a low opinion of my skills.

I jog towards the giant glowing orb.

At the entrance, I marvel at the perfectly smooth wall and wonder how they built it with no visible seams or joints. I also catch my first glimpse of the people in this universe and get a clue as to why I've been brought instead of Kyle. I have more in common with them physically.

My grandmother on my mother's side had been Chinese by blood, Filipino by birth. I have the same dark hair and skin tone as the pair of museum greeters flanking the door. They give Jess, who's darker than me, an extra-long glance but otherwise greet us as politely as their profession dictates.

I, unfortunately, don't understand a word of the language that sounds like Chinese spoken with the throaty, rolling Rs of French.

Jess responds pleasantly. We're directed to the ticket booth. A man or woman is behind wavy glass, which makes it seem like I'm looking at the person from underwater.

Jess speaks into a silver trumpet-like opening beside the glass. A response comes back from the same trumpet-thing. Then Jess leads me through a doorway and into a long dark hallway beside the booth.

It's dark enough that I want to hold her hand for balance and guidance but I dare not. Air puffs over me in short bursts. I pass through two planes of blue lasers. Then we're out of the hallway and at the bottom of a set of wide gray steps leading up to what must be the museum proper.

Jess's shoulders lower, but not by much. Then according to plan, we split up, her heading left to get as close to the employee offices as possible, while I go up the stairs to the main exhibits.

Using computers and technology from his and Jess's home worlds, Kyle had breached the museum security system to see how it works. We aren't concerned about being on cameras; if everything goes according to plan, we'll be gone before they figure out who we are. We did need to know, ahead of time, things to make this mission as quick and easy as possible: escape routes, security patrols, communication with local law enforcement and their response to museum alarms.

The people of this universe have pretty much absorbed their technology in the manner of implants. This has made mass-communication easier, but has also left them vulnerable to miscommunication due to tech-malfunction. Kyle already pre-programmed a scrambler into their communication lines. Triggered by the sound of the fire alarm, the scrambler will take any communication within, or sent from anyone in the museum, find a corresponding response in this universe's database of films, and reply with a line from a movie, written or otherwise disguised by a voice modulator.

All that is supposed to accomplish one thing: buy us time to get Yeh-Shen's DNA and get out.

My footsteps echo in the stairwell. Then I arrive at the second-story level, halfway to my goal. This museum is unlike any I've ever been to, and I'd been to dozens back home, and even more with Jess and Kyle.

They'd always had one thing in common: absolutely controlled environments. Necessary to preserve priceless oil paintings, marble statues, leather helmets, cotton dresses.

But here, it's like an underground botanical garden. From the outside, the building is a pearly sphere like all the other buildings and homes. I'd assumed the interior would have normal walls and rectangular rooms, like Jess's house. But inside, on the second floor, it is one gigantic cavernous space, like a cathedral, with glistening black walls sloping up to converge with the dome-shaped roof.

It's humid but cool. The air smells of moss and something akin to Arabian jasmine. The silence is constantly disrupted by the sound of water, sometimes gushing, sometimes tinkling in a trickle over metal.

There's a white light emitting from within a small grove of trees at the center of this giant space, and sconces illuminate vines and plants covering some parts of the wall, but I can't see much more of anything in front of me except for an entry gap in what seems to be a barrier made of tall hedges.

Kyle couldn't find an aerial view of the span of this room, but from a sketch he'd drawn on one of his computer pads, it looks like a cross between an English garden maze and a room full of cubicles. In lieu of walls to isolate galleries and exhibits in separate rooms and wings, this museum uses hedges and a unidirectional flow to direct visitors from one exhibit to the next.

The exhibit I need to go to is, of course, at the end of the maze.

A chime sounds, followed by a woman's voice speaking in a language that sounds like a mix of Chinese and French. The message seems to be repeated three times, in three other languages, none of which I know, and I can understand five.

For the first time, I feel a prick of panic. I've never been in a world where I had absolutely no hope of communicating with anyone.

I clench my fists around the strap of Kyle's satchel and head into the hedge maze.

That relaxed announcement, mindlessly droned, was probably the usual polite museum warning that it's near closing time and people should make their way to the gift shop then leave. I need to get to the halfway point in the route, where there should be a snack and refreshments kiosk, benches, a small sunken atrium for docent presentations, and bathrooms.

And between those bathrooms, a utility closet I'm supposed to hide in until everyone is gone.

But I can't help it. I stop at the first art exhibit, stunned, confused, but mostly stunned. I'd thought this was a history museum, not a modern art museum, and yet the installation looks like something I would've seen at the San Francisco Museum of Modern Art back home.

Yet, the MOMA would never have had this balance of art and life, transience and permanence. Museums rarely use water because it wreaks havoc with their carefully calibrated preservation systems.

The installation or piece or whatever they're calling it had looked like a painting at first but I realize what I mistook to be brushstrokes are flower petals on orchids. Hundreds and hundreds of orchids portraying a landscape of a valley at sunrise. The colors are so vibrant, the reds feel like they could cut skin, the blues emanate coldness, and I can almost taste the yellow.

Whatever yellow tastes like. I don't know.

It just feels like I can.

Another chime breaks my concentration. Another announcement.

I have to get to the utility closet before a museum docent or security guard comes to escort me out.

Head down to avoid temptation, I stare at the path just beyond my feet and hurry without looking like I'm hurrying. I get to the halfway point and pause at the edge of a circle. To the left of me is another exhibit but I purposely ignore it even though I feel it like a looming presence. To my right is the snack and drinks kiosk thing Kyle had mentioned, though how he knew it dispensed food and drinks is beyond me. It's a plain gray box thing with no pictures of candy or chips or water bottles, no buttons or openings. Nothing to indicate what it's for.

I chuckle to myself. Back at the San Francisco MOMA, this big gray box could've been one of those dumb, pretentious art installations with a title like "Tea and Cop-cakes" or "Golden Gate, Fogged."

Still chuckling, I sidle up to it, pretending like I'm going to buy a snack but Kyle hadn't told me how it worked, so my pretense might actually be more suspicious than me just acting normal.

Look casual. Look casual. Just gotta disappear into the shadow behind the kiosk and strafe over to the utility closet.

BING-BING-WHREEEE!

I jump away from the kiosk, which is now swirling with color like fireworks in a jar. Pictures of food appear, shimmering in time to the beat of what I assume is an appetite-inducing melody which vaguely sounds like Old McDonald Had a Farm. Desperately, I swat at buttons to silence the infernal machine.

The sound of shouting cuts through the din. It's coming closer and there's nowhere for me to go but to the utility closet I should've jumped in as soon as the noise started!

I grab the handle and push down. Locked! What the hell, Kyle?

The shouting is getting closer. Whoever it is, a woman, sounds more concerned than angry. Like a party host who's come upon an injured guest. It could even be just another museum visitor coming to see if I need help choosing a snack, but I'd rather not find out. I open the door on the right and slip inside what should be the woman's bathroom.

Again, I'm disoriented by the vast difference between expectation and reality. The floor is tiled, dark blue like the walls, and there are black sinks and silver faucets, but there are no stalls. Not even anything that resembles a seat-style or squat-style toilet. Just…black water.

I look back at the wall of sinks, at the beveled mirror that spans the wall above the sinks, at the disheveled hair, frizzy from the humidity, of my reflection. Everything is normal on that side of the room.

But where the toilets should be is just something that looks like a long pool of black water. There are feet-shaped grooves at the pool edge, and little steel bars I suppose one could grasp while doing one's business. But then it just goes in the water?

I sniff.

Smells like…stone and earth, not like sewage. The water isn't cloudy, neither still nor too turbulent. But it's so black. I can't get over how black it is.

The sound of someone—two someones—speaking makes me back up against the door and brace it shut. There's absolutely no place to hide now, unless I want to jump in the water of what is, for all intents and purposes, one giant shared toilet.

The desire to avoid such a thing even makes me consider, for a fraction of a moment, "What's the worst that could happen if I get caught?".

Best-case scenario, they escort me out. Worst-case scenario, they escort me out.

Then Jess will be in here by herself, setting a fire to create a diversion for a crime I can't commit.

I won't die. Getting caught wouldn't kill me. The world won't end.

But I would lose whatever meager trust I've built with her. She would come home, take one look at me, and shake her head without saying a word.

My mother dies again and again in those silences.

The voices are coming closer.

I open the flap of Kyle's bag and rifle through the supplies. Protein packets, carb sticks, a rolled up computer panel. Then I find his little pouch of emergency Asset patches. I open it and the lining glows, giving enough light to read the labels on the dull silver squares the size of Nicotine patches. The patches that Kyle has stolen from the Stitchers have complicated codes I don't have time to decipher. The ones he made, however, have labels that are more helpful, handwritten in his cramped print.

Fire-Skin.

Hercules.

Faultless Aim.

Mouse-Feet.

Urduja (Anne).

Ajax.

I'm pleased to see he packs more than strength-based Assets, unlike Jess, and I'm touched he thought Princess Urduja, whose sword my mom had died trying to steal, had a quality that could save his ass at some point.

But the one Asset I need, water-breathing, isn't in the mix.

The voices are right outside the door!

Screw it.

I toe my shoes off and kick them against the far wall. I buckle down the satchel flap as I sit on the edge of the…ugh, toilet-pool.

The door handle clicks open.

I take a few deep breaths then slide into the cold black water as the door creaks open.

Mistake!

I tumble in the cold darkness on a swift current, disoriented, completely blind.

Panicking.

Panicking.

Bouncing against hard walls or ceiling or floor. Tunnel? Broad tunnel?

Can't see.

Panicking.

Panicking.

Lungs starting to burn.

Stop panicking. Tighten your lips. Stop panicking. Deep breath—Wait! Don't do that!

I bounce against something, grab on reflex—a ridge on smooth stone—almost let go then realize if I do that's it.

So the choice then is do I let myself go with the current, which almost guarantees my death?

Or do I fight it, which will probably lead to death anyway.

But there's a chance.

God, how long was the distance between where I am and where I was?

Seems so long. So very long. Why fight it anymore?

My lungs ache and it's starting to be too distracting. Can't think clearly. Soon, won't be able to think at all.

Choose now!

My fingers loosen on the ridge and I slip free.

Fear makes me scrabble blindly, touch-seeking the false salvation of another wall ridge that'll only prolong the inevitable.

But that fear is my answer. This is not what I choose for myself. I find another ridge and grab on with one hand. With the other, I reach into Kyle's satchel, which I secure as well as I can between my body and the wall. I find the Asset patches, carefully rip one open with my teeth, and stick the patch on my cheek.

Please be made from the blood of Hercules or Ajax. Please be Strength.

Within moments, the darkness abates. I can see. I can see! My skin glows orange with heat that would be sweltering if I wasn't submerged under water. I find another Asset patch, open it, and stick it on my other cheek.

Please be Strength. Please be Strength.

The ridge crumbles under my grip and I'm loose again, but now I can see, and now I'm stronger.

I grab the next ridge I see, bring my feet up between my hands by curling my body, and launch myself against the current. Then I grab the next ridge in what's turning out to be a large circular tunnel. Then I do it again. And again. From ridge to ridge, I leap towards a growing point of light.

Then finally, the last ridge I grab is an edge of the toilet-pool I'd jumped into. Not caring if there's anyone in the restroom, I climb out of the water and heave the stale air out of my burning lungs. I breathe in fresh air, hear my blood roaring in my ears, and my vision fills with black spots.

I collapse on the cold tile floor and just concentrate on feeling my sore chest protest with each breath. It's the first part of my body I feel. The roaring in my ears fades to a faint shush. Then I'm aware of a stinging tingle in my fingertips. I lift them to see. They're still glowing orange from the Fire-skin patch, but the ends are scraped bloody. They don't hurt too much so I ignore them and take stock of the rest of my body.

My toes and heels are bloody and, to a lesser extent, my knees and elbows. I feel and look like a stone that's been put through a rock tumbler. I must've been knocked around that tunnel more than I realize.

But no broken bones. And still a job to do. I can't fail or else it'll prove right whatever misconceptions Jess has about me. In her eyes, I can't do anything right. It's not like I'm trying to replace her precious daughter, but if she could just give me a fair chance.

And this mission is by no means a fair chance in any book.

She'd said Kyle was supposed to go with her. He'd had two full days to prepare. He'd even come out and seen everything with her, while I'd had to stay at home for the hundredth time. Those two are always doing things without me.

And then Jess just throws this in my lap.

Of course I'll fail! This is what she expects! This is what she's set me up to do. Fail!

Crack!

All I want is a little compassion. They're not the only ones who've lost someone. What about me?

Crack!

They should consider that I'm the one who's lost the most. I never asked for this. Jess and Kyle, they sought this type of life. Not me. My mom dragged me to work with her on "Take your daughter to work day." This is all her fault.

All her fault. *Crack!*

She's dead because of her own choices. Not mine!

Crack-crack-crack-smush-squish-squelch.

And I'm here because... Lost in an infinite number of alternate universes because... A completely hopeless burden because...

The squelching sound breaks my train of thought and I seek what's making it.

I am. I'd pounded my fists bloody, pulverizing the blue tiles. In my right hand is a large shard, which I'd been using to try to cut through the ramie cloth on my left arm.

But the ramie is wet. And this remarkable cloth is stronger when wet. God, I'd be bleeding out by now, I think. The cloth held, but I'll have a wicked bruise.

What am I doing? What was I thinking? Where did those thoughts come from?

I scrape the Asset patches off my cheeks. Their beating red glow dims as my glowing orange skin fades to my normal tan hue.

It was the Strength-based Asset patch. It must have been derived from Ajax, driven insane, and ultimately to suicide, by jealousy. Guess I should be thankful I hadn't put on the Hercules patch. That one, worn for too long, makes people go on a killing rampage. Jess almost killed me and Kyle the last time she wore it when we were attacked by Stitchers and Cecaelians. I put both patches in Kyle's soaked satchel for incineration later. Can't leave them to be found by native populations.

I wash my hands in one of the sinks and tidy myself as well as I can but who am I kidding. If I get caught, I look like a rat that's just crawled out of their toilet.

Not knowing how much time's passed, I open the door a crack to see if there's anyone outside.

That subtle shushing sound that I'd thought had been an effect of oxygen deprivation or something sounds much louder and seems to be coming from strobing red lines on the floor, directing me towards the exit. The only thing I can think of is that this is the fire alarm that Jess was supposed to set off, the alarm that should've made everyone evacuate, buying me time to break through the protective case over the glass slippers, which would set off another set of alarms.

I book it through the twists and turns of the hall. My shoes squeak against the tile. Blood and water squelches between my toes with every step. I'm chilled but burning with exertion and anxiety. A few more turns and then I'm at the exhibit of Yeh-Shen's shoes.

Unmistakeable.

Kyle had tried to describe it and I'd scoffed at his exaggerations but I was the wrong one.

It's a monolith made of black stone like onyx or a very dark granite. It reminds me of Devil's Tower in Wyoming but the vertical striations, probably made from the water constantly dripping from somewhere in the darkness above, reminds me of El Capitan in Yosemite.

About three-quarters of the way up, water trickles over a clear case that protects Yeh-Shen's glistening white ball gown and sparkling glass slippers, posed on the stone to look as if she's still dancing in them.

What is it with these people and water?

The visible part of the monolith is about fifty feet tall, but its base is hidden in a moat of black water. Probably not the same water that was in the toilet-pool, but similar in darkness and viscosity. I get to the edge of the moat and peer in to judge the depth of the water and see whether or not this one has a current. Doesn't seem to. There are labrador-sized koi swimming lazily among stands of reeds and cattails and lily pads.

I circle around to the other end of the moat where there should be a stone path to get to the monolith so it can be maintained. Though I don't know how much maintenance a giant rock needs.

Five stone steps, in the shape of lily pads, brings me to the foot of the monolith. I start to climb and make my way to the front of the monolith by using the tiny handhold-pools and crevices carved by untold years of water wear. The ascent is not too difficult at first; the base is broad and the hand- and footholds are plentiful. But the monolith tapers at the top, and the water, moving swiftly on the steeper grade, hasn't had as much horizontal effect on the stone's surface. I go slower because I have to grope the smooth stone for the grips and holds that will bear my weight.

But finally, I'm next to the clear case. It looks like the kind of display case that sports bars use to keep signed jerseys in, only ten times bigger. I can't get access to the shoes from the top because they're too far down into the case. The case is too wide across for me to get in front of it—no handholds or footholds. I have to go through the side, a little higher than the shoes because I can't find hand- or foot-holds any lower than this height close to the case.

I take a moment to drink in this once-in-a-lifetime sight. Despite the dimness, the shoes shine like diamonds. And the dress! Though the hem on the wrists and along the bottom edge look as tattered and fragile as shed snakeskin, the dress glitters and glimmers like a sun-struck cloud. My heart swells with the beauty of it all.

But let's get back to work.

From the satchel, I get a swab-tube and Kyle's special glass-cutter-sealer thing. It's a three-pronged tool with a diamond-tipped cutter on one prong, a suction cup on one prong to hold the glass piece, and a glass-fuser on the other, to seal it once I'm done. A tool they've used many times, in many museums, stealing only biologicals and doing as little harm as possible to the native cultures' priceless artifacts.

I put the swab-tube in my mouth, then brace myself for the next few steps in our plan because once the case is broken, I'll have to move quickly to swab the inside of the shoe before enough water trickles in to wash it out.

I draw a triangle to squeeze my hand through with the cutting end.

Now the tricky part. Gotta get in there and swab it without getting the swab too wet, or getting too much moisture into the case, or getting too much water into the shoes.

One. Two. Three.

I suction out the glass piece, exchange the glass-cutter tool with the swab tube from my mouth. Quickly, I thumb the cap up and stab the other end against the monolith's stone face, pushing the swab out of the case. I swirl it up and around the nearest shoe's inner heel and toe area, then bring it closer because it requires two hands to securely cap.

"Hos-ten! Hos-ten!" The cry is loud and comes from above me. I look up and see a white face!

I jump, startled, slip—grab—slipping.

With the fingers on both my hands bearing all my weight, I'm helpless and vulnerable to whoever's looking down at me from the monolith top. It's a small woman with long black hair but I get the feeling she's old. Very old. Even from about ten feet away, I can see her veins through her pale, thin skin. Her eyes are black, not too large, but almost perfectly round. And her brows are thin and gold, with two small wispy protuberances on the ends nearest her nose.

She continues to stare at me with those strange round eyes, expression unreadable, neither offering help nor helping me to my death.

"This is…exactly what…it looks like," I say carefully so as not to disturb the careful balance I've struck on the edge of these handholds.

I'm equally worried about the hole in the case. It had seemed small, just large enough to fit my hand, but the water must be trickling in faster than I thought. Already, there's two inches of water within the glass case. If it gets to the level of the hole, it'll submerge the shoes. And all that humidity can't be good for the dress.

The only things I can move are my eyes, so I flick my gaze over to the dress, Yeh-Shen's ball gown, which is currently being destroyed by water.

The woman speaks again. The language sounds like that mixture of Chinese and French.

I shake my head just enough to indicate I don't understand.

She purses her lips, then tries again in a language that sounds like a mixture of French and Swahili. Again, I shake my head.

The face disappears.

I contemplate how deep the moat really is, and whether or not I'll survive a fall into it. Probably. But it'll hurt. Might even get a few broken bones.

Should I just let go and take my —

A length of black cloth comes over monolith's top edge and descends until it's beside me.

The woman reappears and says, "Come. Up."

I'm relieved to hear English, and grateful for the help. I grasp the black cloth—ramie again—and climb up to the top of the monolith.

The top is flat but not smooth. There are shallow puddles, maybe just three inches or so, here and there, fed by water trickling from the ceiling, and in the puddles are tiny glowing green plants with glowing white flowers that give enough light to illuminate us. The woman, shorter than Jess and slighter than me, is naked and I'm further confused about her age. Her breasts are nearly flat but a little droopy. Her stomach is a bit pouchy, like she's had a few kids. But aside from the hair on her head, she's completely hairless. Either a very good waxing salon, or she's never had pubic hair or leg hair or underarm hair.

She takes back the cloth, undoes the knots, and puts her clothes back on. The outfit is similar to my pajama-chic gray one, but with an extra length of black ramie that she ties around her waist, like a skirt, with a long tail that gets flung over her left shoulder.

"Thanks," I say.

She bows her head and smiles a little. "You are Albion?"

"Sorry, no. Anne. My name is Anne."

She shakes her head, rests a hand with uncommonly long fingers on her chest between her breasts, and says something with the into-nation that it might be her name. But the word has innumerable syllables and throaty Rs and several changes in pitch. The sound is more a song than a name, an entire story; it sounds like a stream and evokes longing, loss, pride, and grief.

My name, in comparison, sounds as blunt as a stone plopping into a serene pool.

Rather than truncate her beautiful name into the first three sounds I heard, I attempt to say it. "Shay-Rin-Lew-Shaland—"

She gestures for me to stop. "Albion?" she says again, pointing at me. "Anne of Albion?"

"Oh. No. Uh…" Albion… Kyle had mentioned it once as an ancient name for England. Maybe she's asking if I'm English. Close enough, if it'll help us communicate. "Yes. From Albion."

She nods. "I know it. In your language," she pats her chest again, "Bianca."

"Nice to meet you." I slowly lift a hand, unsure whether the overture for a handshake will be seen as hostile or friendly.

Bianca solemnly mirrors me but rubs the back of her hand against the back of mine. Her skin feels strange. Smooth in one direction, rough in the other, like catfish skin.

"Listen," I say. "Thanks for helping me, but I have to get going. I am so sorry for all the damage to that dress and I promise I'll never come back."

I head for the back side of the monolith where the holds were dispersed more generously. Bianca grabs my upper arm with a grip I'd expect from a construction worker.

"You vandalized museum property," she says. She speaks slowly but surely, confident in her knowledge of our shared language. "You must pay for restoration."

I try to shrug off her grip but she's damn strong. "Okay. Okay. My mo—… My frie—… A woman I'm staying with will pay. I can ask her for the money. How much?"

"I saw you do something to the shoes. What's in your hand?"

"No damage was done, I swear. It was just a —"

I open both hands, pat my thighs even though I don't have pockets. No swab-tube! Illogically, I check my mouth too, which was the last place I remember it being.

"No. Oh no!" I kneel and empty Kyle's satchel onto the floor. I run my hands over things that suddenly don't seem familiar, looking for the one thing I need. Things roll into nearby puddles and as I see them clearly in the water, illuminated by the soft glow of the aquatic flowers, I realize I must have dropped the swab-tube into the moat.

I run over to the edge to see if I can see where it fell.

Bianca catches me, holds me back like she's afraid I'm going to jump.

"It's gone," I say. And the shoes are full of water. I could try to free the shoes from the monolith face and from their exhibit case, bring the shoes back, and have Kyle dig around for any useable DNA. But water washing over glass... It'd be difficult, if not impossible.

And I loathe the idea of disturbing artifacts that haven't been handled for hundreds, maybe thousands of years.

I let Bianca help me to a sitting position, aware, but only vaguely, of heat on my face.

Tears.

There are a dozen painful reasons why I'm crying but I'll admit to only one: I failed my mission. I failed Jess's unspoken test. I'm sure of it.

And I'm saying all this to Bianca because even though we don't know each other, she reminds me of home. She looks nothing like my grandmother but I still feel connected to her somehow.

But then I keep going. I tell her things we're not supposed to talk about in case the person we're talking to is a Stitcher in disguise, or we unwittingly reveal technology a civilization isn't ready for. I tell her about how we travel from universe to universe, harvesting DNA from weapons or clothes of legendary heroes and using their DNA to create Asset patches. I feel compelled to tell her everything maybe because I'm hoping she'll take pity on me and help me in some way. But mostly, I think I tell her everything because I haven't had a chance to talk to anyone like this since my mom died. Longer, actually.

The last time I felt like someone was truly listening to me, and listening without judging, was when I last talked to my younger brother, Ben. He'd just started college, and I was just finishing it. He'd had no idea what he was doing and I…I didn't either, though everyone assumed I did, so I felt like a failure in that I wasn't living up to their expectations or mine.

I'd told Ben all this, and he'd just kept making our sandwiches, nodding and asking clarifying questions. At the end, I'd gotten no closer to an answer but I felt like I'd made the journey halfway to it.

This time, though, after I finish telling Bianca everything, I just feel wrung out.

"What was so special about the shoes?" she says.

Flabbergasted, I gape and can't speak for a moment. "They were Yeh-Shen's shoes! They're the whole reason for this —" I gesture around us "— this whole museum!"

Bianca is as cold and stoic as Michelangelo's Madonna of Bruges as she asks, "Why does it matter to you?"

I wipe tears and snot away with the back of my hand and take a deep breath. "Transformation. Yeh-Shen went from a servant to a princess. She went from having…"

"No love," says Bianca. "To the love of a Prince. The love of a kingdom. She had no home in her own house, then she found a home in everyone's heart. Is that what you seek?"

I'm taken aback. A prince? What, Kyle? And what kingdom? What home? I'm frustrated by her prying questions. But deep in my heart I realize I'm being defensive because her questions are cutting away all my half-truths and excuses.

"The love of a mother," I say, thinking *Am I being disloyal to my own mother if I want such love from Jess?* "I'm so confused… And tired. And cold. But mostly tired of everything."

Bianca's face softens and she comes towards me. Before touching my shoulder, though, she tilts her head like she's hearing a far-off noise.

"The fire-catchers are coming," she says. "You must leave now or they will question you."

I want to ask a dozen questions, mostly about *fire-catchers!*, but I'd rather not answer questions myself.

"You cannot return empty-handed," says Bianca.

"The shoes are useless now," I say.

"Not the shoes," says Bianca. "What you seek, you will find in the dress."

"The dress?" I say, nearly screeching. This woman hasn't heard a word I said! "It's not the same. Surely, the magic was in the shoes. Some kind of reaction to those specific shoes, whatever they're made of. All the stories specify the shoes."

She doesn't say anything but continues to stare at me with those strange round, almost protuberant eyes, and I get the feeling she's waiting for me to… trust her?

I look down the monolith's face. Though I don't have a huge problem with heights, it's a vertiginous view from the top of the monolith. The rock face looks slick with the continuous flow of water. From this angle, the hand- and footholds look insubstantial.

Bianca slips over the edge before I can stop her. Her ramie clothes get wet and start sticking to her body. She descends with a nimbleness that belies her elderly appearance.

While she's going down, I have a chance to make my escape. The way down on the other side of the rock was drier and looked easier. I'd be gone before she came back up. I'd probably be halfway back to our safehouse before she raised another alarm.

Curiosity gets the better of me. And I'd rather have something to show I'd almost completed my mission than come back empty-handed.

On the monolith face, Bianca snakes her arm through the hole meant for my hand. She reaches up and smoothes her long-fingered hand over the dress until she finds whatever it is she's looking for. Over the dress, not under, which makes me question if she'd not only heard but understood what I was saying. There would be more biological remnants inside the dress, on the surface that touched skin.

Bianca finds an opalescent, pearly white bead and pulls it off the dress. She folds it in her ramie skirt then tucks it into her waistband. When she's back on top of the monolith, she gives it to me.

It's not a sphere, not a giant pearl like I'd thought, but flat and about the size of the top joint of my thumb. It's as flat and as thin as paper. It bends slightly but feels as strong as steel, reminding me of the pliancy and resilience of bamboo. But its smooth surface, slick with water, has me doubting it'll be useful as anything other than a souvenir of my failure.

"Thank you," I say as gratefully as I can.

Her lips twitch into a frown. "Go now."

I'm eager to leave because I feel awkward, but I dread facing Jess.

———— ◦◦◦◦ ————

Jess takes one look at what I brought back, leaves the house, and slams the door with enough force to knock dust loose from the plaster ceiling.

"It's a fish scale," says Kyle, peering into the eyepiece of his microscope. "You were supposed to bring back a biological sample from your childhood hero, and you brought back a fish scale."

This must be how Jack felt when he brought back those magic beans. I don't know what to say. Telling him the whole truth of what happened would reveal all the mistakes I'd made.

Kyle continues to peer into his microscope. Then he grins and, without looking up, says, "Good news is, there's some biological matter. I think enough to be useful."

"Okay," I say.

He finally makes eye contact. The grin evaporates.

"Why does she hate me?" I say. My voice is hoarse from holding back my frustration and sadness.

Kyle shakes his head and wrings his hands. A weird habit he does when he's thinking intensely. "I've never seen her like this," he says. "I wish I could tell you more, and that it'll blow over, but I have no point of reference and I don't want to lie to you."

"Did I do something? Because we come from such similar universes, it seems like it'd be easy to inadvertently do something that's culturally deeply insulting."

"Not that I've noticed..."

"What? What is it?"

"Anne, can I say something and you won't..."

"Fly off the handle?"

"Fly off the what?"

"Handle. Like, an axe head, flying off its handle."

"You and your 'Americanisms.'" He fingerquotes and for the thousandth time, I regret ever introducing that gesture.

"Just say it."

He comes towards me a bit. The grave expression on his face makes my stomach cramp.

"I'm worried about your safety around Jess."

"What the hell. You're scaring me."

"I'm not saying she'll…attack you or anything like that. But she's become…unpredictable. And if she went on a mission with you and she had to use one of the Strength-based Asset patches… I don't know why she's being this way—"

"Only towards me. She seems fine with you. So I'm not imagining it? She's being weird to me, specifically?"

"You're not imagining it. Anne, there might come a time when you have to choose what's best for yourself: staying with us because you think we can get you home, or making a new home for yourself in one of the worlds we end up in."

From his concerned expression, I sense that time as coming sooner rather than later. And there's more to what he's saying but I can't put my finger on it right now.

"What are you thinking?" he says.

"Nothing. I'm exhausted."

"I bet." He lifts his soaked satchel off the counter and puts it into the kitchen sink. "Next time, test the water before jumping in."

"I'm starting to learn that lesson."

I turn on the water to take a shower and for an anxious moment, I expect the water to come out black but it's as clear and sparkling as good sapphires. I take a shower, change back into my normal clothes of jeans and my dance team tank top, which are becoming as threadbare as Kyle's slacks and flannel.

We have a first aid kit but I feel dumb using up all our bandages on my scraped elbows, fingers, and toes, so I just rub on some antibiotic cream and hope I don't bleed all over my sheets.

It wouldn't surprise me if I fell asleep as soon my head hit my pillow made of balled up spare clothes, but something Kyle said keeps bothering me. The elusiveness is giving me a tip-of-the-tongue feeling.

Then I understand. He'd said I'd have to choose between "staying with us" or striking out on my own. The us part. He was saying, in a roundabout way, in a way he probably thought was gentler than saying it outright, that he would stay with Jess.

I'm surprised at the grief this causes.

What did you expect, I say to myself. He's known Jess longer than he's known you. He has more in common with her. They're from similar tech levels; he doesn't have to explain himself to her all the time.

But I'd thought...

What, that he'd keep his promise to help you back to your home-universe? He's probably already forgotten about it. Besides, to them, there's more at stake than helping a lost little girl find her way back home.

Hey, fuck you. I'm not a "lost little girl."

Yeah, but you might be going crazy. You're arguing with yourself. Face it, you're holding them back. They could do so much more if they didn't have to drag your useless ass around with them.

I want the release of crying into my pillow, but I'm too tired to do even that. Lucky thing, too, because I hear the front door open, and I would've been mortified if Jess caught me crying. Again.

Jess and Kyle murmur a long discussion. Their mingling voices sound like the burbling of a stream. Listening to them, the tension uncoils around my heart and I drift off to sleep.

———✺———

I wake to the disorienting feeling that my bed feels different. The house smells different. Things are not the way they're supposed to be.

Like a flash of lightning, it hits me that things will never be the same again.

So I go downstairs to face the music.

Jess and Kyle are at the kitchen counter, eating something that looks like seaweed out of big cellophane bags. They're drinking orange sludge out of pear-shaped bottles.

And…there's a bag and bottle at one end like they've set a place for me at the dinner table.

"Have a good sleep?" says Kyle.

"Yeah. Thanks for asking," I say with automatic politeness. "This for me?"

"Yes." Kyle tips his head back and empties the crumbs out of the cellophane bag and into his mouth. "I've got to get back at it."

He gets up and, with my eyes, I try to plead with him to stay so I don't have to sit alone with Jess, but he doesn't meet my gaze. Actually, he seems to be trying hard to avoid it.

There's something up. He looks…different. Brighter, like he's just taken a shower and scrubbed himself clean of travel-dust. Maybe it's just that—a shower.

No. More. There's a gravity to his movements. He's always been flighty and light on his feet, useful when fighting but almost annoyingly hyper the rest of the time. Now, I notice that his shoulders sag, his feet drag across the floor, his features droop in an expression of profound anguish.

Then it's gone, as quickly gone as if he's stepped out of a doorway and into the light of a noonday sun.

"Sit and eat," says Jess, not unkindly.

I sit as far away from her as I can, without making it obvious. Kyle goes back to doing calculations for our next universe-jump. I want to keep watching him but Jess clears her throat for my attention.

"Did you take some pain meds for those?" Jess says, gesturing her orange sludge bottle at me.

I look down at myself and notice that bruises have developed all around my joints as I slept. "Looks worse than it feels." And I've had much worse bruises and injuries from dance.

She nods and there's a glimmer of something in her eyes. Respect? Surely not. I brush away thoughts of doing something daring—more like, stupid—just to see it again.

"You should eat," she says. "It'll help repair tissue damage."

I almost, almost say, "I know, Mom!" but thankfully, I don't. I obediently open my food and sludge bottle and eat a mouthful of the green stuff—tastes like I'm eating the fake leaves of the synthetic plants at my dentist's office—and wash it down with the orange sludge. Which tastes and feels like fish roe.

Nasty stuff, but she's probably gone to some trouble to steal or buy us food, so I bare my teeth in what I hope passes for a thankful smile.

"You remind me of my daughter," she says.

I nearly choke. I glance at Kyle to see if he can give me any clue about where Jess is going with that bittersweet announcement but he's engrossed in star charts.

"I do?" I say to Jess.

"How she used to be when she was younger." Jess has a faraway look in her eyes. Lost in memory, her usually stern features are soft, nearly erasing the wrinkles that parenthesize her mouth.

I'm both eager and afraid to hear her talk about her daughter. Eager because she's rarely open about her past and her private life. Afraid because, from what Kyle's told me about Jess's daughter, that Anne was badass. Sharpshooter, black belt, marathoner. To Jess, I'm a poor man's version of the daughter she lost.

"Anne was a handful when she was younger," says Jess. "Always underfoot. A late talker but once she got started, couldn't stop her, no way, no how. So whenever it got quiet, I knew she was up to something. Mischievous. But she outgrew it. Kind. She outgrew that too, when the time came to put away childish things."

I want to say kindness isn't childish, but I don't want to break the spell she seems to be under.

"My daughter was my daughter until she became my friend," says Jess, nursing the bottle of orange sludge. "I could trust her with my life, and I grew to trust her with Ben's life. That made doing missions so much easier because I could concentrate on getting in and getting out. Didn't have to worry about them. No looking over my shoulder. No worrying. Absolute trust."

She swigs her sludge, making me think there might be alcohol in it. Would explain her unfocused eyes.

"In the end, that trust was our undoing," says Jess.

She's never been this…emotionally open and I believe, I hope, that it signals we've turned a corner in our relationship. I lean forward. My eyes burn but I dare not blink for fear of breaking eye contact. With my body and face, I signal to her that I am completely and utterly giving her my undivided attention.

"I should've gone back for them," she says.

Kyle had told me Jess's whole family died in his home universe. When he's feeling particularly morose, he says she sacrificed them to save him. Because he'd known where Excalibur, the legendary weapon she and her family had gone to that universe for, was being kept, and he'd known how to get it out.

But she doesn't glance at him, nor radiate any enmity in his direction.

"I thought they could get out without me," she says. "I waited at the rendezvous point. Kyle and I. We were laughing about something when the castle exploded. I'd trusted them to get out and never even thought… It never even crossed my mind that they needed me. That I wouldn't be there when they needed me most."

She crumples her empty bottle in one fist and focuses her attention on me. Her eyes and expression darken like a shadow is passing behind her face.

"My family's downfall was I trusted them too much. Our downfall," she points at Kyle, then herself. "Our downfall will be the same, but in a different way. You see A—…"

She chokes on my name, can't bear to call me the same word as her daughter.

"You see," she says, trying again, "you're like how my Anne used to be. When she was a child, young and immature. You've been too sheltered. I don't know what your mother did to make you turn out this way, whether it's a blessing or curse that you're so… soft. I should resent you for having the safety and security my own daughter never had, but at the same time, I'm grateful she had to go through what she went through to make it as far as she did. I don't think you would've. I don't think you will."

I push away my half-eaten food. "What are you saying?"

"I can't watch you die because of your own…"

"Say it," I say, voice hoarse again with checked emotion. "You want to call me stupid. You did call me soft and sheltered. Naive. I did have a good childhood, and I'm sorry your Anne didn't. But that's not my fault. None of this is my fault, and I'm trying my hardest to prove myself to you."

Jess pounds her fist on the table. "It's not enough!"

"You could try harder to give me the training I need!"

"It'll never be enough."

"But—"

"We'll take you back to the universe where we left your Timid People. You'll have friends to take care of you there."

"I don't need someone to take care of me. I need you to teach me!"

"You're too stubborn to be taught. I told you this was a fool's errand. We wasted almost a week on this daydream, this fantasy."

"You can't be sure—"

"We're wearing the Assets you had Kyle make!" Jess lifts her shirt, revealing her cesarean scar and the smattering of Asset patches on her chest above her worn out, once-white bra. Most of them are perfect squares and drained, black. Half a dozen dim, low. One bright one with irregular edges beating to the calm rhythm of her strong, athletic heart. "It does nothing."

"Give it more time! You can't be sure—"

"That's enough, Anne!"

Her saying my name, lacking all the softness of how she says it when she says her own daughter's name, even though it's the exact same word, is more final than anything else she can say.

"Okay," I say. "If you refuse to listen to me, then there's no way for me to convince you."

I leap up from the table and run from the room, out the front door, sprint up the footpath to the main road, expecting footsteps to follow and bitterly disappointed when they don't. My mind doesn't know where I'm going, only that my heart will burst if I stay to hear any more. My feet seem to know, though, so I let them fly me away from the house.

The land is very different during the day. The sky is aquamarine. The path I'm on is flat but lazily meanders through tall blue-green grass as high as my neck. In the daytime, the round, glowing, pearl-like homes seem even more so with their smooth opalescent surfaces and seamless doors.

The biggest pearl, the museum, looms before me like a moon rising out of the sea.

In the day time there are more museum-goers. A double line of young dark-haired children in simple ramie dresses is approaching the entrance. As are two small groups of people, a cadre of seniors and a quartet of middle-aged women.

I sprint past all of them, run inside, past the ticket booth and the attendant behind the murky glass. No one stops me as I run into the museum proper, which looks completely different during the day.

Last night, the ceiling had been dark and I'd assumed it was partly to conserve energy and partly to encourage everyone to leave. Looking up I realize it had been dark because it had been night; the ceiling is a giant dome made of a semi-opaque cream material. There's no need for artificial light because natural light is plentiful.

Passing through the building material, the light is diffused, making the humid air glow with a dream-like quality.

I pause at the first art installation just as I had the night before, expecting it to look cheaper, smaller, now that it's brightly lit. Far from it. Each color is a dozen times more vibrant, like an autumn forest after a pelting rain.

Then I move on, head down again, on a mission again, to get to the monolith that protects Yeh-Shen's ball gown and glass slippers.

The top is shrouded in glittering fog. In the hazy daytime light, the ebony monolith reminds me of Excalibur and its wavering, undefined edges. It's an illusion on the monolith. It won't cut me. I think.

"Bianca?" I say.

I'm not a hundred percent sure why I'm here, only that it feels good to be somewhere where no one hates me. It's sad that I would rather be with a total stranger than with people that should've been my family.

"Bianca!" I call up the false mountain, into the false cloud.

A breeze parts the clouds and I glimpse the display case where the dress and glass slippers are supposed to be. The case has been destroyed! The case glass surrounds the empty space like a scintillating vignette, emphasizing the fact that they're missing. I'd thought they would be there forever, somehow becoming part of the stone they'd been mounted on. Beyond that space, I think I see Bianca's face but it's hard to tell for sure.

The only way to get answers is to climb. I go around to the back then I toe off my sneakers and climb the rear face, the face away from the viewing area. I don't care if security cameras record me or if a museum visitor reports me. But judging from the three onlookers, staring up at me with rapt expressions, they have no inclination of giving me away. Maybe they're waiting for the grisly show of me falling and shattering on the tile or breaking my neck and drowning in the moat.

Halfway up, I see Bianca's face peeping over the edge.

"It didn't work," I call to her.

Stoically, silently, she stares at me until I continue to climb, backing away only to give me room to pull myself over the edge.

I'm tired and wet with sweat and water dripping from trumpet-shaped tubes strung down from the high ceiling. They'd been invisible last night but in the day, they shine like mercury.

The flowers that had been glowing in the shallow pools and puddles at the top of the monolith are all closed tight and dark, like red pearls yanked off a necklace and scattered across the floor.

"It didn't work," I say again. "The biologicals from the dress must've been contaminated or something."

Bianca slowly blinks her glossy, nearly protuberant eyes.

"It didn't transform them at all," I say. "Kyle extracted the DNA and made the Asset patches. He and Jess put them on, both at the same time or something, for some godforsaken reason. Kyle probably put it on first and when nothing happened, Jess probably— Look, they didn't become…better than what they were. There was almost nothing endearing or…or lovable about them. If anything, I'd say the patches made them worse…"

I can't tell if my frantic rambling is making any sense.

"I thought you said it was for you," says Bianca.

"Wait, what?"

"You said you wanted love. A mother's love. You wanted to belong to someone."

I hold up a hand. "Now wait a minute. I don't belong to anyone. And I don't remember if I said those exact same words but… Yeah,"

I finish lamely. "That's what I wanted. Only that's not what I got. They were terrible to me."

Bianca purses her lips and nods like she'd known this would happen. She steps aside, revealing a glittering white pile in one of the shallow pools. I'm drawn to it.

Yeh-Shen's ballgown. In the case, it had looked fragile, almost damaged. Bianca must have mended it somehow, or replaced the hems with bright white satin. But why toss it into a puddle?

When I lift it out of the water, it's magically, completely dry. And when I hold it up against me, it looks like it would fit well.

"Do you want to try it on?" says Bianca.

"I couldn't," I say, but I'm nodding.

"It flatters your darker skin," she says.

"Really, I couldn't," I say. "It's a priceless artifact." And I think I keep politely declining but suddenly I'm wearing it.

The bodice hugs me comfortably, not too tight and not too loose, like a good diving wetsuit. The skirt part drapes smoothly to the floor like an upside-down calla lily, but when I do a couple of pirouettes, the cloth flares up and out, as light as spun sugar.

Bianca laughs and claps her hands. "Again! Oh, my daughter used to dance but not like you. Not in the Albion way."

I oblige her and do a part of my Swan Lake routine atop the monolith. I pirouette and leap, leap and pirouette, so happy that I can dance again that I attempt to spin the routine's thirty-two fouettés while spotting Bianca's face.

She claps with delight, but over the sound, I hear something that makes me lose my concentration and wobble to a stop.

"That was wonderful," says Bianca. She reaches for my face, stops short of touching it. "May I?"

I look at her questioningly. She reaches out again and brushes my hair, damp with sweat, off my cheeks.

The sound comes again, but this time, I discern a word.

"Anne!"

It's my mom's voice but with Jess's impatient hardness. I don't want to answer.

"Are you here, Anne?" she says. "Anne!"

There's a commotion down below. Clanking sounds of something metal being hurled against the tiled ground. Curious, I sidle towards the edge.

"I see you, Anne! I'm coming!"

My hair, swinging forward, gave me away. I jump back from the edge and look to Bianca, who has undone the length of ramie from around her waist.

"Stay back from the edge," she says calmly. She loops the long swatch of black cloth between her hands. Then she tosses it up and it unfurls like a tendril, like a tentacle, reaching for the water trumpets above our heads.

"Anne!" says Jess, closer now. She must be scaling the monolith face.

"What are you doing?" I say to Bianca.

Bianca has a water trumpet in a loop of cloth. She pulls on the cloth. The water trumpet inches towards her. Metal squeals above us, echoing in the cavernous building.

Bianca pulls on the trumpet. It goes to her willingly like a gooseneck faucet. As long as it's held firmly, it can be aimed. Bianca fiddles with something on the trumpet's base and the water increases from a trickle to a gush. Nothing as strong as a firefighter's hose or even a power washer, but a healthy spray that could wash off a driveway.

"She gave you up, didn't she?" says Bianca.

"I'm not something to be 'given up'," I say.

Bianca looks at me. Her round eyes glisten like fresh yolks. "I meant it as how one would give up a puzzle they could not solve."

"I'm almost there, Anne," says Jess. She's so close, she doesn't have to yell. That was quick. Must be wearing one of her Strength-based Assets, of course. The madness would come soon. The frightening, destructive insanity with the power of Hercules behind it.

I back away from the edge, which gives Bianca room to maneuver the water trumpet and look over the edge. She sprays water down the monolith's side before I can stop her.

The sound of gasping and choking reaches me. Jess!

"Stop, Bianca! You'll make her slip!"

Bianca keeps spraying. She moves the trumpet slowly side to side and the gasping and choking continues. Jess can't strafe fast enough to avoid being waterboarded.

I go to Bianca and pull on her shoulder to get her attention. She doesn't budge.

"Bianca! Stop!"

People below are screaming now. I chance a peek over. There are people dressed in official-looking uniforms, with batons or something at their hips. I think the whole museum is down there, watching Jess trying to climb up as Bianca tries to wash her off.

"Bianca, don't kill her," I say. "Please stop."

She ignores me. The blank look on her face frightens me because she's having no qualms about what she's doing. I can't trust someone so cool about taking a life.

I grab the water trumpet and try to pull it out of her grasp. She holds tight, so I pull and pull. She changes her grip to pull it closer to her body. I change my grip to pull it away. It's slick! I take a step back to catch myself from falling, only to step on nothing. Arms wheeling, I feel myself fall as if in slow motion.

But Bianca catches the skirt hem of my dress.

We freeze, balanced precariously on the monolith's edge.

I'm almost perpendicular to the monolith's face and wholly at Bianca's mercy. She is red-faced with the effort to hold on at this angle.

The odds of me succeeding in anything I do at this very moment are razor-slim.

But I would rather die while trying to do something than just let myself fall.

I break eye contact with Bianca so I don't telegraph my intent. Then, keeping my legs locked straight, I bend at the waist, grab skirt fabric at my knees, and yank Bianca towards me as I bend my knees, which pulls the rest of my weight over the fulcrum of the edge as Bianca falls towards the space I'd occupied.

We switch places except she doesn't have a skirt I can grab. I look away and wait for the screams and a splash or thud.

There are screams but they're cut off abruptly. Then the clapping starts.

I look over the edge. Jess has Bianca by the ankle.

Quickly, I take Bianca's length of ramie and the clothes I'd been wearing. I tie everything together into a makeshift rope, which I lower over the edge.

When Bianca takes the end, I feel her weight strain my shoulders and neck muscles. I brace my feet against the driest, tallest outcrop on the monolith's top but I can't hold the pose long. My strength is in my core and my legs, not so much my arms and shoulders.

Fortunately, the weight eases off. I check over the edge to make sure they didn't kill each other. Both of them are ascending steadily.

I pull up my hasty rope and struggle with the knots so I can have my clothes back but, soaked with water and pulled by Bianca's weight, the knots are difficult to tease apart.

I've gotten my tank top loose and I'm working on getting my pants and Bianca's skirt apart when both Bianca and Jess come over the edge at the same time.

Without warning, as if choreographed, they launch at each other and grapple.

"Stop it!" I say, going to them but hesitating.

They look nearly matched in strength. If Jess is wearing a Strength Asset, she could go nuts any minute. But to take it off would give Bianca the upper hand over both of us.

A flash of green against Jess's hip catches my attention. She brought my sword, Urduja's blade!

"Jess!" I say.

She understands and dances back, reaches over with her right hand, pulls the sword out and tosses it in my direction. It skitters to a halt in a puddle several feet away. I open my hand to call it into my grasp then remember I'm not wearing my Urduja Asset patch; the sword won't respond without it.

As I run towards it, Bianca takes advantage of Jess's vulnerable, arms-open position and strikes her between the breasts. Even where I'm standing, I hear Jess's forced exhalation. She stumbles back while trying to gulp in air.

With each backward step, her face darkens and purples, not for lack of oxygen but the rush of blood and adrenaline. Her brows descend, her eyes squint into narrow points of soul-consuming hatred.

The madness is taking over.

"Bianca," I say softly. "You'd better come over here."

Bianca, maybe thinking she still has the advantage, rushes towards Jess, who backhands her with a well-timed smack. Bianca reels back.

I grab her by her hair and yank her behind me before she can rush Jess again.

"For god's sake," I say to Bianca, "calm the fuck down. You too, Jess!"

Jess advances with a snarl frozen on her face.

"Get out of the way, Anne," she says. Her voice is as coarse as salt.

"If you want her, you have to go through me first." I wave the sword between us.

Confusion flickers over her face, but the crazy sneer returns as she stalks forward. "You nearly killed her a second ago. Why protect her now? Give'er here."

I back up, feel Bianca's hard but cool body against mine briefly, then she backs away too.

"That was to save my life," I say. "And now, I'm saving your life by saving hers. You're not in your right mind right now." I wave Urduja's blade again, this time between our faces to show that I mean to use it to the best of my paltry ability.

While I wave it, I whisper hastily to Bianca, "Get that cloth. Gotta bring her down. I can fix her. Count of two. One. Two!"

We both run towards the cloth. I cover Bianca while she takes the sopping length into her arms.

"And now?" she says.

"Uh…" I shake my head. No time to plan complex things. "We rush her. On two. One. Two."

Bianca lets loose a roaring scream that startles me. I fall behind a step. Fortunately, it also startles Jess, who focuses her attention on Bianca. I toss my sword away—don't need it—and tackle Jess around the waist.

A second later, I feel a dense, cold weight land on my back and shoulders then rub across, chafing my nape as Bianca wraps the cloth around Jess.

Jess struggles, almost carrying the weight of two grown women. Then little by little, the struggling abates but doesn't cease. We get her down to the floor. I wince as the back of her head bounces against monolith stone. She doesn't even seem to feel it.

Her nose and the furrow between her eyes are crimson but the rest of her face is as white as the foamy froth erupting between her pale, taut lips.

"Gerrof me!" she says, along with a few curse words in several languages, two of which I understand. One must've been pretty gross or offensive, for Bianca spits in her face.

"Okay, okay," I say more to myself than anyone else. I feel like I'm violating her personal space but she's forced me to do it, for everyone's safety. I climb up her body until I'm practically straddling her. Her strong legs continue to kick and stomp on the ground. She's as wild and crazed as a cat in a wet pillowcase.

Bianca, not knowing my plan, has bound what remains of my makeshift rope around Jess's chest. It also secures Jess's arms against her sides. But it prevents my access to her chest, where the Asset patches are.

"I'm real sorry 'bout this," I say, right before I dig both hands between the cold, tightly wound cloth and Jess's fever-hot body. I form fish with my hands, and wriggle them up toward the area between her breasts. There are, as usual, several patches. I scrape them all off as gently as I can.

The struggling abates further until, finally, Jess seems to shrink and her face returns to its normal tawny coloring.

And then I realize the flaw in my plan. Jess is bound and Bianca is not. And I'd let go of my sword so I could grip both of Jess's wrists. I look up to meet Bianca's gaze and suss out where we stand.

We stare at each other and I realize that people have made it up the monolith. Official-looking people, some armed with batons, are ready to take us all into custody. But frozen in place by something. I trace their stares to a pale, remarkable long finger on a pale, slender hand. I trace the hand up an arm, across a shoulder, to Bianca's face, and finally meet her gaze once more. She holds everyone at bay with one finger.

I start to understand.

"Yeh-Shen was your ancestor?" I say.

Bianca smiles softly. "She was my daughter, as I'd wanted you to be."

My eyes feel like they're going to pop out of my face. "You look damn good for your age."

She bows her head in thanks.

"I'm sorry for all of this," I say. "I know it's nowhere near an explanation or excuse, but I had…" I take a deep breath and blurt out my lame excuse anyway. "I had good intentions."

Bianca nods. "I saw."

The way she says it makes it seem like she means something different than my understanding of that word. Patiently, she waits for me to figure it out. Then I do.

"It was never the shoes!" I say. "Oh my god, duh. For god's sake!" I pound the heel of my hand against my forehead. "It wasn't a Transformative power," I say to Jess. "Was it?" I say to Bianca.

To Jess again, I say, "Have you ever run across anything like this?"

To both of them, looking from one face to the other, I say, "It's something else. Hold on, I'll come up with a word for it. Okay, maybe not right now. The best I can compare it to is…"

I say to Bianca, "It was never the shoes because it was the dress. It doesn't transform, it reveals."

Bianca nods and her large round eyes glisten with, what I hope and assume is, pride.

"It wasn't about making her prettier or changing anything about her," I continue. "It was because her stepmother and stepsister kept her secluded and hidden, made her doubt her own worth. That dress revealed who she was by…" I can barely keep up with my own thoughts. "Changing brain chemistry, probably. Loosening inhibitions, like alcohol or cannabis. Letting her speak without second-guessing. Giving her the courage or confidence to be herself.

"It was your dress," I say to Bianca, remembering specific details of the story my grandmother told me: the magic mother, who 'died' and was reincarnated as a fish, who gave her fish scale skin to her daughter so her daughter could wear it as a dress to go to the ball. "The dress was your…skin? It was your *power* all along."

"It can do harm as well as good, Anne," says Jess. "It can make you say things you think about, but would never say to a person you…care about."

"You should be honest to people you care about," I say.

Jess shakes her head. "There's a difference between being honest, and revealing something you yourself are fighting against. I said things to you. I…revealed that I fear for your safety and the consequences of your… Can you guys take this off me now?"

"Right. Sorry." I unwind the cloth, with Bianca's help.

"I was saying," Jess says when the cloth is gone. "The patch made me say what I feared. But I was fighting that fear. I would never have said those things to you because…Lord help me, I like having you and your ideals around, and if we can't tolerate the faults of people we…care about, then what's the use of fighting for them?"

She takes a deep breath. "That's as much as I'm going to say on this matter. Even though I still believe you might end up killing all of us, I also believe that…your place is with us."

I duck my head and busy myself with unknotting my pants from Bianca's cloth.

"Thanks," I say. "We should get back. Kyle is probably waiting for us."

They both look at each other, then at me, and I don't want any more talking because I want Jess's words about having a place with her, with them, to echo in me a little longer. In silence, Jess helps me free my pants while Bianca dismisses the museum staff. Then I change back into my clothes while Jess and Bianca speak in Bianca's language. Out of the corner of my eye, I see Jess give Bianca something. It looked like a key, but I can't be sure.

Surprisingly, we're free to go. The museum workers are actually even smiling at us as we pass, and the two flanking the entrance wave goodbye.

Back at the house, I notice that all our things are packed and already on top of Kyle's transport pad.

"One last night here," Jess says. "We can't jump to the next universe tired and be unprepared for whatever we encounter on the other side."

"Okay," I say. I remember what she said on top of the monolith but I still shower with the door open and listen for any indication that they're preparing to make the jump without me. I still listen as I get dressed. I listen as I lie down. And I'm so tired from everything, and from listening, that I'm asleep as soon as I close my eyes.

–––◦◦◦–––

The realization that I'd fallen asleep, and that they could very well leave me despite what Jess said, jolts me awake to complete darkness. A cramp shoots up my right leg, making me cry out.

"Hush," says a familiar voice. A warm hand cups my heel and helps my foot into a dorsi-flexion while another warm hand eases the cramp in my calf muscle.

"Ow-ow-owie," I say, whining. "Sorry if I woke you. Ow-ow-ow."

"I was awake," says Jess. "Anne—my Anne—used to get leg cramps too. Whenever she was over-tired."

She was waiting for me to have a leg cramp?

"It's fine now," I say when the pain is manageable. "Do I have time to go back to sleep?"

"Yes. But first, I have something to ask of you."

"Okay…"

"You can stay with us, with me, but I have to ask you to do one thing."

"If I can, I will."

"Don't get involved with Kyle."

I furrow my brow to show her I don't understand but then I realize it's too dark for either of us to see each other clearly. Too dark to really see Kyle sleeping just a couple of yards away, though I can make out his outline, limned by moonlight.

As much as I want to agree with anything she demands of me, I can't keep quiet when someone puts limitations on my life. It's more the principle of the thing than the possibility that something will develop.

"We're two grown adults, Jess."

Jess makes a sound that could be a laugh. "You guys will always be kids to me."

I want to catch that sound and that sentence and bottle them up. After a few minutes, I say, "I don't make promises easily. Especially if I don't know why I'm making them."

She's quiet for a long time. I wonder what she's trying not to say.

Then, "We'll be working together for a while, sometimes in tight quarters. I don't want you to get involved because that leads to strong emotions. Strong emotions have a way of feeding off each other."

I think of that scene in Hamlet, about appetites and insanity and unrequited love.

"I understand," I say. "I'll comply."

She shakes my foot. Then I feel the floor tremble a little as she adjusts her position. "I'll wake you when it's time to go. Goodnight, Anne."

The end.

About the Authors

Dawn Del Sontro

Dawn Del Sontro lives in Virginia with her husband of sixteen years, three children, dog, and immortal rabbit. When she's not writing, Dawn likes to play video games where she can pretend to be Batman, shoot people in the head without repercussion, and solve puzzles to feel smarter than she thinks she is.

As an avid runner, Dawn tries to increase pace while improving distance, all while pretending to be the lone survivor in the middle of the zombie apocalypse. Despite this fascination with zombies, she is certain the world will end when the Earth tires of humans' shenanigans and destroys us all, not unlike what happened to the dinosaurs.

Dawn has been writing since the moment she learned to hold a pencil and still prefers the handwritten method. She has a bachelor's degree in English with a concentration in Creative Writing from California University of Pennsylvania. When the typical gift won't do, Dawn writes poetry and personal stories instead. She has written TV reviews, short fiction for entertainment blogs, and non-fiction stories about children, family, and everyday weird life occurrences. She sometimes uses her writing to moderate an on-line game of Werewolf, where the story is almost as fun as the players.

You can find Dawn on Twitter at @DuttyDawn and on Facebook at facebook.com/dawn.estusdelsontro.

Dean Fearce

Visit Dean at facebook.com/dean-fearce, or follow him on Twitter @deanfearce.

Gordon Hilgers

Gordon Hilgers is a poet who also writes short fiction. His poetry has appeared in many magazines including Edgar Allan Poet Journal, Red Fez, Boston Literary Journal, Texas Observer and others. He has written a number of short fictions under a variety of pseudonyms.

Ernest Ortiz

Ernest is a U.S. Air Force veteran and private investigator living in the heart of Silicon Valley. He specializes in surveillance and workers comp insurance cases, and has worked throughout California, Nevada, Arizona, Colorado, and New Mexico. When Ernest is not chasing insurance cheats, he likes to watch smooth jazz concerts, go car cruising, and try insane hot sauce challenges. An aspiring writer since elementary school, Ernest is working to make his mark in the sci-fi and mystery writing world. He is currently working on a sci-fi thriller called *Homing Target* and a young adult dystopian called *Eternal Courier*. Ernest is a co-founder of the Black Hats Writing Group, a bi-weekly Mountain View based writing critique group, and video producer for Chophouse Books' YouTube channel. You can read his latest blogs on his website ernestortizwritesnow.com where you can find monthly updates, upcoming projects, writing wisdoms, politics from an anarcho-capitalist perspective, and his short comic series, *High School Life* and *Liberty Brew Crew*. You can also reach Ernest on Twitter @ErnestOrtizWN.

Joan Reginaldo

I was born in the Philippines, grew up with all its creepy superstitions, somehow ended up in Silicon Valley afraid to put pillow cases on my pillows at night.

I blog about being a mom to an introverted kid who wants to be called Grimlock, and taking care of aging parents that are afraid of yogurt, their smartphones, and anyone not Filipino. My partner, Futurehusband, is white.

I write from the point of view of these intersections, a point of view shared by many but portrayed by few.

In terms of reading, I have so many books that they've become load-bearing structures in my house. I enjoy all genres and one of my keenest joys is to talk about books, movies, and writing.

Pet peeves:

– Migraines

– The "Reply All" feature

– People who excuse meanness as "snark"

– Asshole drivers

– The genre label "chick lit"

– Group Text

Things we can bond over:

– Animals

– Science

– Books and stories and writing

– Crafting, gardening, and baking techniques

– Twitter quips

– Tech and gadgets

The best way to contact me is through Twitter: @JoanWIP

Dan Tompsett

I was conceived on a Princess Cruise liner back in '53 by two strangers who met on the topmost deck. The man was from New Hampshire. The woman was from Seattle. After the cruise, they each went home. While the woman gave birth, she had her condo painted. The man never heard about me.

Raised by homo beat poets until the age of seven, I was then handed off to a tee-pee of hippies in Pescadero, California, where I lived until the hippies turned into junkies and either went to prison, found God, or died. Vietnam was going on, so I went to Canada in order to avoid having to spend night and day with snakes, bugs, and a bunch of sweaty, well-armed men.

Nothing happened in Canada.

On my return to Pescadero, California, I went to work on an artichoke farm, where, after about three months I became virtually invisible. All most people could see were my ass and hat.

The strangest thing on the farm was a wishing well in the center of the hobby graveyard kept by the farmer's wife and kids. I tossed a penny into it, once. Sometimes I wonder what happened to that penny.

Now, at the age of sixty-two, I'm pretty much dead. Seems like it has taken forever to get here. I'll keep this autobiography short. I'm not famous, so no one will read it, anyway. As a matter of fact, I think I'll just end it here.